Against the background
century, Dello Iacono has written a compelling novel of enduring love, honor, friendship, and betrayal. *Rebellion* unfolds within the story of Wat Tyler's ill-fated peasant revolt of 1381. Thoroughly researched, *Rebellion* brings to life a time in English history ravaged by plague and war. Ruled by nobles and an uncaring church, the common man had few if any rights. In this world Albert meets Elizabeth.

Dello Iacono skillfully weaves together the story of their love and the revolt of Wat Tyler as a rebellion against the corrupt and abusive social and political structures of their time. He captures the feel of the fourteenth century. The characters become alive in your mind. You will care about them both good and bad. It provides a glimpse into a time that from the pen of Dello Iacono is not too different from our own. This very enjoyable book is for anyone who loves his or her history wrapped around a well-told story.

—Joseph Seery,
retired teacher

I had the privilege of reading the book *Rebellion*. It was not only very well written, but once you started reading it you could not put it down. It was filled with great many historical happenings and places of interest, especially in London. I have traveled in Great Britain many times. The book brought back many memories of places visited and the best part was that I could visualize where the action was taking place. The historical aspect only adds to the reader's interest especially for me. I had forgotten a lot of the historical aspects. It was good to have my mind refreshed. *I* was sorry when I finished reading it. I wanted it to go on, to continue to refresh my memory of historical happening years ago! Every thing is very vivid.

A couple of months ago I was given the first two books written by Charles Finch. They are murder fiction that take place in London and vicinity. Once you started reading them you cannot put them down. I found the same with *Rebellion*. You're waiting for the next book to be published.

—Graham A. Long,
retired bank manager for Dedham Cooperative Bank

I recently had the privilege of reading *Rebellion* by Dello Iacono. In all honesty, I found the reading of this novel quick and absorbing. The characters were well developed, and I found myself drawn into their lives and caring about their mishaps, triumphs, and defeats. I love historical novels, and the author balanced his tale within an historical event without having the facts overpower the story. I will highly recommend this book to my friends and to anyone who enjoys being transported to another time and place and has been touched by the power of love.

—Thomas J. Grudinskas,
branch manager of Needham Bank

Rebellion is excellent. I might be biased as I love historical works, but *Rebellion* really is one of the best in this genre I have read in a long time. The way the story is interlaced with real historical events and people is brilliantly done. The overall style of the book reminds me of *The Pillars of Earth* by Ken Follet.

—Mark Angel,
Chief Editor, Angel Editing

Rebellion! I loved it, especially the characters. They were so well rounded that it was hard to separate the fact from the fiction; the interaction was totally believable. Just enough romance to keep the ladies happy, and just enough action for the guys. I am looking forward to a sequel or at the very least a second novel. Maybe more.

—Brenda Berardinelli,
mail clerk at Brandeis University

An excellent love story during medieval times that kept me amused, excited and glued to *Rebellion* until the end.

—Thomas Conneely,
stone mason

Rebellion!

Rebellion!

DELLO IACONO

TATE PUBLISHING & *Enterprises*

This novel is a work of fiction. However, several names, descriptions, entities, and incidents included in the story are based on the lives of real people.

The opinions expressed by the author are not necessarily those of Tate Publishing, LLC.

Published by Tate Publishing & Enterprises, LLC
127 E. Trade Center Terrace | Mustang, Oklahoma 73064 USA
1.888.361.9473 | www.tatepublishing.com

Tate Publishing is committed to excellence in the publishing industry. The company reflects the philosophy established by the founders, based on Psalm 68:11,
"The Lord gave the word and great was the company of those who published it."

Cover design by Kellie Southerland
Interior design by Joey Garrett

Published in the United States of America

ISBN: 978-1-61566-507-5
1. Fiction / Historical
2. Fiction / War & Military
09.11.17

DEDICATED TO MY GRANDCHILDREN,
ABBY AND JACOB HART,
AND MY GODSON, AIDAN CONNEELY.

Introduction

The smell of burning flesh permeated the air, but Albert had grown accustomed to the sickening odor months earlier when he was in France. It brought all the horror of that time back into his mind. That was when he was a knight fighting battles in a foreign land. Now he was in England, searching for a future as elusive as a dream.

The night sky could be seen as an orange and yellow glow for a good distance up the Thames. There, the merchant vessel, *Mary*, sailed into what would be one of England's largest uprisings.

"Sir Albert!" called Master Sims, spraying saliva through missing front teeth taken out by a Genoese sword years earlier. The gap in his teeth added to the overall facial appearance of scars and pockmarks from a lifetime of combat. "The city is ablaze, sir! I cannot unload the cargo, but I will set you ashore." Albert clutched the rail as the sweat dripped from his face and palms.

He was not listening. The screams and bloodshed mesmerized him as he stared at the chaos that was taking place before his eyes.

"Sir Albert," shouted Sims. "We are nearing the wharf!"

Sims' shouts brought Albert back to his senses. Coming out of his daze, he turned and looked at him. He reached into his satchel and took all the coin he had and handed it to Sims.

"Take this, and await my return if you can. I must go and find Elizabeth and her brother, but if you find yourself or your ship is in any danger, by all means, sail away immediately."

Sims stepped forward and placed his strong hand on Albert's shoulder. "I will try to maintain as long as I can, and God be with you, sir."

Albert thrust his hand out to shake the seaman's hand. He thanked him and started down the gangplank. His heart pounded, and he sweated profusely as he looked around nervously. He was well aware that the king's men would be searching for him, but that wouldn't keep him from his search.

From Paul's Wharf he ran up Thames Street. The stench filled the air with a vile odor as he passed mangled, lifeless bodies and bits of body parts that littered the streets and alleyways. His pace slowed as he approached Castle Bayard, and he stopped now and again to examine various corpses of the indiscriminate dead. He was hoping he would not find any loved ones among them, especially Elizabeth. Merciful God! He prayed that he would not find her among the dead. He continued to search as ragged men, women, and children rushed past him, fleeing for their lives. As he bent down to examine the body of a woman, a shrill cry got his attention, and he looked in the direction of the sound.

Just as he stood to get a better view, he heard a groan coming from the same direction, and he moved toward the body he thought the cry had come from. He stood above a man lying face down. As Albert knelt down beside him, he saw the man's fingers move. He gently turned the dying man over and gazed into his eyes. Albert looked down and noticed the huge gash in the man's stomach, exposing some of his innards. He knew from his experiences in battle that this was a slow and excruciatingly painful death.

"Please, sir," the man cried. "Finish me!"

With pity, Albert looked back upon the battered face.

"Please, sir," the man begged. "In the name of our beloved Savior, end my suffering!"

Albert slowly drew his dagger. He hesitated for one moment, looking into the man's face and hearing him whisper, "Please!" Taking a deep breath and placing his dagger on the man's chest, Albert closed his eyes and whispered a prayer as he plunged the dagger into the man's heart. He felt the cracking of ribs as blood spurted out, covering his hands. He heard the man's final gasp of air as he withdrew his dagger. As he rose, Albert looked down at the man's face again to see that he was finally at peace, and Albert felt a rush of relief for him. He stood, wiping the blood from his hands with his sleeves. He made the sign of the cross and began to walk away, resuming his search.

He arrived at Black Friars Convent, noticing that its sanctuary had been destroyed, presumably by an angry peasant mob. He passed St. Paul's to West Cheap Street where he encountered a small group of fleeing commoners. Believing Albert was one of the king's knights, they knelt down at his feet.

"Have mercy, my lord," one cried.

Albert motioned them to rise. "I am not one of the king's men. You have no need to fear me, but I'm hoping you can help me. I'm looking for Wat Tyler. Does anyone here know of his whereabouts?"

One man stepped forward to speak. He looked at Albert with sad eyes, and Albert steadied himself for bad news.

"His head rests on London Bridge with that of Jack Straw's," the man replied.

"Oh God," Albert cried softly. His eyes filled as he lowered his head. In an unsteady voice, he asked, "What of his sister? Does anyone know what became of her?"

"We know not, sir," one replied hastily as the group started off again, making their way toward the city gates and the freedom of the countryside.

Albert turned and continued on his way. His search seemed to last an eternity. Finally, his pace slowed. Feeling exhausted and discouraged, he decided to surrender himself to the king's forces.

After all, he was a fugitive, and with Wat dead and with little hope of finding Elizabeth, it was his only choice. He would first return to the vessel and set Master Sims on his way. He began retracing his steps back through the city. Many peasants continued to pass him, running with horse and infantry companies not far behind. Through the fray he walked, oblivious to his surroundings, and by some miracle, not recognized by anyone in the companies of men who were pursuing the rebels.

Sounds grew distant; there seemed to be a lull in the action, followed by a momentary silence. He was lost in thoughts of Elizabeth. Tears filled his eyes and rolled down his cheeks as he walked head down toward Paul's Wharf. He feared that the worst had befallen her. He tried to console himself with the thought that perhaps she had escaped and returned to the safety of the convent, but he also knew that she would try to protect her brother and be caught up in the melee. As he passed an alleyway, he heard a soft cry coming from within.

His first thought was to avoid the situation, but as unpleasant as it could be, his conscience and curiosity would not let him walk past. He turned and entered into the darkness, stumbling on what were the bloated remains of some poor wretch. He took a step forward. It was hard to see at first, but his eyes were beginning to adjust to the darkness; and he noticed something at the far end in the corner of the alley. It looked like a pile of old rags, but he couldn't be sure. He waited and called out, but there was no reply. Again he waited, beginning to think that he'd imagined it. As he turned to leave, he heard a whimper and looked back. Someone was there! Albert thought it might be a child, but then he heard the loveliest sound.

"Albert!" called a soft, familiar voice.

Without a word, Albert rushed toward her. He

leaned forward to touch her outstretched arms and drew her toward him.

"Elizabeth," he whispered as he held her.

They looked at each other through teary, unbelieving eyes.

"I thought I'd lost you forever," he cried as they both tried to smile. They held each other for a long moment. In the moments they stood together, Albert thought about an earlier time, a time of hopeful youth. It was a time before the rebellion.

Chapter One

The year was 1369. Europe had just begun to shake off the talons of the horrible Black Death that had decimated one third of its population. The Hundred Years War, which had begun thirty years earlier and had been lying dormant, now threatened to reignite. England was about to go through a rebellion; the causes of which began with the feudal order and the want of its abolishment by the peasant class. The Black Death had diminished much of the labor force, making the lower classes more valued as there were fewer to be hired for menial work. Therefore, they were demanding the abolishment of laws that fixed minimum wages. Tile workers and other builders were among those who were most affected by these unfair laws.

For the Tyler family—Peter, his daughter Elizabeth, and especially his son Wat—the laws caused much animosity between them and those who hired them. Such was the case of the Deaconsons of Sudbury. John, his wife Sara, and their son Albert, who owned and operated a business in the wool trade, were despised by the lower classes as much as the nobles were. So it was that they hired the Tylers to remove the old thatched roof of their home and replace it with tile.

"Tile is better than thatch," John had discussed with his wife, "because it is not as likely to catch fire." This conversion of thatch to tile was becoming a trend among the wealthier classes as awareness for safety was becoming more prevalent. For Wat's family, the work was their salvation and an escape from grinding poverty.

Only the silhouettes of the three workmen could be seen against a morning sky as Albert watched from below. He noticed that each one had a particular job—an applicator, a laborer, and a man who did both. The work was hard, especially when the sun rose to its highest point in the often-unforgiving summer sky. He thought about this for a moment and even compared it to his own work.

Albert was the son of a wool merchant and his father's apprentice. He wondered if his strength and agility would match those of the workmen if he were required to do similar work. This thought disturbed him a bit, but he was not sure why. Looking down, he turned and walked toward the barn.

He had to ready the horse and cart and bring it to the front of the house in preparation for the journey to Peterborough. He and his father were to meet an associate, Thomas Hawkins, on the way, and the three would continue on to Peterborough together. There they would pick up their staple of wool of which a portion would be brought home to Sara for household use.

The rest would be shipped to Calais where it would be sold at market.

Calais was an English-controlled port city located on the north coast of France. It was the center of trade for one of England's largest export commodities, wool. It was a very lucrative business, and John Deaconson was among the most successful merchants in the trade.

However, John had not always been a wool merchant and not always an Englishman. He was born Giovanni Dello Iacono, in Florence, Italy and grew up amongst all the political strife that existed there. While his family's party was in power, they enjoyed a lifestyle that was reserved only for the wealthiest classes. However, when that party fell, Giovanni's family lost everything. The only saving grace that Giovanni had was his position as a bodyguard for an English prelate, Simon Sudbury, Bishop of London.

The bishop traveled extensively in Italy, and one of his journeys took him to Rome. There the roads were thick with outlaws who saved their banditti tactics for small groups of travelers and pilgrims. On one occasion, while entering the Papal Marches, the bishop's small retinue was attacked by a band of such outlaws who let their bravado tactics get the best of them. Although they were outnumbered, the escort fought bravely, but it was Giovanni's physical strength and fighting skill that overpowered the outlaws, leaving a few dead and sending the rest to flight. The bishop was so impressed that from then on he had the utmost respect and admiration for this Florentine cavalier.

As politics again changed in Florence, Giovanni became an outsider; therefore, it became too dangerous for him to remain there. Following the bishop's advice, he decided to leave Italy and go to England. Upon entering England, he anglicized his name from the Italian Giovanni DelloIacono to the translated version of John Deaconson.

With the support of the bishop, he entered the wool trade. It was a trade he was not accustomed to, but he rose to the challenges of his new life. A short time thereafter, he met and fell in love with Sara Crecy whose family had been in the wool trade for two generations. They were married, and soon after, they had their only child, Albert.

The time was drawing near to leave for Peterborough. After leading the horse and cart to the front of the house, Albert climbed into the seat to wait for his father to finish up the small details for the journey. As he sat, again he watched the workmen on the roof. One of them, the older man, appeared to be the master and did most of the application of the tiles. The younger man, the apprentice, was also applying tiles, but did some of the laboring work as well. The third man seemed to have the most strenuous job of all. This workman had to fetch the materials for the other two.

Suddenly, one of them stood up, and in a bold voice,

he called from the rooftop, "Would you have any ale for three thirsty workers?"

Albert waved to him and jumped down from the cart. He went into the house and returned with a large pitcher of Sara's brew. He called to the workmen, and the three stood and started down the ladder. The two younger workers waited respectfully while the master roofer quenched his thirst. He thanked Albert and passed the pitcher to his apprentice, who seemed to be the friendliest of the group.

"A fine ale your mother brews, friend. I'll be thankin' ya," he said, wiping his mouth with his sleeve. He passed the pitcher to his laborer. This one was the quietest of the lot, and Albert thought he was a bit strange. He had his head covered with an oversized hood and was much smaller than the other two, and when he reached for the jug, Albert noticed small delicate hands. He may have been just a very young boy, but those hands looked more like a girl's hands than those of any boy, however young he was.

"I don't believe we have met, sir. My name is Wat Tyler," said the apprentice, thrusting his hand out toward Albert. "And this is my father, Peter."

Before Wat could say any more, the third man dropped his hood, and Albert was looking at the most beautiful young girl he had ever seen!

"And this is my sister, Elizabeth."

Albert stared in disbelief as the tumble of long light auburn hair came loose and fell on her shoulders. It took him a moment to regain his composure. He reached out to shake her hand as he bashfully introduced himself.

"How do you do, miss," his voice croaked out.

She smiled with an angelic perfection that took his breath away. Touching the girl's hand and seeing her incredible smile sent Albert's senses reeling. He was sure he had never met anyone quite like her.

"What be *your* name?" asked Wat, bringing Albert out of his trance.

"Albert Deaconson," he answered.

Wat noticed the look in Albert's eyes. It was a look he had been seeing a lot of lately. Elizabeth was blossoming into young womanhood, and every man, young and old, was noticing it. He gave Albert a knowing smile as the others started back toward the ladder.

"She's quite fetching, my sister, isn't she?"

"Yes, quite," said Albert as he lowered his eyes, ashamed of these new stirrings he was experiencing of late.

"Better not let your yearnings get the best of you, my friend," Wat said. "My sister is not one who will be used by uppity merchants as their whore."

"I had not thought of your lovely sister in that way at all!" Albert snapped.

"Then what did you have on your mind?" Wat countered.

Albert's anger calmed as he explained what his true feelings were. "I was taken by surprise by her beauty, is all."

Watt let out a bellowed laugh, Albert understood, for he knew the traditions of his times. For him to have her for a night would be acceptable, but for marriage, it would be completely out of the question. He looked into Albert's eyes and found that spark of truthfulness.

His demeanor changed completely toward his new acquaintance, and he knew he could become a trusted confidant.

Albert wondered what their lives were really like. Wat seemed pleased with his lot and showed a ready smile and friendly manner, but there was another side to him that could be very explosive. His father was quiet but seemed strong and confident. And most importantly, to Albert, the hard work and strife hadn't seemed to affect Elizabeth's disposition or physical appearance.

On the contrary, she seemed very sweet. Her face had a lovely glow, and her body was slender and delicate. She walked with grace; her manner was quiet and demure—she seemed almost regal. He wondered how this lovely and gracious girl could be of such low birth. She was very unlike any of girls Albert was used to with their painted faces and low-cut bodices, always flaunting their overly plump bodies. After meeting Elizabeth, these girls seemed shameless and vulgar. Sensing Albert's curiosity, Wat gave a brief description of his family's history.

"You know, we originated in Colchester, and there were once five members of our family. Peter and Emma, my parents, and us three children; I'm the oldest, then Thomas, and lastly Elizabeth. Shortly after Elizabeth was born, Mother came down with a fever and was dead within a week," he said, bowing his head.

"At first, it didn't seem to be at all serious, but as the week wore on, she broke out in horrible welts that turned a nasty purplish color. Father tried hard to save her. He prayed every day that the illness would pass, and that God would have mercy on our family. But it was not to be, and when he realized she was going to die, he tried to get a priest to give her the last rights. That was not to be either, for many of the priests had left the area for bigger and better paying parishes, and among the less greedy ones, which were few, just one would agree to come. He was William, a parish priest who dedicated his life for the good of others," he continued. "Less than a week after Mother passed on, Thomas showed signs of the illness. Even though he was only a child, he knew that he was about to face the same fate as Mother. He put on a very brave face and told Father not to fret because he was being called to go to heaven to take care of his mother. When he died, we were overcome with grief."

Wat carried on with the tale. "More than ever, Father relied on me to help him take care of Elizabeth. Finally, we moved on, desperate to flee the sickness and sorrow that had devastated our family." Wat took a last drink and handed Albert the pitcher. "Thank you, my friend," he said. Albert took the empty pitcher and looked at Wat.

"How long has this been your family trade?" Albert asked, looking up at the roof.

"We began when tiles were created for the purpose of roofing," replied Wat.

"It seems grueling to work at this every day," said Albert.

"Well yes, I suppose it would seem so, but at least we're able to work and earn a living for ourselves, which is more than we could claim a few years ago."

Albert wasn't sure what he meant and questioned Wat.

"You see, at one time, we worked for the bishop of London, Simon Sudbury." Wat's face took on a sickened and angry look. "He thought he was God, but he was a lecherous bastard!"

Albert looked incredulous. "He's a man of God! Watch what you say!"

"Ha! A man of God, indeed," Wat retorted. "You wouldn't think so if I told what he tried to do to my sister."

"That is blasphemy! Watch your tongue!" Albert cried.

Wat looked at Albert with a smirk that irritated him. "You need to open your eyes and ears to the world, my young friend," he said. "Some people, especially those in power, aren't always what they seem to be. They put on a pious face to hide all their sinful doings."

"Surely you don't really believe that!" Albert said.

"Surely, I do!" Wat snapped back.

"What could this holy man have done to your sister then that would cause such hostility?" asked Albert.

"I cannot say. I only know that she was quite upset when we were finally able to leave Simon's house."

Their conversation was interrupted by Peter's call for Wat to come back to work. He looked up to see his father waving from the roof and turned back to Albert. "I am sorry," he said, placing his large cumbersome hand on Albert's shoulder. "I just get a little carried away sometimes. I have no ill feelings toward you or your family, and please thank your dear mother for the ale."

Albert watched as Wat walked away, still struck by his words. A shiver went through him as he felt for Elizabeth, for what *did* happen with the bishop? He found Wat's story hard to believe. He looked up at them working on the roof, and his eyes fixed on Elizabeth. She was lovely, and he could understand how a man could lose all sense of propriety.

He walked back into the house just as his father was coming out and handed his mother the empty pitcher. He kissed her cheek and walked out the door behind his father, his mind still full of the conversation. Father and son both climbed onto the cart with Peter at the reins. As the cart pulled away, Albert turned and looked up at the roof again. He sat quietly as they traveled through the heavily rutted town road, dodging pigs and fowl that were feasting on discarded garbage that littered the way.

They passed into the surrounding farmlands, and Albert looked out over the field at the peasants hard at work. He watched as they passed a workman standing close to the road. The man looked up as they passed, and Albert could see his face clearly. His thick unkempt growth hid his leathery skin. He was just one of many working in the fields. Albert looked at him for a long moment. Although he had passed by this field many times, it was the first time he'd ever really looked at any of the people working there, and he thought of the Tylers.

As their cart made its way past the farmland and into the forest, Albert asked his father if he had noticed the men working in the fields, especially the one closest to the road.

"Yes, of course, I saw him, and why is he different from the others?"

"Well," said Albert. "Looking at him made me think about his lot in life. Most of them are indebted to landlords who don't treat them as kindly as they should. Like that man, they are pitiful creatures that are driven hard by their masters."

John looked at his son for a long moment. "Albert," he said with a chuckle. "What you see here is just the way of the world. It's the natural order of things. These people are low born," he said, his voice trailing. "There are those, however, who are able to accumulate some wealth and raise their station in life. They become able to purchase a small tract of land and rent it to those who can pay. It's not an easy situation as they must pay the nobles and churchmen their taxes and tithes, but some still manage to make a profit. But we have passed by that field and those workmen many times; why do you now ask about them?"

"I spoke with the lad who is working on our roof," Albert began. "He told me about a time when he and his family had worked for Simon Sudbury." Albert's face turned red as he looked down at his hands.

"What was it he told you?" John asked.

Albert looked at his father's face and could not find the words to explain Wat's story. It was too embarrassing, and he wished he'd never brought up the subject. But John knew Simon; therefore, he didn't push for an answer. "You can't always believe what you hear, son," he said simply. He thought it best not to discuss what Albert had suggested because he knew the power of the clergy and how it could affect his son's well-being if he should repeat what he'd heard. It was a mortal sin to speak ill of a man of God! It was blasphemy!

Still, he remembered many times when Simon had engaged in less than holy affairs with certain young girls and boys he had invited to his palatial residence. They were, at first, excited to be there until they found out why they had been summoned. They always left with tears in their eyes, returning to families who had no recourse for the holy man's lascivious behavior. John later learned that one girl had died by her own hand after her visit. The villagers found her days later, floating face down in a nearby pond.

Albert sat quietly thinking about Elizabeth. She was very young, and a man as prominent as Simon could be quite forceful when he wanted something. He wondered what effect Elizabeth's encounter with Simon had had on her. She would have been little more than a child at the time.

However, what Albert didn't know as yet was that Elizabeth was much stronger than she appeared. She had the intelligence of a much older child, and although slender, she was quite strong physically.

Once again, Albert summoned the courage to tell his father what he had learned about Simon.

"Father, if what Wat says is true, then, what kind of man is Simon? Is he really as godly as he presents himself to be?" he asked.

"I will not have you speak of the bishop in such a way!" he said, his voice rising in anger. "He is a very pious man and would never do what you are implying!"

Albert looked at his father's face and saw it turning as red as his had been earlier, and he knew that his father didn't have to be told what Simon had done to the Tylers.

"You know about Simon, don't you, Father?" he said.

Without another word, John drew back and slapped Albert's face hard enough to send him reeling almost off the cart.

Albert regained his balance and straightened himself as he held his hand over the red stinging welt. He was confused and hurt by his father's behavior. He had always believed his father was a good and decent man, but that being true, how could he defend a scoundrel?

For the remainder of the journey, the two spoke very little. Albert stared at the road ahead and again thought of Elizabeth. She was so very beautiful, and he was quite taken with her; but he knew he would never be allowed to pursue her. He wondered why his father didn't see the unfairness of it all. Why were some people privileged and others downtrodden, and where exactly did he fit into the scheme of things? What was it that was so fascinating about Elizabeth and her family?

The two rode on silently as John kept a watchful eye out for highwaymen as they headed into the forest. Traveling alone could be dangerous as many victims who had survived could attest. John was aware but not afraid. He had been involved in a few roadside encounters but managed to survive.

Peterborough was twenty leagues (eighty miles) from Sudbury and required at least three overnight stays at local inns. The weather and time of day in which a town was passed would determine the number of stops that were made. The general rule was not to be traveling at night. Robbers and animal predators were sure to be about, and even the most seasoned traveler could get lost. The roads were unmarked, and they all looked alike after dark.

Chapter Two

The inn was a welcome sight for John and Albert. After their evening meal of warm ale, cheese, and bread, they would rent one of the few beds that were provided. Retiring for the night, they found themselves in the same bed with another weary traveler along with a host of microscopic patrons that dined on them as they slept.

The sounds of morning came with the ringing of the Angelus bells. John and Albert as well as the other guests that had stayed the night rose for the day. They started down the stairs, scratching feverishly and yawning loudly as they entered the public room for their morning meal. After paying their bill, they prepared the wagon and started off in the morning rain.

It wasn't long before the fog and rain forced them to get out and lead the wagon through the rutted road. Albert reached in for a hatchet, which he used to chop branches that had randomly fallen in their path. This time he used it to cut saplings for probing puddles, making sure they were not deep enough to overturn the cart. John took the reins and led the horse as his son walked ahead.

After a while, Albert encountered a gaping hole in the road that appeared quite deep. Measuring its depth, it seemed to be bottomless. Albert motioned to his father to come closer. As John approached, he could see the apparent problem at hand. It looked like a pond. He gently pushed Albert away from the edge. "You never know how big this could be," he said. "This is not an ordinary puddle. It could be as deep as ten feet. From the look of its boundaries, it could be quite deep indeed."

It was a rare thing to see one this big, but John was aware that it was possible that when a road was not traveled regularly like this one, people may not give a thought to digging up and removing the clay to repair their mills or houses. The heavy rain added to the problem, making the holes bigger and eventually collapsing into a very large crater.

They noticed another path cut through on the side of the road by other carts who had passed by earlier, so they followed the tracks. As they approached the other side, John noticed something protruding out of the water. He jumped down, taking Albert's hatchet to cut down another sapling. He walked to the edge of the hole and prodded the object. John quickly made the sign of the cross, for under the water he saw a lifeless corpse trapped under his overturned wagon.

"What is it?" Albert called.

"A man's body," cried John.

Albert walked over and stared wide-eyed. Upon

looking closer and deeper into the water, they noticed the horse further below the surface. Apparently, an inexperienced traveler, underestimating the depth, tried to cross. His horse had stumbled and fell in, dragging the cart and the man in with it. John returned to the wagon.

"Let us say a prayer for the poor man's soul," he said. They resumed their journey and planned to report the incident to the clergy when they reached Cambridge.

Soon it had stopped raining, and it looked as though the sun would appear. John hoped to regain some of the time lost at the delay. As much as he hated to push his horse, he knew he had to in order to reach Cambridge by nightfall. They arrived just as the bells began ringing in Compline at 9 p.m. They jumped down from the wagon, tugging at their semidry clothes that stuck uncomfortably to their bodies.

They stood at the Hawkins' front door, and John gave a heavy-handed knock. Within moments the door swung open, and standing there was a large barrel-chested man sporting a thick black beard. He smiled broadly, showing the gap between his two front teeth.

"John! How are you?" he bellowed as he grasped John's extended hand and pulled him into an embrace.

"I'm well, Thomas, but the trip was a bit trying," he said as he motioned to Albert to secure the horse and wagon. "We would have arrived a little earlier but for the rain."

Albert soon followed his father onto the doorstep.

"Hello, Albert!" bellowed Thomas as he thrust his hand toward him. "It's good to see you, lad!"

Albert smiled and accepted Thomas' hand.

"How are you, sir?" he said.

"Very well, indeed," Thomas replied.

His wife Anne came from the counting room in the rear of the house to greet her guests. Anne was a pretty, petite, dark-haired woman with a full figure. She held her hand out to John and smiled.

"Hello, John," she said, kissing his cheeks. She turned to Albert. "My, my, Albert, you get more handsome every time I see you."

Albert blushed red, and that made her chuckle. She was followed by the Hawkins' children, Margery and Peter, who had taken leave of their carding for the moment to greet their friends.

Carding and spinning had recently become a new extension of the trade for the two families. While Thomas and John shipped and sold wool on the continent, their families had become involved in the growing industry of spinning the wool into thread and selling it to the local weavers who would then work the threads into cloth.

In the past, England had provided wool to Flemish and Italian merchants who in turn would produce and sell cloth for a great profit. Eventually, Edward III noticed and began cloth production in England. In time it would become England's primary industry, overshadowing the Flemish and Italian producers and adding great wealth to England's economy.

Margery held her hands out to Albert and kissed both his cheeks. "How are you?" she asked, smiling.

"I'm well," he replied, smiling back at her.

"It does my heart good to see you, Albert," she said, still holding his hands and looking at him adoringly.

He gently removed his hands from hers and turned to greet her brother as John told the family about their ghastly experience on the road. He asked Anne if she would kindly report it to the parish, and she readily agreed.

Thomas and Anne escorted their guests to the table where Anne served ale. In between the beck and call of her husband, she prepared a meal of salt fish and vegetables. As the men drank, they discussed their impending journey to Peterborough and other important issues of business. By that time Anne was serving up the evening meal. They began by saying grace before enjoying the fair. Soon after, all retired for the night. The three men would have to be off early to avoid the congestion on the busy narrow road that would take them out of town.

The morning bells of the nearby churches and university woke the household. Thomas and Anne awoke first, and John heard them waking their children. He gave a tug to Albert, pulling him back from his world of dreams. They all dressed, took their turns using the privy, which was off the sleeping room, and went downstairs. In the kitchen, Anne served up eggs, brown bread, and cheese with hearty ale she had brewed the day before. They quietly ate the morning meal, and soon they said their good-byes.

Albert, John, and Thomas readied their wagons, filling them with all that they would need for the journey to Peterborough including some dried meat, cheese, and ale to have on the way. The wagons pulled away and had gotten only a few feet when a sudden screech gave testimony that Thomas' wheel had killed one of the many chickens and other fowl that wandered through the streets. It wouldn't be long before the poor creature would be a meal for other critters that roamed the same town.

As they turned the corner, a dung cart making its weekly rounds was slowly proceeding toward the gatehouse. A swarm of flies and other flying insects had formed a small cloud above the cart. In an attempt at public health and for safety of the traffic, they would clean the streets of animal and human waste and garbage, all of which had been thrown indiscriminately out of windows and doorways.

Upon reaching the gatehouse, a cast of characters began collecting to await entrance into the city. The sound of their voices was loud, and words were garbled as each engaged in their own conversations. All were coming into Cambridge for various reasons, some seemly and some not. There was a friar, his gray robe draped around a rotund belly that jiggled as he gave an uncomfortable nudge to the man standing in front of him. A colorfully dressed knight stood with his young squire and waited patiently. The fishmonger was also present with his cart of salted fish, waiting in hopes of selling his catch to the large populace, so he could return home richer than when he came. And then there were the Italian moneylenders. They were sleek, dark-eyed, and crafty, and they gestured verbosely with their hands when engaged in conversation. They were sometimes looked upon as suspicious due to their financing of the king and their role as collectors of Papal tithes.

They also had monopoly on the finest wool, which they traded with many of the great abbeys.

These were just a few of the many who awaited entrance. The gatekeepers watched as the wagons approach from inside the gate. They signaled all to stand aside to let their wagons through. They passed a hostile crowd overly eager to gain access to the city. They hurled insults and spat at the men as they passed. Even the reverend friar gave a less than holy gesture.

The wagons continued through the crowd and out into the countryside where they were greeted by the serene coolness provided by the morning fog that shrouded the low-lying field. Their first stop of the journey was St. Ives, which was the halfway point between Cambridge and Peterborough. Also, St. Ives was a village well known for its international fair that drew merchants from everywhere from Scandinavia to Italy.

The journey for the first league was uneventful. They crossed paths of various vendors and fellow merchants that were making their ways to towns near and far. The kidney-shaking ride would force the three to stop periodically to relieve themselves. It was not long after one of their nature stops that they came upon a congestion of traffic on the roadway. John gave a tug on the reins to slow the horse. He turned to motion to Thomas behind him to stop.

"What's the holdup?" Thomas bellowed.

John jumped down and walked back to the other wagon. "I'll go and see what it is," he said to Thomas.

"Goddammit!" Thomas grumbled. "Wait, I'll go with you."

They passed a couple of wagons and carts where some drivers waited patiently while others waved their fists and shouted obscenities in frustration. The merchants walked up to the source of the delay. It was a wagon driven by a parish priest and his entourage of fire and brimstone religious zealots who where returning from St. Thomas à Becket in Canterbury.

"Need any help?" asked Thomas.

"Good morning to you, sirs," said the priest as he held out his hand. "We are just about to finish repairs," he said smiling. Soon the wheel was repaired and placed back on its axel. The group climbed back onto the wagon, and the priest gave a brief benediction to all and promised they would spend eternity in paradise. He climbed aboard the wagon and made a hasty departure.

They arrived in St. Ives during vespers at 6:00 p.m. and found an inn where they spent the night. The three decided to enjoy the ale served, and after a while, Thomas began to get boisterous. With a leering grin, he pointed at Albert. "When are you going to marry my daughter, lad?" he bellowed. He laughed uproariously at the look on Albert's face.

Albert never expected such a question. He was at a loss for words and looked to his father for an answer. John just smiled sheepishly at him and shrugged his shoulders. Years earlier, he and Thomas had betrothed the two, and now John knew he should think of a way to tell Albert about the plan. It had never occurred to Albert that there would be such a plan, and he certainly never considered marriage to her.

Oh, Margery was a nice quiet girl, and she was

pretty in a modest sort of way; but Albert was definitely not interested in her in that way. He liked her well enough, but in the same way he liked her brother. He never thought of her as a wife.

John had other ideas about his son and Margery. He thought they were a good match. "As soon as your lovely daughter becomes of age, sir," he fired back much to Albert's amazement. Albert thought about what was said for a long moment and reassured himself that it was just talk between two semidrunken friends.

Finally, the three decided to turn in for the night. The sleeping accommodations were less than desirable, but they were lucky to get shelter at all. The summer shearing season had just begun, and there were many merchants in town. This left John, Thomas, and Albert as well as many other late arrivals sleeping on the dormitory floor. They didn't mind the hardness of the floor as much as having to sleep with the rats that were attracted by the vomit, urine, spit, and rancid food that was seldom swept away by the innkeeper. Many who laid their bodies down would pay no heed to the disgusting varmints as the ale flowed freely, and most were too drunk to care about what they were sleeping with.

It was late when one of the drunken patrons and fellow merchant stumbled out the door into the darkness. He was brought back a few hours later by the night watch beaten and robbed. It remained a mystery as to who was responsible for the assault, but it was well known that a wise person didn't wander the streets at night. He could very well become easy prey for bandits who lurked about waiting for a hapless victim who was too drunk to fight back, or it could even be the night watch himself who under the guise of protector would attack as soon as a back was turned.

To Albert's misfortune, the man was dropped beside him. He lay there groaning loudly, and Albert thought it best to get him some water. He felt sorry for the man, but he also knew that if he didn't help, he would be listening to it all night. He got up and walked to the back of the establishment where the innkeeper was tallying his earnings for the evening. Startled by the intrusion, he rudely asked Albert what he wanted.

"Sorry to bother you, sir," Albert said politely. "Could I have some water and a cloth?"

The man pointed to a bucket in the corner. Albert picked up the bucket filled with vile smelling water and brought it to the man, who had by now fallen asleep and was snoring loudly. Not wanting to wake him, Albert rested the bucket on the floor nearby in the event that he would need it later.

Finally, he laid himself down and thought of the beautiful peasant girl and her brother. He fell into an exhausted sleep, trying to understand the meaning of what Wat had said. He had never heard anyone speak in that way, and thoughts of Wat's lovely sister danced their way into his mind as he drifted into sleep. Soon the innkeeper's candle went out and the sounds of snoring and only an occasional belch or fart broke the silence.

The morning bells ushered in a new day, but they were ignored by many of the guests. The innkeeper made his rounds, waking the patrons whose night of hard drinking made them as helpless as babies. "Up with you! Up you, bastards!" he yelled, giving a hard nudge to anyone in his way. Everyone began to rise, stretching and scratching themselves unceremoniously. Soon everyone was on their feet—all but one.

The battered merchant who had wandered out during the night lay motionless at Albert's feet. He motioned to the innkeeper. As soon the innkeeper's foot made contact with the man, he knew that he was dead. He could tell by the familiar stiffness of the body.

He got down on his hands and knees for a closer look.

"The damn fool is dead," he said, looking up at Albert.

Albert looked at the dead man as the innkeeper walked away, grumbling unsympathetically about how he would have to dispose of the body. Some of the patrons, including Albert, John, and Thomas, quickly made the sign of the cross and said a silent prayer. Those who knew the man would bring the sad news to his family if he had one.

The overcast skies of the morning were as somber as the patrons' moods. John and Thomas paid the innkeeper for the evening and were on their way. This was to be their last stop before their final destination. Even though the skies were cloudy, there were no heavy rains to hamper the journey. The roads too were in much better condition than the one they had previously traveled.

They reached Peterborough by early afternoon. This was the leading wool center of the day. It contained large monasteries, which produced the finest wool in the world. Unfortunately, John and Thomas could not buy this wool because it had already been sold to large Flemish and Italian firms. They would have to make contact with the small peasant growers that provided lower quality wool to the smaller independent merchants. However, there were times when the peasant flocks were combined, and the grazing would be comparable to that of the larger monasteries giving the smaller merchant a choice of the best quality wools.

This time they went to William Wallsingham, a grower with a flock of about fifty sheep to make their purchase, only to find that Wallsingham had raised his prices to ten shillings per sack. John and Thomas were outraged. Thomas, a man who would not let his thoughts be contained, voiced himself quite strongly.

"What? Ten shillings for this rubbish?" he yelled.

"You know this wool is not the same quality as that of the abbeys," John said in a more reasonable tone.

Wallsingham avoided looking and speaking to Thomas and appealed to John.

"However," he responded. "These sheep graze alongside the lord's in the same field."

John and Thomas examined the wool again, and after much bickering over price, they finally agreed on nine shillings. They spent the next day as they did this one, shopping and bargaining for wool. On the morning of the third day, their wagons were loaded to capacity, and they began their long journey home.

Chapter Three

The gentle morning breeze was a welcome relief from the hot, sticky days of summer. As they rode out of the town and into the quiet countryside with Thomas not far behind, both father and son were quietly thinking their own separate thoughts. Of late, John had been concerned about his son ever since he learned that Albert had had troubling thoughts about his own future. He didn't like the turn Albert's ideas were taking.

This made John think about his own youth, and he struggled to remember how it felt to be young.

"Albert," he said suddenly.

Albert startled by the sudden abruptness of his voice looked at his father.

It took John a long moment to begin, and Albert looked at him expectantly. Finally, John began. "Son," he said hesitantly. "Have I ever told you about my youth?"

"No, sir," he said as he listened intently.

"Well, I was very young when I became a knight."

Albert's eyes widened.

"I was a knight of the eminent city of Florence," he said. "And I'm very proud of our Lombard heritage. We were one of the strongest of the Northern Italian cities," he continued. "Our merchants and bankers amassed such wealth that we even provided financial assistance to the English king's wars in France."

"Why did you leave to become a wool merchant here?" Albert asked. John looked at him, and Albert could see the sadness in his father's eyes.

"Italy is a strange land," he said, looking back at the road. "The Italian people have been divided since the days of Rome. When the sixteen cities of Northern Italy united, they defeated Holy Roman Emperor Fredrick Barbarosa in the battle of Legnano. Unfortunately, petty differences and squabbling between regions and cities even differences within the same parties have left much of Italy a land where its people are divided. It was the reason I came to England. I was banished," John said sadly.

"Banished! Why?" asked Albert.

"You see, the Guelphs was the party to which I belonged and the one that supported the Pope. The Ghibilines was the opposing party and gave its support to the emperor. At the time of my banishment, my party controlled all of Florence. The fighting began within the party, and it fractured into two, the White Guelphs and the Black Guelphs. I found myself on the side of the White Guelphs, who were beaten. I was then without a party, and the only choice I had to maintain my dignity and wealth was to come here and start a new life."

They continued to talk about John's past and, more importantly, Albert's future until John noticed a disturbance in the road ahead. His eyes grew wide as he yanked on the reins, and the wagon began moving faster toward the commotion. As he gained speed, Thomas struggled to keep up. He didn't notice the disturbance at first and wondered why John was going so fast. He quickly looked behind and to the sides of his wagon, checking for highwaymen and then moving ahead again. Now, he was close enough to see the reason why John had sped up his pace.

It appeared to be an outlaw attack on a small group of knights. As they drew closer, they could hear the sound of heavy double-edged swords clanging and the screaming curses of the combatants. Thomas stood with reins in hand, trying to keep up.

Going as fast as the horse would run without toppling the wagon, John raced with Albert hanging on to the sides of his seat. He looked over at his father. John's face was rigid, his eyes glinting, and there was a hint of a grin on his lips. *He is no longer a merchant,* thought Albert as he watched his father. *He is a knight!*

Within the next few moments, both wool carts were thrust into the melee. John reached back behind his seat and pulled out his sword, which he kept with him at all times, but it had been a very long time since he'd had to use it. He ordered Albert to get into the back and hide between the bales of wool. John leapt off the cart even before it stopped moving, and Thomas was not far behind, wielding his dagger.

Disregarding his father's orders, Albert grabbed the reins and stopped the wagon. He jumped down and reached into the back for his ax. He started running toward the fight on trembling legs with his ax raised in a shaking hand. As he approached, one of the knights blocked his path, so Albert pushed as hard as he could past him. He stood helplessly as he watched his father's skilled use of the sword. The knights were outnumbered, but with John and Thomas' help, they began to gain on the enemy.

As Albert watched, one of the outlaws approached his father's back. Albert shook violently but managed to raise his ax. He yelled as he ran toward the outlaw and drove the ax deep between the man's shoulder blades. He heard bones cracking and saw blood gushing. He stood trembling as he watched the massive hulk of a man collapse onto his knees, and then his large torso hit the ground with a sickening thud. Suddenly, Albert's stomach lurched, and he quickly turned from the scene and violently vomited onto the ground. He had witnessed people die before, but it was the first time he had actually caused a man's death.

John turned around after dispatching his opponent to see his son wiping his ashen face with his sleeve. "You've got knighthood in your blood, son," he said with a wide grin.

Suddenly, his grin turned to a grimace as a wounded outlaw came from behind him to deliver one last blow. He caught John's side, grazing him with his sword. John staggered as Albert raised his ax to finish the outlaw, but Thomas was quicker.

He threw his dagger, which hit its mark with exact

precision. The outlaw dropped his sword and frantically tried to remove the knife that was stuck in his lower back. His body now sapped of strength stumbled backward, pushing the dagger into his back up to the hilt. He lay on the ground wreathing in agony.

As the victors surveyed the bloody sight, they noticed four of the outlaws lay dead and one was mortally wounded. There was also one knight on the ground with a large crease in his helmet made by the vicious blow of a battle-ax, which was enough to cause his demise. One of the knights stood leaning on his sword,

"Thank God you arrived when you did, sirs," he said, breathing heavily. "Our cause appeared to be lost. We had dispatched our squires to Peterborough to announce our arrival at the monastery. We did not expect to be waylaid so close to the city. Pardon, but I'm forgetting my manners. My name is Sir Richard Stury," he said, then pointed to the other knight. "And this is Sir Robert Wellingham, and what are your names?"

"John Deaconson," John said in his accented English. "This is my son Albert and my associate Thomas Hawkins. We are wool merchants and were visiting Peterborough on business; we're now trying to make our way back home."

"You handle yourselves quite well for merchants," said Sir Richard. "Where do you come from then?" he asked.

Just then they heard a groan issued from one of the men on the ground. Sir Richard looked around at the bodies and noticed an outlaw who was slightly writhing and moaning in pain. He picked up his sword and quite calmly walked over to him.

Looking down at the man, he dug his gold spur into the side of the man's head. The outlaw let out a loud groan. Sir Richard then planted his feet firmly on the ground, vertically raised his sword, and without a moment's hesitation brought the sword down through the man's ribcage. The outlaw gasped his last breath of air and then lay motionless. Sir Richard kneeled down beside the body and wiped his sword clean on the man's clothes. He stood and returned his sword to its scabbard before walking back toward the group of men.

"Please excuse the interruption," he said nonchalantly as if it was nothing to end another man's life.

John's wound was still bleeding, and he was beginning to feel faint. He held onto his side and began to answer Sir Richard's question when he started to topple forward. Sir Richard and Thomas reached out to hold him up. They picked him up and carried him to a grassy clearing where they gently laid him down with Albert following close behind. Sir Richard raised John's tunic and examined the wound. He turned to Sir Robert and ordered him to tear a piece of cloth from one of the dead outlaws, which he folded and handed to Sir Richard who placed it on the wound.

"Albert, hold this firmly," he said.

Albert put his hand on the cloth and pressed gently to stop the bleeding.

"He's lost some blood, but it hasn't affected his innards," Sir Richard said, taking notice of Albert's concerned expression.

Albert kneeled, tending his father as Thomas and

the knights unceremoniously began dragging the bodies of the outlaws to the side of the road. They were dragging the last when Thomas looked up the road to see someone approaching in the distance.

"Who's this now?" he asked, alerting the two knights.

All three stood, looking curiously as the rider approached. As he drew closer, they realized that he was a friar on his way to Peterborough. He stopped his mule as he gave a glancing survey over the bloody scene and offered services for the dead.

"Yes, Father. Please, we have a fallen brother," Sir Richard replied, pointing to his noble comrade. The friar gently dismounted his mule, walked over, and with a dubiously dramatic flare, knelt down beside the body. His head bowed, he gave his benediction as the others watched his fine theatrical performance.

"This brave knight is already with the Lord," he announced gracefully.

"Father, we also have a man wounded. We would be most thankful if you would say a prayer for him as well."

The friar made his way to John and Albert, bowed his head and prayed aloud in Latin. Concluding his prayer, he turned and gave Sir Richard a look that was all too well known.

"Thank you, Father," Sir Richard said as he took out his money pouch and handed the so-called man of God a coin. The friar gave a wide grin and a bow of gratitude as he departed a bit wealthier than when he arrived.

Albert looked on as the whole scenario unfolded

and wondered if the good friar would have wasted his time on a poor peasant who could not pay. Thomas and the knights completed the gruesome task of removing the bodies of the outlaws to the side of the road, leaving them to rot.

"Albert," Sir Richard called. "Remove the compress and see if the wound still bleeds."

He did as he was told. The wound looked better, and the bleeding had subsided. He replaced the blood-soaked cloth with another and tied it on with a rope he had retrieved from the wagon.

Sir Richard recommended that John return to Peterborough to have the wound tended and asked to use their wagon to take his comrade there for a proper burial. The three merchants agreed, and in return the remaining knights would escort their wagons into the city.

As Sir Richard and Thomas lifted the knight's stiffened body into Thomas' wagon, Sir Robert went to the clearing to retrieve their horses.

"Sir Richard," he called. "Come at once!"

Thomas and Richard started toward him. Sir Robert stood with his head bowed, but he looked up as they approached.

"I'm afraid your horse is lame, sir," he said sadly.

Sir Richard took the reins and walked the animal forward to find that it was true.

"Sweet Jesus," he murmured as he bowed his head.

He looked into his stallion's eyes and cried out. The tears filling his eyes blurred his vision, and he wept openly. Thomas stood silent as he watched this strong, brave knight whose prowess in battle was widely acclaimed break down at the untimely loss of his most treasured possession.

The knight knew what he had to do. He took a deep breath, and with all the courage he could muster, he drew his sword. He made the sign of the cross, grasped the sword with both hands trembling, brought it to the horse's shoulder blades, and with a heavy heart, thrust the sword into the proud beast. The horse neighed loudly and collapsed to the ground.

Sir Richard paused over his fallen steed, removed his mantle, and covered his noble companion with it. He called on Thomas and Sir Robert to remove all accessories from the animal as he could not bear to do it himself. He took the reins of the remaining horses and walked back toward the wagons.

Finally, they were ready to begin the trip back to Peterborough with one knight leading the wagons and the other bringing up the rear. When they arrived at the gatehouse, the gatekeeper gave the entry signals as soon as the royal standard had been recognized. They headed toward the abbey where Sir Richard, being a king's knight, was able to quickly secure the services of the monks.

John's wound was not life threatening, but even a slight wound such as his was subject to infection. Albert and Thomas remained with John as he received treatment while the two knights left to make arrangements for their fallen comrade.

Their squires had arrived much earlier and met them at the abbey. When they heard the news of Sir David's death, they lowered their heads in prayer, and his own squire was overcome with grief.

The monks unloaded the body from Thomas' wagon and brought it into the infirmary. They laid the body on a wooden table. Albert who had never seen this procedure before took a keen interest as he remained with his father nearby and watched as the monks prepared the body for burial. He was amazed to see Sir David's limbs in such an odd position. The left arm remained upward above his head, and his left leg was bent. As he remembered, the limbs were perfectly straight and flexible when the body was loaded onto the wagon.

However, unbeknownst to him, the jarring wagon ride and rigor mortis setting in, which usually occurs within several hours after death, would account for the odd position of the limbs.

His condition would surly present a problem when they tried to bury him; therefore, the two monks prepared to remedy the situation. One man held on to one side of Sir David while the other pulled the arm down. They did the same to straighten his leg. The sound of cracking bone made Albert wince and turn away. The monks continued by stripping the body and washing it down with perfumed water. They anointed Sir David with balsam and balm, encased him in a linen shroud, and sewed him in deerskin. Finally, they laid him into a burial pier and carried him to the chapel.

As John lay being treated by Brother Sebastian, a fever was beginning to take its grip. The brother was not very skilled, but he was the best the abbey had to offer. John had lost a fair amount of blood, and the wound was deep. Brother Sebastian carefully removed the compress. He examined the wound and felt John's forehead. He asked Albert to go to the kitchen for egg whites, which he spread on the wound as gently as he could and covered it with a clean cloth. He then tied the cloth on with the rope just as the dinner bell rang. With his stomach erupting with hunger pangs, the brother wasted no time finishing up his job on his patient and was on his way before Albert and John could thank him.

Thomas reentered the infirmary and was walking toward them. "I've finished feeding and watering the horses," he said. "How is your father faring?"

"I suppose he will be all right. The brother didn't take the time to explain Father's condition. He rushed off to dinner," said Albert.

Thomas let out a hearty guffaw. "Ha! So it was the dinner bell then," he said laughing. "These monks would brave the demons of hell for food and drink, which reminds me that we should go and have something to eat ourselves."

Albert agreed, looking down at his father.

"He'll rest until we return," said Thomas reassuringly.

Albert nodded, and he and Thomas started toward the dining hall. They soon returned, bringing food for John, but he had no appetite and was still feverish. He asked for water, which Albert fetched from the well near the rear wall of the grounds. As he approached the well, he heard a multitude of squabbling voices outside the wall. Curious, he climbed on the rim of the well and peaked over. He watched as one of the monks tossed scraps of food to a group of beggars and outcasts. With every toss, the monk let out a burst of laughter as the pitiful rabble clawed and scratched one another for every morsel. The monk's eye caught sight of Albert.

"Come over the wall, my son," he said, inviting him to join in the carnival-like atmosphere. He let out another roar of laughter that caused tremors to ripple over his portly physique. Albert shook his head in sad amazement as he climbed down from the well. *Everyone throws scraps to the beggars,* he thought, *but never before have I seen it done with such little regard for human dignity.*

As Albert walked away from the well and the disgusting display he had just witnessed, once again he remembered Wat's words and was beginning to understand his contempt for the clergy. But he knew that not all members of the clergy were like the one making sport of the beggars. Some were decent and good—true men of God.

He brought the water to his father and wet his forehead and lips with his fingertips. Soon John took a sip of water and quickly fell asleep. Soon the friars appeared and assisted in carrying John to their sleeping quarters.

Chapter Four

All slept soundly and were awakened the next morning by a light tap on the door. Albert awoke and stretched as Thomas groaned, feeling the aches and pains from the previous day's battle. He looked over at John who was still asleep. Albert got to his feet and went to his father to wake him, but John's condition was not improving; and he needed help to sit up.

"How are you feeling this morning?" asked Thomas as he and Albert helped John to his feet.

"I'll be fine," he said, trying to stand erect.

They spent a few moments shaking the sleep from their bodies before leaving for their morning meal.

Sir Richard and Sir Robert sat with their squires at a long dining table eating heartily when the merchants entered. Sir Robert looked up from his plate with bread dangling from his mouth and waved for them to join him and his party.

"Move down, good brothers," he said to those who

were sitting beside him. "Make way for these brave and noble merchants who saved our lives," he said, cheerfully. "It takes a lot of grit for a man to do what you three did yesterday, especially when you're not in the business of war."

As they ate and talked, a monk entered the dining hall with some urgency and approached their table. "Prince Edward has arrived!" he announced. The knights sprang to their feet, wiping food, and drink from their faces. Sir Richard looked down at the merchants who were still seated.

"I think you'd best come along," he said.

Albert and Thomas stood without hesitation and helped John to his feet. They followed the knights into the courtyard where they were struck by the lofty appearance of a grand figure clad in royal attire and sitting on a most graceful black mare.

They stood before their lord, Prince Edward of Wales, the Aquitaine hero of the French wars and next in line for the throne. All the men bowed graciously as Edward gazed at his subjects.

Sir Richard stepped forward, "My lord, may I introduce Thomas Hawkins, a merchant from Cambridge, John Deaconson, and his son Albert, also merchants from Sudbury, whose courage is of the most heroic virtue, even the lad's bravery is equal to that of his elders."

The prince dismounted and held his arm forward; the three merchants bowed and kissed his hand in turn. "My lord," they said as the bowed their heads. A cheer went up in the courtyard as they looked up at the prince.

Edward raised his hand to quiet the group. "To these loyal men of the realm, my deepest gratitude," he said. "In times of danger, there are many who could not maintain composure. They become paralyzed with fear and do not know what course of action to follow, but gentlemen, you were able to keep a presence of mind in spite of the danger and managed to save two of my knights from certain death. Your courage befits the most noble of knights," he continued. "I am eternally grateful to you and offer you my services if at any time in the future you are in need. To insure your safe journey, I will order Sir Robert and Sir Richard, their squires, and a small troupe to escort you to your homes," he said.

Another cheer went up as the prince remounted his horse, and he and his entourage made their way toward the chapel to pray for the soul of their fallen knight, Sir David.

With Sir Richard, Sir Robert, and a small company of men, the merchants left Peterborough. As they exited the city walls, Sir Richard pointed to something a few paces ahead. In the grass as they passed, a young couple lay, making love among the tall grain stocks, and were completely oblivious to the company passing by.

"Look yonder," said Sir Richard with a chuckle. "We should be so lucky."

They all gave a hearty laugh and cheered as the couple looked up in surprise upon hearing their approach. Albert craned his neck to see what the couple was doing. At first he didn't see the humor, but as he drew closer, he began to understand. He laughed with the others but with a red face. The older men turned to see his reaction, and that made them laugh all the more. For the lovers, this was a minor intrusion on their privacy. Making love in a grain field was far more private than being in their own home where privacy was nonexistent.

On the road they passed a small number of merchants, farmers, and ecclesiastics making their way to Peterborough. Soon they approached the place where the melee had taken place the day before. Sir Richard looked out over the field where his steed's carcass lay in tatters and with bits scattered about by wolves and birds that fought over the grizzly remains.

The troupe now caught the stench of the rotting flesh of the fly-infested remains of the outlaws and turned away, disgusted at the sight of them lying in the ditch on the side of the road.

Albert looked down at the bodies also, but his thoughts were different from those of the others. *What made these men become outlaws?* He wondered. *Was it greed? Was it adventure? Or was it as Wat Tyler would say—desperation?* He tried to see the situation from the point of view of the outlaws and agreed that it was the will to live in spite of their station in life.

Deep inside him he began to realize that churchmen and nobles didn't give many of the poorer folks any alternative. He turned and looked at his father's pale face as he lay in the back of the wagon with his eyes closed. Although John never complained, he knew his father was in pain. He couldn't bear to see him this way, and it frightened and angered him. His mixed feelings about the whole incident confused him, especially since he had also killed one of them, but he had no choice. It was a perfect stranger or his father. Still, the thought depressed him, and he prayed God would help him to find the right way.

The wagon rolled along as Albert's mind drifted. His eyes were fixed on the back of one of the escorting knights. With each parting of the tree branches, the sun's light glistened through, reflecting off his helmet and sending blinding light into Albert's eyes. He noticed the knight's blue mantle how it flowed gracefully from his shoulders and gently draped over the backside of his black steed. To Albert he looked quite regal sitting atop his horse. He imagined himself as a noble knight with the glory of battle and the romance of heroism. He thought again of Wat and his contempt for nobles and churchmen. Yes, they did have it all at the expense of the downtrodden. Did he really want to be a part of that? He wasn't sure. He knew in his heart that all would be justified when everyone got to heaven, which those in power would have to pay for their abuses. What would Wat have to say about this? He wondered. Perhaps he would agree.

A large rut in the road brought Albert back to reality as the wagon bounced uncomfortably. He turned to see if his father had been affected. "Are you all right, Father?" he asked.

John did not seem disturbed as he lay among the bales of wool. His eyes opened, and he gave a smile and a nod. Reassured, Albert turned his attention back to the road.

Two days of uneventful travel brought the party to Trumysing Gate in Cambridge where the royal escort and the merchants parted company. "We'll bid you farewell, now," said Sir Richard. "May God go with you all. I shall dedicate a Mass for your father's speedy recovery," he added, looking at Albert.

"Many thanks for your escort," said Thomas. "And may God go with you also." Albert nodded a thank you to Sir Richard as they started toward the bustling town and Thomas' house.

At the Hawkins household, the wool spinning was slowed by Anne, who nervously interrupted her work to walk to the window at the slightest noise that sounded like the wheels of her husband's cart. Over and over again, she had been disappointed until finally, with a sigh of relief, she watched the two wagons roll to a stop in front of the house. She stepped back quickly from the window so that Thomas wouldn't see her and rushed back to her spinning wheel.

"Is that father?" asked Peter.

"It is," answered Anne.

The sound of Thomas' heavy footsteps brought a sense of elation to Anne who always worried whenever he was away. Thomas opened the door and stood looking at his wife with a large grin, but she knew there was something amiss. As the children jumped up and ran into his arms, she looked into his eyes.

"Is anything wrong? Why were you delayed?" she asked.

Still looking at her, he picked Margery up and kissed her soft cheek. He put his arm around Peter and hugged him.

"I will explain later, but first, we have need of treatment for John as he is wet with fever," he said, turning back outside to help Albert with his father. By now the fever was soaring, and John could barely walk even with help.

Anne hurried to the second floor to prepare a cot for him. She had just completed the task when Albert and Thomas carried him in and laid him down. He shivered with small tremors as Anne removed his tunic to examine the wound. She sent Albert to get a basin of warm water and a knife to cut the bloodstained bandages that had been applied earlier. With it she cut the rope that held the wraps in place. She attempted to remove the bandage, but it had stuck to the wound. She plied it with warm water and gently pulled it free. As she did, John jerked in pain.

She examined the very swollen wound that dripped with pus and blood and became outraged at the callousness with which he had been treated.

"To whose incompetence do I attribute this medical travesty?" she asked indignantly.

"It was a brother at the abbey," Thomas said.

"Those monks know less than a common housewife when it comes to medicine, and they couldn't care less," said Anne in disgust. "This is beyond my realm of knowledge," she said. "We must find a surgeon to help."

Thomas nodded and without a word was out the door to summon one. Albert stared down at his stricken father with concern.

"Will he be all right?" he asked.

Anne, not wanting to cause any undo worry for Albert, assured him that his father would be fine.

It was not long before Thomas secured the service of one of the many medical men in Cambridge. When the surgeon arrived, his first task was to set his sand glass in order to take John's pulse.

John, although feverish, was still conscious and aware of the doctor's presence. He asked John to urinate into a mug, which he took to the window to examine in the bright daylight. He then sniffed it, dipped his pinky into the cup, and gave his diagnoses of a serious infection. His remedy was simple; he would pierce the wound and drain it of its poison. He reached into his satchel for a lancet, and with his steady, healing hand, he punctured the infected wound, which began a steady flow of puss and blood.

He gently pressed the area to quicken the process. Everyone save the good doctor winced as John gave a loud groan. Turning to Anne, the doctor asked for a bottle of wine, which he poured over the wound.

"This will help in the healing process," he said, answering the puzzled look on everyone's face.

Anne and Thomas, not taking much stock in his explanation, stared as the expensive French import dripped from the bed and formed a pool on the floor. But if the doctor thought it would help, they supposed it had been used for a good cause.

Now the wound was ready to be bandaged. The surgeon called on Anne once more to bring some clean rags. Then he employed Thomas to help hold John still while he wrapped the wound as gently as he could.

Finished, he prescribed a diet of herbs, chicken

broth, and the milk of pulverized almonds. "It's now in God's hands," he said.

"Will you sup with us?" asked Anne.

"No," he said as he picked up his instruments and returned them to his satchel without the care of washing them. "I have others to tend, but thank you for your kind offer. Now, I must ask for payment," he said smiling. Albert immediately reached into his father's money purse and paid the good doctor his fee.

The doctor left with Albert and Thomas following close behind to tend the horses and carts. Anne remained with John who was still feverish and beginning to fall asleep. She knelt beside his cot and offered prayer for his quick recovery. She then left the room and headed outside to talk to Albert. He and Thomas were unloading bales of wool for the household.

"Albert," she said. "I believe we should try to get word to your mother about your father's condition and tell her why there is a delay."

Albert nodded in agreement as Thomas asked how she would forward the message.

"I shall go to the Holy Seplicar Church," she replied. "If there is anyone going to Sudbury, I will ask if they will take the message to Sara."

Albert again opened his father's purse to pay for an offering for the church services.

The next day John's fever had subsided, and he began taking nourishment. By the fifth day, though still weak, he was able to ride the cart. He and Albert said their farewells to the Hawkins family. Thomas went with them as they had planned to go on to Flanders to sell the wool after John had rested for a day.

The journey home took two uneventful days. The wagons reached Sudbury on the afternoon of the second day. Sara heard them stop in front of the house and rushed out the door as Albert and Thomas helped John from his cart.

"I prayed for your safe return," she said, kissing Albert and gently holding her husband.

She greeted Thomas with a kiss on both cheeks. "I heard the news of your ordeal by a passing friar and have been saying the Rosary every day since."

"Not to worry, dear wife," said John. "It was just a slight wound, but I'm sorry to remind you that we have only a day here. Then we must continue on to Flanders."

John saw the look of sadness come over her face. She knew that they would have to make up the time by leaving within the next two days in order to get to Flanders before the fair ended.

"Fear not, my lady!" Thomas said in mock chivalry. "I shall take care of both your good men," he said with a broad smile. Everyone laughed at Thomas as he bowed at the waist with his hat in hand.

"Why thank you kind, sir," said Sara with a curtsy that matched his performance. Thomas' humor had relieved her somber mood and made her feel a little better.

The evening meal was filled with Sara's good food and drink. The dinner conversation was of the heroic deeds the three had performed. Sara sat with her cup in hand and listened, cherishing every moment. She knew that tomorrow they would be gone and that she would be alone once again.

The next morning they shared the breakfast fare and said good-bye.

"God's speed," Anne said sadly. She stood with her rosary held tightly in her hand and waved to them as they rode away. She prayed to the Blessed Virgin to see them through their journey and a safe return home. She worried that John was still too weak to travel, but her biggest concern was for Albert as this would be his first time sailing. She gave another hearty wave as the carts rolled off into the morning mist.

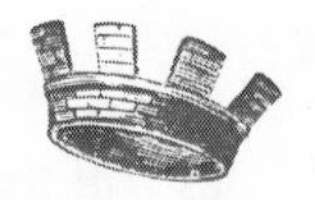

Chapter Five

Colchester was a port city, which handled a great deal of exports and imports, especially the exporting of wool. From there, it would be sent to the English-held city of Calais. Some merchants had agents that sold the wool for them, but others, such as John and Thomas, would sell the wool themselves at the fairs and markets. Their journey to Colchester was a pleasant one until a caravan of merchants who were passing in the other direction warned them of the gruesome sight they were about to encounter.

As they approached the scene, there were two men with a wagon near the severed torso of a monk, which was recognizable only by the shaved area at the top of the head. John, Albert, and Thomas stopped not only out of respect, but out of curiosity. They jumped down from the wagons, each making the sign of the cross as they approached the two men and the body. John and especially Albert were quite disturbed by the scene, but Thomas seemed not to be as affected by it. After he had dismounted, he turned to the wagon wheel and nonchalantly relieved himself. He walked toward the two men who were picking up the lower half of the body.

"What happened to him?" he asked one of them. One man shrugged and the other ignored the question entirely. Neither seemed impressed with the grizzly sight.

"Who could have done this to a holy man?" John asked.

"Could have been the Lollards, followers of that John Wycliffe," replied Thomas. "Preached at Cambridge, he did, and fell out of favor with the church but not with the nobles," he continued. "Wycliffe believes that no more tithes should go to Rome when money is so badly needed here. Nobles like to hear that. I think we can safely say they are responsible for this," he said, nodding toward the body. "Poor bastard," he mumbled as they departed the scene.

"My God!" John interjected. "It must have been someone half-crazed!"

"Surely was," said Thomas dispassionately.

They finally reached Colchester and headed for the docks. As they passed the great Guildhall of the Weavers, a call rang out through the crowd.

"Albert! Albert!"

Hearing his name, Albert looked around quickly. John and Thomas also heard and slowed their wagons.

"Over here!" They all turned in the direction of the caller.

"Over yonder!" yelled Thomas, pointing in the

direction of a wooden scaffold that clung to the weavers' building.

"Who's calling you, son?" John asked.

"I don't know. The voice is not familiar," Albert replied. He jumped from the wagon and headed for the scaffold just as a broad-shouldered youth descended with extraordinary speed.

"Remember me?" he said with a boyish grin.

"It's you!" Albert said in pleased surprise. The two grasped hands vigorously, and Wat Tyler laughed at the look on Albert's face. He scanned the rooftop and scaffolding for any sign of Elizabeth.

John, anxious to be off, called to Albert.

"Please excuse me," he said and hurried back to the wagon.

"What's holding you up?" John asked a bit annoyed. "We must be off!"

"I will be quick, Father," said Albert. "I've met Wat Tyler, and I would like to give greeting to his family."

"Is that the same young man that replaced our roof?" said John, a bit concerned.

"Yes, sir," he replied.

John wasn't sure Wat was a good influence on his son, but talking for just a moment would be acceptable.

"All right then, but be very quick. We'll wait there," he said, pointing to the docking area. He knew not the real reason Albert was pleased to see Wat, or why he wanted to take the time to give greeting to his family. But soon, they would be at sea, and all would be forgotten. Albert started back toward the scaffolding as John and Thomas headed for the docks.

Wat met him at the bottom of the ladder, and they

shook hands again. "I would like to give greeting to your family," said Albert after a brief bit of small talk.

"Yes," said Wat knowingly. "She is here too."

Albert's face turned crimson. *It is uncanny how Wat can almost read my mind,* he thought. *'Almost' being the important word here because if he could actually read my mind, he might not take kindly to my thoughts.* He followed Wat up to the scaffolding, stumbling as he reached the top. As he righted his footing, he looked up and was suddenly staring into Elizabeth's warm, green eyes.

The feelings she invoked were a mystery to Albert, but surely not unpleasant. She smiled and held out her hand to him. He drew it to his lips and kissed the small delicate knuckles, and it was obvious that she was quite impressed with his chivalry. Indeed, he was impressed by his own behavior! Never before had he felt the urge to kiss a girl's hand, and he did not want to stop there. He flushed at the thought of kissing her mouth. Elizabeth must have been feeling the same way as she was blushing too. Wat laughed at the expressions on both their faces. Peter noticed and smiled too, but he knew that such a match could mean trouble. Albert turned to him and held out his hand.

"It is good to see you again, sir," he said. "Indeed, it's good to see all of you."

He looked at Elizabeth and thought it would be wonderful if he could speak to her alone. He wanted so much to tell her how he felt and find out if she felt the same. "I leave for Calais soon," he said, taking her hand again. "I hope I will see you when I return."

Elizabeth looked down and then nodded. This

pleased Albert very much, and he looked forward to that day.

Wat cleared his throat loudly. "Did you come up here to court my sister or to give me news of your doings?"

Albert turned back toward Wat, looking embarrassed.

"I'm just making light with ya," Wat said with a chuckle. He put his hand on Albert's shoulder. "We have heard of your adventures at Peterborough," he said with a broad smile.

"How could you have heard of that so soon?" asked Albert, amazed that the story had reached Colchester even before he did.

"We were leaving your home when your mother got word of your father's injury. As I heard," he continued, "it was the prince's entourage, and had you three not arrived when you did, they would have been cut down."

Albert nodded. "Yes, that's the way it happened," he said proudly.

"Well, with due respect for your bravery, you should have passed on by and let them all die," said Wat, and this time he looked at Albert without smiling. He picked up another tile and resumed his work as he talked.

"Why do you hold such resentment for our prince?" asked Albert. "He is one of the most magnificent soldiers of the realm!" he continued. "He was able to secure all of the family's royal lands in France."

"You are right, my friend, but how does that help us commoners?" Wat interrupted. "Do we share in that wealth?" he asked. "Not at all!" he said, answering his own question. He stopped working for the moment and looked at Albert.

"Wat!" said Peter, raising his hand to quell his son's hot temper. "Perhaps, it would be better to keep your political thoughts to yourself. The boy has loyalties that you should not try to interfere with," he said.

"Well, he should know the truth," said Wat defensively.

Indeed, Albert wanted to know the truth, but he was not sure it wasn't tainted by Wat's resentment.

"You see, all the prince does is tax the people for a war that means nothing to common folk," explained Wat. "In victory we pay for troops to remain in conquered lands, and in defeat we pay again for troops to fight to regain lost territory. And did you know that it is out of our hard work that the nobles maintain a life of frivolousness and waste?" He continued.

"Wat!" said Peter. "We must stop the talk and get on with work!"

"All right, sir," said Wat. He looked back at Albert and smiled. "Well, that should give you something to think about."

"Yes, I will certainly, but now I must be going," said Albert, looking toward the dock. He looked at Elizabeth to find her looking at him too. "It was good to see you again," he said as he nodded toward her. "And it was good to see you, my friends," he said, looking back at Wat and Peter.

"I have a feeling that it won't be the last time," said Wat as he stood to bid Albert good-bye. He placed his hand on his shoulder, and they looked at one another. "Your eyes may be rather blinded, but your heart is brave and pure and one for which I hold the utmost respect. God's speed, my friend."

"Your sentiment is returned," said Albert. He walked toward Elizabeth for one last farewell. "My father awaits me," he said, taking her hand. "And I must go, but if it is my destiny to perish, I shall go to life eternal with you in my heart. And if I return, our hearts will find one another one day, and our two worlds will become one." He brought her hand to his lips and kissed it again. She looked into his eyes, searching for any mockery and found none. She knew he was smitten, but she hadn't realized that he was so taken by her. She bowed her head as Albert turned to go. She watched him as he climbed down and ran toward the dock. He turned and looked up at her, waving his hand. She smiled and waved back.

He turned and continued running down toward the docks, dodging the carts, people, and the mean ruts that pitted the road. He slowed his pace as he approached and gazed at the many ships that were docked, some being unloaded of cargos from across the seas while others waited to disembark on voyages that would take them to distant lands. He walked in the direction of the customs building where he knew his father and Thomas would be. They would have to pass through the king's customs agents where their wool would be weighed, marked, and assessed.

Standing on tiptoes, Albert was able to catch a glimpse of his father and Thomas waiting in a line. Shuffling through the crowd, he made his way through, finally reaching them.

"Come along, Albert. Our wool will be loaded over

there," said John, pointing toward the English merchant vessel, *The Christopher*. Albert looked with curiosity in the direction of the ship. "It has a crew of twelve sailors, a boatman, and a cook." John explained. "It not only carries wool but other goods such as beer, wheat, fish, and small loads of English cloth. Also, crossbow and darts are provided in case of pirate attacks."

"Pirates?" asked Albert, looking wide-eyed as he scanned the massive hulk.

"It's a fine, pirate-dodging vessel, though." His father added.

"Are there many pirates in the channel?" asked Albert.

"Ha!" snorted Thomas. "The channel is full of scum."

"There is nothing to fear," said John reassuringly. "We travel in convoys and have plenty of protection."

It was already early evening by the time they had finished loading their cargo, and the wind had begun to pick up. The clouds rolled in quickly. *The Christopher* was now loaded to capacity, but there was no room for Thomas and his cargo. He would have to sail on *The Michael*, which was a similar vessel and would be crossing with the convoy. They were informed they would all sail as soon as there were favorable weather conditions. Hopefully, it would be in the morning. Being a busy seaport, accommodations would be difficult to find, so they decided to bed down aboard ship. Before retiring, they visited one of the many bawdy inns that dotted the shore to dine.

These establishments were as uncivilized and as filthy as any could be. The pickpockets and prostitutes took full advantage of everyone from the drunken sailor to the wealthy merchant and anyone else who ventured into their midst.

As the three men neared the inn, Albert noticed a woman smiling at him. She looked strangely different from any woman he knew. She acted differently too. Many of the prostitutes were applying their trade, and Albert noticed the peculiar way they carried on with the patrons.

Prostitution was much more common along the waterfront than it was in inland towns, and it was more accepted. After many weeks and sometimes months on a ship with nothing but men to keep company with, sailors were in dire need of a woman. This made prostitution a very lucrative business for women who were alone in the world and who would otherwise be indentured to some lecherous nobleman or landlord who would take their liberties for free.

One caught Albert's attention, looking and smiling broadly at him. He smiled back self-consciously, and she took this as an invitation. Before he knew it, she was standing beside him clutching his arm.

"You're a fine-looking lad!" she said seductively.

John had gotten all the way across the room before he noticed that Albert was no longer behind him. He looked back and saw him standing awkwardly next to a rather shabby, not-so-young-looking woman. He quickly walked back and grabbed Albert's free arm.

"Those are not the kind of women you would want to spend your time with, son. They are of questionable reputation," he said, glaring at the woman.

Albert turned and looked at his father. John knew

he understood immediately what he meant, but Albert was not as knowledgeable as John hoped.

Albert wasn't sure exactly what took place when a woman did this. He knew that she and a stranger would spend an evening together, but he wasn't aware that she took money in return for sexual favors or that it could be a risk to a man's health. The look of her both intrigued and frightened him at the same time.

"Why don't ya mind your own business, ya old sod?" she yelled.

"Take your filthy hands off my son!" John shot back.

"Oh! He's your son, is he?" she said in a high-pitched whine. "How about I show ya both a good time? I could do ya for half the price just 'cause your boy is such a fine-lookin' lad."

John gave her a disgusted look and pulled Albert away. Albert was still looking at her when she lifted her skirt to give a view of her wares. The sight both surprised and embarrassed Albert, and he tripped over his own feet as his father pulled on his arm to get him away from the woman.

"What's the matter with ya? Ain't ya man enough to handle a real woman? Ya uppity, old bastard!" she yelled.

They reached Thomas who had witnessed the whole affair from across the room. He stood, waiting and smiling as they approached.

"Nearly took you both for a ride, did she?" he chuckled.

Neither one answered. John just glared at Thomas, and that made him laugh out loud. Finally, they all sat and filled their plates with the fare that was placed in the middle of the table. Anxious to put the incident with the whore aside, John began talking about the impending journey, but Thomas was still smirking as they talked. They ate quickly and removed themselves from the premises. Returning to the vessels, Thomas bid them good night and boarded *The Michael* as John and Albert headed for *The Christopher*.

As they lay on makeshift beds among the cargo and other merchants, Albert gazed up into the night sky. All his thoughts centered not on the voyage but on Elizabeth, whose image danced in his head. Soon the fatigue set in as sleep overtook him, leaving him to dream of a day he would see her again.

The morning brought a crystal blue sky void of any clouds and a warm and gentle westerly breeze. Upon awakening, John sported a wide grin. "'Tis rare to see such a perfect day for sailing," he said, wiping the sleep from his eyes. He took a deep breath and looked at Albert who didn't care a fig about the weather. His concerns were not so much with the uncomfortable accommodations aboard ship as with his dreams and how they were rudely interrupted by his father's nudging. As he rose, a morning meal was being served accompanied by a stern warning from the master.

"Take heed of the amount you're eating, and don't let the calm weather mislead you!" he called.

Albert, now more alert, looked at his father in question.

"When the ship leaves, we are in open sea, and there is a chance the weather could change. When it does, few men can keep down even water, so eat light."

Albert nodded and took his father's advice. He wasn't very hungry anyway as he had eaten a lot the night before. While most heeded the master's warning, some continued to eat heartily. With fine masters and crews, they would brave the unforgiving sea for the sake of commerce and the three powerful wooden cogs with their heavily laden cargos of merchants and goods set sail for Calais.

Soon they were on the open sea, and Albert watched as the landmass faded ever so quickly. A dense fog overtook the pristine skies of only a few moments past. Torches were lit on each vessel to prevent one from straying off course and to avoid collisions. These were not the only challenges that the small convoy would face.

Although the English fleet controlled the channel, there was much open sea in which French and Scottish pirates prevailed and would frequently wreak havoc on maritime shipping. As the fog abated and the morning slipped away, the seas began to swell. A large wave lashed the side of the ship, sending Albert's body into flight and landing him onto the solid-oak decking. He pulled himself up quickly, hoping no one had noticed and rubbed the part of his posterior that had made contact with the deck.

Aside from the dangers of pirates and collisions, it was now Neptune who would mete out the wrath of his vast, watery domain to all intruders. The seas tossed and turned the vessels in a violent rage. Passengers and crew held on for dear life, and a good many stomachs' early morning fare lay strewn over the decking. But it did not remain there for long as a mighty burst of water from the furious god cleansed the deck of all debris and at least one elderly merchant whose hands had failed him at an unfortunate moment. It was at that time that the seas began to subside as if being appeased by the human sacrifice. All three ships had remained within view of one another.

Everyone was gathered topside as Master DeCrigul led the prayers for the lost merchant's soul after which he announced that the merchant's cargo would be entrusted to fellow merchants who would deliver it to the poor fellow's family. Slowly, things began to settle back to normal, and by afternoon the skies were as clear as if nothing at all had taken place.

An easterly wind began to blow in earnest. Hopefully, the landfall would be close to Calais, for there was no way to tell how far they had been blown off course. By late afternoon there was a land sighting, but as the master's experience had taught him, they were not headed for Calais. He gathered the merchants as well as the crew on deck to explain their exact position.

"Fortunately, we are between Calais and Boulogne and still within the king's realm."

But there was still cause for concern because although both ports were controlled by England, the land between was in French hands, and the waters were infested with pirate ships just waiting for any wayward merchant vessels laden with booty.

They sailed the coastline without incident to within a short distance of Calais when a signal was given by the watch of a French pirate vessel that appeared to be gaining steadily on the convoy. The crew was raised to action as Master Richard fired off orders in preparation of battle. From the starboard, all watched in nervous anticipation as the pirates raced toward *The Michael.* John gasped, and Albert's eyes grew wide as they witnessed the ship being overtaken and two other pirate vessels heading quickly toward the remaining merchant ships. The chase was soon abandoned as an English fleet coming from port appeared a short distance away. They were in time to save the first two vessels, but *The Michael* had fallen into French hands.

John's eyes filled as he watched *The Michael* fading in the distance, and he lowered his head in despair. "My dear friend," John said sadly. "Lord, have mercy on his soul." He let out a sob as Albert put his arm around his father's shoulder to console him.

Master DeCrigul noticed and walked toward the father and son. "Did you lose someone on *The Michael*?" he asked.

"Yes," John replied. "A dear friend and associate, Thomas Hawkins."

"My deepest sympathy, sirs," said the master respectfully. As the vessels neared Calais, he called the ship to order. "A moment of prayer to all lost on the voyage," he announced, "and a prayer for all those present for a safe return home."

The two remaining ships made their way into Calais. Here the Rule of the Merchant Staple applied to all wool merchants. The rule gave them guaranteed room and board at one of the many homes in Calais, but John and Albert would stay with the family of their friend, William Paxton. It was late afternoon when they arrived at the Paxton household. Warmly welcomed, they relayed the tragic news of *The Michael* to the Paxton family.

Many aboard were friends and acquaintances of William and even a few relatives. "Even having control of the seas does not insure the safety of our merchant ships," he said sadly. "And it is not just the French and Scots, we must contend with, but the Genoese and Castilians are raising hell with our ships as well."

"Yes, it's difficult and dangerous." John agreed. "What are your thoughts on that, William? Do you think things will improve?" he asked.

"I believe a new offensive is being planned for there are more troops than I've ever seen in the city," said William. "And there is talk of a campaign to be launched by King Edward." John had heard similar rumors about the planning of a campaign and believed it to be true also.

Soon the evening meal was being served, and they all sat down to eat. Afterward, John and William sat with snifters of brandy and talked sadly of the lost *Michael*. The evening wore on with John and Albert being the only guests that the Paxtons received. Late evening arrived with the sounding of the Compline bells, and John and Albert retired to their room.

The next morning, the business of the merchant staple was foremost. It would be a hectic day as the city bustled with a multitude of merchants from all over Europe and beyond, bearing a large variety of goods from English wool to Arabian spices. Added to this diverse influx of population were the vast cohorts of English soldiers marching off to war.

John and Albert's first order of business was unloading their wool from a wagon borrowed from the Paxton household. They slowly made their way toward the docks, stopping and dodging every few minutes around the hordes of people and animals not to mention other carts and larger wagons that could barely pass when confronted by one another. With much patience, they finally reached their destination, and the wool was loaded onto their wagon.

Before they could begin the business of selling their goods, they would have to pass through the king's inspection officers who would check the sacks for correct labeling. Next, the sacks were disassembled by professional packers looking for any wool that was less than good quality or stones that may be hidden in the bale's center to increase the weight. Lastly, they were repacked, labeled, and sent to The Fellowship of the Staple who would collect a sum for the king and another for the mayor of Calais.

After their bales were returned to them, John and Albert moved on to join a gathering of merchants who had assembled in the town. Some merchants chose not to sell their goods in Calais but to move on to the fairs at Flanders where they believed they could receive a larger profit. Even though the Flemish truce with England was fragile, there was still a large demand for English wool. Before leaving for Bruges, they went to The Staple Chapel of Our Lady to pray for the souls of fellow merchants who had perished on the lost *Michael.*

John and Albert were joined by five other merchants who had also decided to sell at Bruges. The merchants not only sailed on the same wool fleet, but John remembered them from past business transactions. There would be few concerns along the way, except the weather, as the roads were in fine condition and robbers were all but nonexistent during the daylight hours. The local authorities made this a priority as it brought much revenue to the area and was of the utmost concern. Knights on horseback could be seen frequently policing the roads, and workers on carts passed them with spade and gravel ready to repair the slightest blemish.

They were now ready to transport their goods to the fair. The road wound through the lush, green forest as the sun shone through the trees, giving the world an almost idyllic appearance. As they continued on, the forest yielded to newly cleared areas, which would later become farming and grazing land. Reaching a gentle knoll, Albert looked up and saw the city of Bruges ahead. As the carts and wagons rolled closer, the road became more congested with people waiting to enter at the city gate.

Once inside, the freshly cleaned streets held a host of people; among them were merchants who had come from near and far and townspeople dressed in their brightly colored costumes. The smells of the various sections of the city gave hints as to what business was conducted there. The pleasant aromas of the bakeshops and cookeries would soon give way to the pungent smells of the fish market, and further on, the more undesirable smells of the butchers shops and tanneries. Albert held his nose as they walked by.

"Did you think the whole city would smell like roses?" John asked with a chuckle.

Albert looked at his father and smiled back. They finally reached their destination and entered the large, wool hall where they would sell their goods to the general population. They had just begun to unload their wagon when the collector of the taxes and his armed retinue approached.

The bales were counted, and a monetary tax was levied to be paid before the wool could be sold. Being of good quality and fairly priced, their wool sold quickly, earning them a substantial profit with which they would purchase goods to bring home. It was a moment Albert had waited for, and his excitement could hardly be contained as he and his father roamed through what seemed like endless rows of tents, stalls, and buildings.

Each tent was a different color and sold a variety of goods. Brightly colored silk from China came via the Levant and was sold by the great Venetian traders. The tent of the Hanseitic League's merchant sold an array of soft, luxurious furs of varying colors brought from the vast forests of Russia. The multitudes of people filled the air with all sorts of babble that added a bit of charm and wonderment to the already colorful scene.

John purchased spices for Sara's kitchen from an Arabic trader and silk from the Venetian stall. And he thought of Anne and the children and bought spices and silk for them as well, vowing to help them through what would be extremely hard times. This had been his constant preoccupation since he lost his dear friend, and he dreaded the time he would have to face his family with the tragic news.

While he and the other merchants conversed, Albert stole away to the Spanish ironmonger's tent where he bought a lovely iron ring which he planned to present to Elizabeth and hoped with all his heart she would accept it. Speaking no Spanish, he handed the man some of the coins that his father had paid him. The merchant took his due, and the purchase was completed. Albert walked back through the crowd to where his father was finishing up his purchases after which they would leave for Calais and head for home.

Chapter Six

For Albert, Colchester was a welcome sight. Sailing back from Calais was depressing. He thought of Thomas, and how sad it will be to have to inform his family of their loss. It was a relief to be able to leave the ship, and as he stepped off onto dry land, he thought of Elizabeth with the anticipation of seeing her again. After leaving the ship, they headed for the livery where the wagons and horses were stored. Each took the reins of a horse, attached the wagons, and walked them to the docks. After unloading their goods from the vessel's hold, they said good-bye to the other merchants and headed for home.

The road took them past the guildhall, and Albert looked up at the roof and remembered Elizabeth's lovely face and Wat's rebellious words. Where, when, and if he would ever see them again was uncertain, and his heart sank to its lowest depths as that reality set in.

Soon, his thoughts turned to more immediate matters as the journey from Colchester brought them home.

As they pulled up in front of the house, Sara rushed out to greet them.

She burst through the front door and threw her arms around them. "I was sick with fear," she said, looking at them through teary eyes. "I heard the news of *The Michael.*" She looked over John's shoulder at Thomas' cart. "I wasn't informed of who was on board, but now I know." She looked into John's eyes sadly. "God, speed his soul to heaven," she whispered.

That evening was quiet and somber, but John and Albert were glad to be home with Sara; and they were all safe and sound. John explained what happened on the journey and gave her the goods he had purchased. He explained that he had made purchases for Thomas' family and stated that they would all have to do what they could to help. The three of them bowed their heads in prayer for the Hawkins family and the soul of their beloved friend.

The next morning John and Albert departed for Cambridge. After the day-and-a-half journey, they reached Thomas' house. As they walked up to the door, they could hear Anne's conversation with Margery through the partially open shutters.

"Father will be home; don't you worry," Anne said, but without her usual confidence.

John looked at Albert sadly and shook his head. They stood on the front stoop for a few minutes while John mustered the courage to knock on the door. Taking a deep breath, he knocked.

Within a moment, the door opened, and Anne

stood looking at the two as if she already knew the sad news they were about to share. She held out her hands to John. "Welcome," she said. Without another word, he took her in his arms as she wept. "I heard the news of a merchant vessel being attacked. I could only hope and pray that none of you were on it," she sobbed.

She led them into the house, and they sat at the kitchen table as John gave details of the ill-fated journey. Their conversation was overheard, and Margery left her spinning wheel and rushed into the kitchen.

"What's happened to Father?" she asked nervously.

Anne rushed over to embrace her and explain. "Father won't be coming home, child," she said. "We must pray for him." Margery sobbed uncontrollably in her mother's arms. "Please go, and find your brother. Finally, the girl regained her composure and went to look for Peter. She found him in the barn where he was carding the wool and called to him.

"What do you want?" he asked without turning to look at her. She was always bothering him when he was busy. She didn't answer right away, and he heard her sniff. Finally, he turned around, and his annoyance immediately turned to concern.

"What is it?" he asked.

She burst into tears again.

"Is it Father?"

She looked up into his eyes that were already filled with tears and nodded.

"Is he dead?" Peter whispered.

She nodded again, and he put his arms around her trying to console her. "Margery, you know father warned us about that possibility. Do you remember what he told us?" he asked.

She thought for a minute and nodded. "We should take care of Mother and be good children," she answered.

"And that we were not to mourn any longer than necessary," he added.

They turned and walked hand-in-hand toward the house, wiping tears. Peter was now the man of the house, a big responsibility, but he was determined to do his father proud even if he had to work night and day.

The entire household was engulfed in sorrow as the children entered the great room. John and Anne sat talking about future plans. Albert entered shortly after storing Thomas' horse and wagon.

"I must prepare the supper; please excuse me," said Anne, looking at Margery who took the cue and followed her mother into the kitchen. The three men stood as the ladies left the room. John asked Peter to help unload the wagon and bring the goods he had purchased into the house. They were most grateful to John and his son for all their help.

"Whatever your needs be, my family and I will be glad to provide," said John.

They stayed with the Hawkins for two more days, helping with household affairs and attending the Mass they had arranged for Thomas. Finally, it was time to go home, and Albert went to the barn to prepare their horse and wagon for the trip. John stood at the front door with Anne and her children.

"I do wish you didn't have to go so soon, John," Anne said sadly.

John embraced her one last time. He knew she was afraid to face the future without her husband.

"We will be in touch often," he assured her.

She looked longing at him as he turned to go. John boarded the wagon and took the reins. He and Albert waved to them as they pulled away and started down the road toward home. John also wished he could have stayed a while longer, but there was much work to do. There were the business finances to tend to, and foremost in John's mind, he believed it was time that Albert met with the Simon Sudbury, who was by this time the new Archbishop of Canterbury.

It had been many years since they last met, and now that Albert was growing up, John wanted to introduce him to the archbishop, as it is always wise to have connections in high places. He also wanted to sway Albert from his interest in Wat Tyler. The journey would be a long one and would include a passage through London. Albert was excited to go on a trip that included a visit to the great city; however, he was apprehensive about meeting with Simon as he remembered Wat's story of Elizabeth's encounter with him.

As they arrived in London, Albert was awestruck by London's vastness and diverse population as well as the many large buildings that housed shops selling everything from domestic products to articles imported from near and far. After a short stay, it was time to move on to their final destination.

As Canterbury came into view, the first sighting was of the enormous cathedral and its steeple, which towered above all else. They soon reached the newly constructed Gate of St. Dunstan along with a massive crowd of pilgrims coming from all over England to visit the shrine of St. Thomas à Becket. It was an important religious pilgrimage that consisted of holy men, peasants, cripples, beggars, and even outlaws. All came in search of miracles that would heal their broken bodies and souls.

John stopped the cart just a short distance away from the cathedral, and they both gazed at the massive edifice. "Did you know that the first archbishop was Italian?" said John. "His name was Augustine, and he became a saint," he continued.

Albert listened to his father and marveled at his infinite historical knowledge. "And, William the Conqueror's first archbishop was another Italian by the name of Anselm. However, neither of these men occupied the great cathedral, for construction was begun by William and to this day remains incomplete."

Albert nodded as they sat for a moment to reflect.

Finally, they dismounted from the cart and led the horse through the large wrought iron gates that led into the close of the cathedral. This close consisted of an enclosed tract of land that contained the cathedral city and included the houses of the dean and clergy. It also included the monastic cloister and, finally, the archbishop's palace.

They approached the large, oaken palace doors, which were adorned with fearsome-looking gargoyles and other hideous creatures.

Albert peered intently at the doors. "Why do

they embellish the sacred church with such demonic images?" he asked.

"They believe it will keep evil from entering the holy domain," John explained.

Albert looked in wonderment and thought of Wat. He would most likely believe that the evil they were supposed to divert indeed existed inside the church. Albert wasn't sure what to believe, but he wanted to believe what his father told him. John gave a heavy-handed knock on the door. They waited only a minute when a very rotund, placid-looking priest opened the door.

"May I be of assistance, sir?" he asked in a soft voice.

"Yes, I would like an audience with His Eminence," replied John.

The priest asked their names after which he graciously bowed and walked down the long dark corridor. Within moments, he returned with permission for an audience.

As they walked to the archbishop's study, they passed expensive tapestry and richly carved wooden moldings that decorated the walls. As they were ushered into the study, Albert observed the grandeur of the finely woven, silk curtains that adorned the windows. The gothic style furniture behind a large marble-topped desk displayed several golden, inlaid chalices. Albert's eyes were mesmerized by the sheer opulence. Never before had he been in a more stately room, and again he thought of Wat's words.

Chapter Seven

Simon held out his hand. "John!" he said with a condescending smile. "It has been many years since we last met, and who might this young man be?" he asked, turning his attention to Albert or more to the sable that Albert was holding.

"Your Eminence, may I present my son, Albert," said John proudly. "He is holding a gift for you. It is a fine sable stole that we purchased in Flanders. Please except it with our heartfelt respect."

Simon smiled as he took the stole into his hands and stroked it lovingly.

"Thank you," he said, bowing his head in gratitude. "You have never forgotten me, John."

"No, Your Eminence," John replied.

Simon motioned for them to sit and turned his attention, again to Albert. "Would you care to see the shrine of St. Thomas?" he asked.

Albert, whose attention was on the magnificence of the room, looked at the archbishop. "Yes, of course,

Your Eminence," he said, somewhat startled at the sudden invitation.

Simon reached for a small, ornate, silver bell and gave it one delicate shake. Almost immediately, as if by magic, the priest who had showed them in earlier reappeared.

"Please escort Master Albert to the shrine," he commanded.

The priest nodded and held the door open. Simon thought it best to talk to John privately, and John was in agreement. They wanted to talk about the past and thought Albert too young to listen; besides, most of the conversation would not be of any interest to him.

As the priest and Albert walked to the courtyard, the priest introduced himself as Father George. They walked outside the gate where there was a large crowd gathering. Albert had visited other shrines, but none so large and crowded as this one.

"This is England's most sacred shrine," Father George explained. "The body of St. Thomas à Becket lays entombed here. He was the Archbishop of Canterbury who was killed in the year of Our Lord 1170." He continued. "Although he was chosen by his friend, our second King Henry, to be archbishop, a quarrel irrupted between the two over which court would bring clerics to trial, church or secular."

"What happened? Who won out?" asked Albert.

"The quarrel led to a deadly feud. The king made a comment in jest, but it was taken seriously by four of his knights who carried out the deed and assassinated Thomas while he said Mass at the cathedral," he answered. "Only three years later, he was canonized a saint. Now, sir, I will let you roam at will," said the priest as he turned and walked back through the gate.

"Thank you," Albert called out after him. He was completely rapt in the story when a tap on his shoulder startled him back to the present. He turned quickly and found himself face-to-face with his old friend. Wat laughed at the surprised look on Albert's face, and he laughed too.

"We were working on the roof of the house yonder," he said, pointing to the cluster of houses a short way up the road. "We have completed the job, and I found a moment to try to see my friend John, who is being detained by the archbishop."

"You mean, your friend is in jail?" asked Albert.

"Jail is such a harsh word, but frankly, yes," replied Wat.

"Who is this friend of yours, and what wrong did he do to end up in jail?"

"Detained," Wat corrected with a smile.

"Yes, of course, detained," Albert repeated. "But who is he?"

"His name is John Ball; an ex-cleric; they have *detained* and excommunicated him for condemning the wealth of the lords and clergy and demanding that the clergy return to evangelical poverty. Someday John and I will march together!" he said with a look of determination and pride. "And you, my friend, what, may I ask, are you doing here?"

Albert looked a little sheepish. "I'm here with my father who is visiting with the archbishop," he said. "They have been friends for many years."

Wat gave a disgusted look. "I'm sure your father is

an honorable man," he said. "But it is too bad he must keep company with such a scoundrel."

"Yes, I must agree now that I've met him. It galled me to have to kneel before him and pay respect to such a man. I believe your feelings are justified; he is arrogant down to his very soul."

"If indeed he has a soul," said Wat. "Why are you standing out here then if you were given audience to the Almighty?" he asked sarcastically.

"I suppose they had business to talk about and feared I would be bored, so they excused me much to my relief I might add," replied Albert. "Though it is quite distressing to watch all these people standing and waiting to rid themselves of whatever misery they are enduring. I do admire their faith and courage," he said as he looked around.

Wat let out a loud guffaw. "They are fools!" he said unsympathetically. "Look there," he said pointing. "Do you see that man yonder selling holy relics?"

Albert looked in the direction indicated.

"The so-called 'holy relics,' which every one of these fools believes to be the bones of the saints, are nothing more than the bones of a chicken and various other animals," Wat continued. "Look at the poor bastards crawling up the church steps on their hands and knees. They're praying for a miracle that may never come. What is needed is less prayer and more fight, which is brewing at this very moment and will come to pass one day."

Albert looked at his friend and knew he told the truth. He saw the look of determination in his eyes and knew that Wat would play a major role in the battle for change. He wondered what would become of his friend, and it worried him. His thoughts turned toward Elizabeth, who was always in the back of his mind.

"How is Elizabeth faring these days," he asked, trying to sound nonchalant.

Wat gave him a knowing smile. "Ah, I wondered when you would ask for her. Alas, she is not with me this day," he said bowing his head in mock sorrow. He raised his eyes to catch Albert's reaction and saw a look of concern. "No need to worry," he said more seriously. "She is quite well and in her usual good health. She stays at the cottage of friends in Maidstone. Our father is ill, and she is caring for him."

"I'm sorry to hear that," said Albert. "What is it that ails him?"

Wat was a little reluctant to answer because he wasn't sure and hoped it wasn't the deadly sickness that had claimed his mother and brother so long ago. He had heard that it had again made its ugly appearance. "I think it's not at all serious, and he will recover soon." He lied.

Albert grew sad as he thought of Elizabeth because he also knew that there was a return of sickness, and he was beginning to know his friend well enough to know that he was lying about their father's condition. It frightened him to think that Peter might be infected and that Elizabeth may have been exposed to the horrible illness. He said a quick silent prayer for them both. At the same time, he reached for his money pouch, which held the ring he had bought for her, and squeezed it tightly.

"Come with me to visit my friend," Wat begged.

"Would the guards not throw us both in jail if we asked to see him?" asked Albert.

"Oh, my young friend, you are naïve," said Wat as he put his arm around Albert's shoulders. "You're not to tell them that you're there to see John Ball! You say you're there to see your drunken father who was thrown in last night for being disorderly," Wat explained. "Once you are inside, they pay little attention to you. There are so many drunken sods in there that they don't even know which one you're referring to and couldn't care less."

Albert was tempted to go, but he knew it was best not to. "I'm sorry, but I must await my father's return," he said.

"Very well," said Wat a little disappointed. "However, there is another preacher I would like you to meet later. He is in Sudbury and was also excommunicated. You could come with us and listen to his lectures."

Albert looked a little skeptical.

"Before you decide not to go," Wat said reading Albert's mind, "consider that he preaches for free. He asks for no fees or donations. You just go to wherever the meeting is being held and listen. Meetings are usually held in public places or in somebody's home."

Albert wasn't sure he wanted to be a part of the group, but he didn't tell Wat. "Well, if there is an opportunity for me at any time, I will surely go and listen," he said.

Wat knew his friend would need a bit of prompting. "Did you know that most of the church's wealth comes from dying parishioners who are trying to pay their way into heaven?" he said. "Various orders of clergy compete for this wealth and will go as far as placing their sacred vows aside. They will go to any lengths for money. Albert, what do you say to that? Will you come?" asked Wat.

Albert hesitated, and several images ran through his mind. One was the image of a disapproving look on his father's face and a sad look on his mother's. He knew they would both be disappointed if they knew he'd even considered going.

"Elizabeth will be joining me when my father recovers," Wat said.

Albert dropped his head in thought. This was one he could not resist, and he reluctantly agreed to go. "We will meet at the fair during the next Lammas (August) holiday," said Wat. "I'm glad you will be joining us, friend," he said, clapping Albert's shoulder. "You are a fine, young man and will be a good addition to our group. And Elizabeth will be proud of you," he said with that same knowing grin. The two walked back into the cathedral city where they parted company with a strong embrace. Albert turned and looked for his father. Soon he spotted him exiting the palace and waved.

The fair at Sudbury was a welcome break from the daily routine to enjoy a day of leisure. It was one of the hundred holidays enjoyed by both nobles and peasants alike. It was a day of celebration that included entertainment, such as staged plays, wrestling, dancing, bowling, and an abundance of food and drink. But with all the activities and merrymaking, one needed to be aware of the pickpockets and con men that infiltrated the crowd. Most of these were children, street urchins, who had been abandon by parents who had died or just didn't have the wherewithal to care for them.

Albert could hardly wait for the week to pass. Finally, the day arrived, and he rushed off early, worried that Elizabeth and Wat would not be there. Visions of them both lying sick and dying flooded his mind until he spotted them. The sight of Elizabeth took his breath away, and he wasted no time rushing to her side. Seized with emotion, he grasped his friend's hand and pulled him into an embrace. Trying to hide his joy and relief, he turned to Elizabeth and reached for her hand. He looked into her eyes as he raised her hand to his lips. He feared that it was all a dream, and he would soon awake, alone and sad. He stood staring at the vision before him, taking in her soft, brown hair, partially covered by a light blue wimple (veil) and her mysterious green eyes. He noticed the lovely girlish figure that could not be hidden under the simple white frock she wore.

"We should be leaving, right away, as Brother William will be waiting for us," said Wat.

"Yes, of course," said Albert, still looking at Elizabeth.

They turned and walked from the fair grounds toward a path that led behind a very large cornfield. Soon they reached the edge of the forest and walked toward what looked like the end of the path. Then Wat pushed aside a low-lying tree branch, and the path continued deeper into the forest. Albert was surprised and a little apprehensive as they were now stepping into the king's forest, and although he had lived in the area all of his life, this part of the forest was unfamiliar to him.

"Where are we going? Isn't this the king's forest?" he asked, concerned.

Wat turned abruptly and stared into Albert's eyes. "This forest belongs to no one! It belongs to the earth! We have as much right to it as the king or anyone else. We hunt here out of need, and they call it a crime," he scorned. "And it is the king who commits the crime by forbidding us our keep and by killing for pleasure and sport. Albert, this is our plight, you see," he said in a softer voice.

"Yes, of course," said Albert apologetically. "I do understand. It's just that it is hard for me to break from old beliefs."

Wat smiled and placed a hand on his shoulder. "Yes, but you will soon learn, my friend."

They continued farther until they reached a clearing and the largest oak tree Albert had ever seen. At its base, among the huge root system and blending into the background, a friar knelt in prayer. Albert hadn't noticed him until he moved when he sensed their approach. He raised his head and struggled to gain his footing, gripping his staff for support. He groaned as a thousand clicks sounded off in his joints as he stood and turned to greet them.

Brother William was a thinly built man with a crop of wild, dark hair that didn't match the gray in his beard. His eyes were deep set and filmy gray in color. His wild and unkempt appearance was betrayed by a soft, intelligent voice. "Welcome," he said as he raised his hands out to them. "I'm afraid my eyesight isn't as sharp as it was," he continued. "What are your names, my children?"

"It's me, Wat."

The friar's face lit up at the sound of Wat's voice.

"I've brought my sister, Elizabeth, and my dear friend Albert Deaconson," Wat said.

"Wat! My young friend, how good it is to see you!" exclaimed Brother William. "And I'm very happy to meet you, Albert Deaconson," he said shaking Albert's hand. "And lovely little Elizabeth," he said, turning his attention to her. "I'm happy to see you again, my child," he said, taking both her hands in his. "And how is your dear father?"

"He is doing well, sir," she answered with a smile.

"Fine, I'm happy to hear that, my dear. How can I help my three young friends today?" he said.

"We've come to hear your words of wisdom, sir," Wat answered.

"Ah!" said the friar, stroking his beard and smiling. "Then you shall!" Turning back toward the oak, he took a seat on one of the large roots sticking up out of the ground, and the three sat on the grass before him.

"I think I shall begin by giving Albert some of my background if you don't mind," he said, looking in Wat's direction. Wat nodded in agreement, and the friar continued.

"You see, I was a parish priest in the town of Broughton. My colleagues and I took our vows very seriously. However, many of them, as well as the higher clergy, cared not for the poor and downtrodden.

Disgusted with the direction which the church was taking, many of us began following an Oxford priest named John Wycliffe," he continued. "We were taken with his idea that a man's relationship with God is direct, and it requires neither church nor priest to act as intermediary. In essence, all Christians are priests and can converse with God directly. Our belief is that God is everywhere and available to all, peasants and poor folk, kings and nobles, and everyone in between,"

"Why, then, do we have churches?" Albert asked.

"The church has the purpose of providing sanctuary for anyone in need but should not own property or excessive wealth," he answered. "John's doctrine seemed to be sound logic, and he began to acquire a following of priests who spread his doctrine. However, there was a serious breach of trust among the faithful." He continued. "Brother Wycliffe began to side with the nobles against the church and ignored the poor. This left them defenseless and at the mercy of the clergy. I and others left the following and devoted our lives to championing the plight of all those who are powerless," he said. "As the others, I look upon my flock as 'my people' who are trying to improve their lives which are mired under the heavy taxes and tithes imposed by both the clergy and the nobility.

"It posed a question about the so-called faithful. Do they truly believe, or do they just say they do in order to convince others that demanding money from even the poorest folks is God's law and must be obeyed? You see, some use the fear of God to increase their wealth and force believers to bend to their will. Some people, such as yourselves, can see through them and rebel."

"Damn the lot of them!" Wat yelled as he jumped up from his seat, startling everyone. His face flushed, and he threw his arms skyward. "I will get back at those bastards if it's the last thing I do in this life!"

"Calm yourself," said William in his soft voice. "Remember what our Savior taught us, my son: 'Vengeance is mine, sayth the Lord.' We must remain peaceful and continue to spread this knowledge. It is not for us to condemn." The calmness in the good friar's voice brought Wat back to his senses.

"Yes, please excuse me," he said as he sat down. Albert stared at him for a long moment and then back at William.

The friar pointed his finger at Wat. "Our Father judges man by the goodness in his heart, not by the coin he holds in his purse. And we need not get revenge as those who harbor evil in their hearts will pay with their very souls on judgment day. It is a waste of our time and good conscience to retaliate, my son," he said. "This is my message," he concluded as he folded his hands in a prayerlike fashion around his staff. "What questions might you have, Albert?" he asked.

"I have one, sir," he said. "If God is everywhere and with everyone, where was he when people were dying of horrible illnesses? Indeed, where is he when there are countless injustices brought against helpless, innocent people who are only trying to survive and serve him? Where is he then?" he asked.

"Yes, my dear Albert. Of course, you would ask that for there are many good folks who have suffered for no other reason than being poor, but there is a reason for everything that comes about in this life. God has a master plan, you see, and it is not for us to question. Sometimes he shows us what his reasons are, and sometimes he does not. We shall find out why things are as they are on judgment day. Until that day, neither I nor anyone else can answer your question. One thing is certain, though, and that is that God is fair and just, and if you treat your fellow man as you would be treated, he will have a place for you in heaven. Now, my children, I must depart," he said as he stood to leave.

Chapter Eight

Wat looked at Albert, who was looking at Elizabeth. "What do you say about our friend?" asked Wat as they started back through the woods.

"He is extraordinary," Albert replied. "He seems almost too saintly to be so rebellious."

"Being saintly is strength, Albert, not weakness," Elizabeth interrupted. She smiled at him, and he agreed.

"Yes, of course," he said, smiling back.

"My, this power my sister has over you, my friend," Wat laughed. "She has only to smile, and you're groveling at her feet. How I wish I had such power!" Albert looked at Wat and smiled bashfully.

As the sounds of the fair grew near, Wat quickened his step, leaving Albert and Elizabeth momentarily alone. Albert seized the opportunity to speak privately to her. Before saying a word, he drew the ring from his pocket and presented it to her. Her eyes lit up, and the pink in her cheeks grew darker. She quickly looked up at Albert as he drew her into his arms. Her legs grew weak and shaky as he bent his head to kiss her. The scent of her was intoxicating, and her lips were soft and yielding. He knew in his heart that this was the girl he was going to marry.

"I cannot find the words to tell you how I'm feeling," she whispered. "But I think it must be love."

"Yes," Albert whispered back.

They turned and walked to the fair hand in hand—both realizing that their attraction was no longer just an infatuation.

During the coming months, the three grew very close and spent time together whenever possible. The love between Albert and Elizabeth grew stronger as they emerged into young adulthood. They visited Brother William who along with his sermons would tell the old tales of Beowulf, King Arthur, and a new and favorite one about a band of outlaws living in Sherwood Forest, Nottingham. As the story goes, the leader had been a deposed earl. This earl and his men would rob the nobles and give their booty to those in need. This was Wat's favorite. He saw himself as that daring young outlaw who called himself Robin Hood.

Brother William's following became larger over time as he preached and weaved his yarns to anyone who would listen. Albert, Elizabeth, and Wat grew more and more fond of the scruffy, old friar with each new sermon, and he became their spiritual guide and mentor.

Albert's family knew nothing of his love for Elizabeth or of his friendship with Wat and Brother

William. He continued working as his father's apprentice, but he knew someday he would have to reveal his secret life to his parents. John planned to have Albert eventually take over his business, so he could retire; and Albert could marry into the Hawkins family, which would secure the next generation of Deaconsons. He knew his son was bright and strong enough to do the job. However, Albert had plans of his own. He had a similar dream of following in his father's footsteps, but his plan included marriage to his lovely Elizabeth.

He often dreamed of their wedding day in which he would see himself dressed in a white tunic and tights with a golden crown on his head. He would be standing before Brother William among the lush, green trees and flowers of the forest. He would turn and see his lady dressed in a magnificent white gown and veil, holding a small, fragrant bouquet of white and blue wildflowers. Then, it would all disappear, and in its place he would hear his father's angry voice. "You've broken you poor mother's heart, son," he would say.

It had been three years since Thomas' death at sea, and John had kept his promise of financial aid to the family. Now Anne was preparing for her marriage to a silk merchant. She informed John and his family and invited them to the ceremony, which was to be a small intimate affair. Just a few close friends and family members would attend.

Her intended was a small, quiet man, just the opposite of Thomas. Leonard had been married before and had two children, who Anne accepted with open arms. Her own children were older and could help with their younger stepsiblings; at least Margery could, as Peter would be attending St. John's in Cambridge soon to become a priest.

Margery remained home with her mother and new family. From the time she was born, she had been betrothed to Albert, an arrangement that was completely unknown to him. His parents had not anticipated the possibility that he would have ideas of his own. He had always been a hardworking, obedient child. However, John knew he would have to tell him of their plans for his marriage to Margery very soon. It seemed that lately Albert was looking and acting more like a man than a boy, and John felt the time for marriage was drawing near. It wasn't until Anne's second husband died suddenly that the truth came out.

A message reached John in the late fall just before his journey to Peterborough for the sheep fells (skins) of the winter kill. John and Sara discussed Anne's problem with husbands dying prematurely. Although she had enough funds to tide her over, it would not be sufficient for the long term. It was then that Albert was informed of the betrothal. A look of shock and disbelief came over his face.

"She's a child of twelve!" he exclaimed.

"Then she will be ready for marriage in two years," said John.

"But I won't be ready for her. Father, I'm very fond of Margery but not enough to marry her," Albert explained.

"You would learn to love her, dear," Sara said, trying to soothe the tension between father and son.

"I don't want to learn to love anyone," he yelled.

His father reached over and slapped him hard

enough to send him reeling, but he stood his ground and looked definitely into his father's eyes. "I shall not marry her, Father!" he said in a quiet, threatening voice, "even if you try to beat me into it."

"We will talk about this again when we are all more coolheaded. For now, you will begin to get used to the idea that we are your parents and know what's best for you, and you *will* marry Margery. She is a fine girl who comes from an exceptional family!"

Albert's eyes filled with tears as he stared at the floor. He felt as though he was in a bad dream and wanted badly to wake up and find himself with Elizabeth. He couldn't give her up; he wouldn't, no matter what happened!

John and Albert left for Peterborough later that week. On their way to the winter fells, they stopped to visit the Hawkins family as they had always done before. They arrived in front of the family's barn, and John asked Albert to put the horse and wagon in for the night. He was pleased to learn that Anne was making an effort to continue on with her latest husband's business, having a measure of success with it.

It meant that she needed less financial support and that she was recovering from yet another love lost. Although she was not as close to her last husband as she was to Thomas, she still missed him terribly after he died. After all, he was a kind man and very good to her and the children. During the visit, she and John talked about Albert's betrothal to her daughter. "She's a very obedient girl and is looking forward to being Albert's wife," said Anne.

"I'm sure she is," John replied. "But I must be honest,

Anne, and tell you that we only just informed Albert of this agreement a few days ago. He was surprised and very nervous about it."

"Why did you not tell him sooner?" asked Anne.

"I'm sorry; I can't answer that. I just supposed he would learn about it eventually either from Margery or even Peter. I know now that it was a mistake to keep it from him all these years, but I'm sure that when he gets accustomed to the idea, he'll come around."

While they discussed their children's future, Albert took his time tending the horse. As he fed and groomed him, he thought about his troubles. He knew in his heart that to marry Margery would be unfair to her. She was a sweet girl and deserved a husband that loved her. He did not. And he wondered how he was going to escape his fate without hurting her and both their families. After a long while, he decided he could no longer put off facing Anne and her daughter. Much to his relief, all except John had already retired. Without a word, they both went to bed.

Albert lay awake until the early morning hours when exhaustion took over, and he fell into a deep sleep. It seemed he had just dozed off, and it was time to get up. After dressing, they went to the table for Anne's morning fare. Finally, it was time to leave, and they said their good-byes. They were soon on their way to do their business of buying the wool at the fells, after which they started for home. The journey home was awkward and silent. Albert tried to think of Elizabeth, but he was too worried to get any pleasure from his thoughts. Finally, they arrived. Without a word, John jumped down from the wagon and headed into the house while

Albert stabled the horse and wagon. As he unhitched the wagon, he heard someone running outside.

"Albert!" Wat cried frantically.

Albert ran to the open barn door. "What is it?" he replied. "You look terrible! Is there something the matter with Elizabeth?"

"No, she's fine. It's Brother William," cried Wat. "He's been arrested by the archbishop!" His voice cracked as he put his forehead against the wooden doorframe, trying to catch his breath. "I went to talk with him and saw the guards leading him away in chains."

"Did they see you?" Albert asked.

"No, I don't think so," Wat replied, sadly. He started to sob, taking Albert by surprise. He had never seen his friend in such a state before. It was so far removed from his usual overly confident manner.

"The archbishop is here in Sudbury then?" Albert asked.

"Yes," replied Wat. "He came here in search of followers of John Wycliffe. He knows that people will listen, and he's afraid it will lead to dissention in the church. Brother William was charged with heresy! He will burn at the stake!" Wat cried.

"What shall we do?" Albert asked.

"Your father is friends with the archbishop, is he not? He could speak on behalf of Brother William."

"Yes, but I'm not sure if it would be wise for me to ask him. He is already angry at me." Albert stopped himself from saying any more. He didn't want the news of his betrothal getting back to Elizabeth. He paused for a moment as he stared into Wat's eyes, and he knew he was not going to turn his back on his friends. "I will ask him and do what I can. I only hope it will be enough."

Wat roughly embraced him. "Albert, my dear friend, I thank you for whatever effort you put forth," Wat choked out. "May God go with you," he said as he left with guarded optimism.

Not sure of how he would present this matter to his father, Albert pondered his thoughts. He feared his father's anger, but with the thought of Brother William being led to the gallows and the possibility of his friends and himself being associated with his activities, he mustered the courage to approach him.

His plan was to try to convince him that Brother William was a good man and would pose no threat to Simon or the church. He also knew that he was not supposed to even know of Brother William, never mind defend him. He walked quickly into the house and stood before the closed door of the counting room. He took a deep breath and opened the door to see his father sitting at his desk engrossed in his bookkeeping. He looked up as Albert entered.

Albert stood, looking at him in silence.

"What is it? Why do you interrupt my work?" John said impatiently.

"I'm sorry, Father, but I must speak to you on an important matter," said Albert.

Seeing the look of concern on Albert's face, John put aside his books to listen. Albert went on to tell him about Brother William's problem and that he was being held by the archbishop there in Sudbury.

"How in the world did you ever come to meet this person?" John demanded.

"I met him through Wat Tyler," Albert replied.

"I had not known that you became so friendly with Wat Tyler, but I do remember warning you about getting involved with such people."

Albert listened in silence as his father lectured.

"They will bring nothing but sorrow to you, Albert, and I say this with great concern. I realize I cannot watch over you every moment; after all, you are approaching manhood. I cannot choose your friends for you. I can only warn you that some people are not good for you. However, I will help this Brother William if you promise to make distance between yourself and Wat Tyler. Do you understand me, son?"

"Oh, yes, thank you, Father!" Albert said excitedly.

"Go, take care of your business, and mark my words, Albert," he said.

"Yes, sir," Albert said as he stood on trembling legs. He turned and left the room, closing the door behind him as he breathed a sigh of relief.

It was after vespers when John went to visit the archbishop at the rectory of All Saints.

Entering the church grounds, he encountered the archbishop's retinue encamped there. At the entrance, a guard stepped in front of him.

"What is your business here, sir?" he demanded.

"I wish to have a meeting with Archbishop Simon Sudbury," John replied.

"Have you an appointment?"

"No, sir, it is a matter that has just now been brought to my attention. It concerns the prisoner, William," he said.

The guard gave John a sidelong look as he called for the village priest to escort John to the archbishop's chambers.

"I shall announce your presence," said the priest. "Wait here." He turned, walked down the hall, and gently rapped on the door. He then opened the door and walked in, closing it behind him. After a moment, he came out and waved to John to come in.

"Giovanni!" said Simon, calling him by his old name. It made John think of his youth and the old days. "Or should I call you John?" he asked as he held his ringed hand out for John to kiss.

"Whatever you are at comfort with, Excellence," said John.

"Oh, but the name Giovanni brings back fond memories of that lovely city of Florence. It's splendor and beauty lingers within," said Simon wistfully. "Come in, Come in," he said, motioning his hand toward the chair. "Do sit down. It is good of you to stop by and visit. How is your family?" he said with a wide grin.

"They are all well; thank you, my lord," said John.

"Very good," said Simon. "Now, what is it that brings you here?"

"I've heard you hold a prisoner by the name of Brother William," John replied.

The charitable look on Simon's face darkened. "Yes," he said somewhat colder. "What of the scoundrel?"

At this point in the conversation, John knew he would have to choose his words very carefully.

"I know this man. He has absolutely no power within the church. He was excommunicated years ago. He now spends his days telling fables and entertaining the younger folk, including my son. He is no more than a charlatan, and no one takes him at his word," he continued.

"Why is his welfare your concern then?" asked Simon.

"Well, as I said, he is harmless and quite helpless, and he is a casual friend. I feel it would be a mistake to hold him as he really hasn't committed any crime, and prosecution could make him appear as a martyr, giving him more credence than he deserves."

Simon looked at John intently. "Let me tell you something John, and listen well, my friend!" he fired. "In the years 1209–44, a group of heretics occupied Southern France. They were known as the Albeginsians. This small, seemingly *harmless* group of heretics gained so much power that our Holy Father, Pope Gregory IX, launched a crusade against them. It took years to extinguish the flames of that one small candle!" ranted Simon.

"You see, John," he continued in a calmer voice. "This man I have is not only a follower of that madman John Wycliffe, he is even more radical. Do you know of this Wycliffe?" he asked. Before John could answer, he continued with his lecture. "He leads a small band of renegade priests that are roaming all over England and corrupting our children with their dissidence. And I have captured one of the most dangerous of the lot. He will be made an example!"

John stood before the archbishop. "What will become of him?" he asked.

Simon clinched his fist and pounded his desk. "He will be tried, convicted, and burned at the stake, sir!" he bellowed. "John, I must say that your son's association with this man is serious," said Simon with a look of concern on his face. "He should be advised to separate himself from him immediately!"

"Yes, my lord, I have advised him so," replied John.

"What of William's followers, has he had anything to do with them at all?"

"No, Excellence, nothing at all. He's a respectable boy. He has never been involved with any renegades or rebels of any kind in his life," said John.

"I must speak to your son at once. Please send him to me," said Simon. He held his hand out for John to kiss his ring and waved him away.

John arrived home and walked into the kitchen where Sara was preparing their evening meal. "Where is Albert?" he asked.

Seeing her husband's face so pale concerned her. "What is it?" she asked.

"Where is he?" he demanded.

"He is in the stable. What is the matter?" she asked.

Without answering, John rushed through the house and out the back door toward the stable where Albert was preparing the wagon for the trip to Colchester.

"Come here, son," said John.

Albert walked over and stood before him.

John put his hands on Albert's shoulders and looked into his son's eyes. "I've spoken to Simon, and he was quite furious with my request. Now, he has demanded to see you."

Albert's face dropped.

"Tell him that you have only met this man once and that it was by chance. He happened to speak to you at the fair and that's all. Do not mention Wat Tyler's name or the names of anyone that he is associated with. Do you understand?"

"Yes, sir," said Albert. "But what will become of Brother William?"

John looked at his son. "This is a very serious matter, son! My concern is what will become of you! The church gives no quarter! I know not what the outcome will be! You are my only son," he said more softly. "Please do as I say, and don't make more trouble."

"Yes, sir, I will try," Albert said sadly.

Chapter Nine

Upon arriving at the rectory, Albert was quickly ushered in without delay. The archbishop stood facing the window when he entered. He turned quickly with eyes blazing.

Albert's first instinct was to turn and run, but he held fast, determined to face his fears. He knew he was looking at the real Simon and not the sickening sweet charlatan he had met before. Without the formality of a greeting, the interrogation began with an unrelenting barrage of questions.

"What do you know of the so-called Brother William?" he demanded. "Where does he come from, and who are his followers?"

"I know not were he hails from, and I know of no one else who has spoken with him. I have met the man only once, Your Eminence, and I know he could not break the laws of the church. He seems a good man, sir," said Albert in a surprisingly confident voice that only fueled Simon's rage.

"Damn you, boy! You say you have only met him once?" he yelled. "How is it that you know so much about him?"

Albert stood quiet for only a moment and looked Simon in the eye. "I don't know very much about him, sir. I'm only telling you that he seems a good man. What possible threat could he be to a man as holy and powerful as His Eminence?" he said, trying to appeal to Simon's vanity.

Simon gave a sly smile. He knew that Albert was very much like his father. He could not be threatened or intimidated so easily. In spite of his fear and anger, he had to respect the boy. He could see that his line of questioning and yelling profanities would only make it harder to get the information he wanted.

Simon took a deep breath and spoke to Albert in a quiet voice. "What do you know of Wat Tyler?" he asked.

"He was the lad who replaced our roof."

"Is that all you know about him?"

"Yes, sir," he lied.

Simon stopped his questioning and started to formulate another tactic. He turned and gazed out the window and then turned back to Albert.

"Perhaps, your Bother William is as harmless as you say and should be spared. After all, we would not want to make a martyr of him would we? That would give him more credibility than he deserves."

Albert immediately became hopeful, but cautious, and he measured his response carefully. He wondered why Simon had made this complete metamorphosis from raging tyrant to angel of forgiveness.

"Jesus forgave his persecutors," Simon continued. "I'm sure the church can find it in its heart to forgive Brother William."

Albert held back a sigh of relief. "Yes, thanks be to God," he said as he bowed his head.

"That will be all," said Simon as the conversation came to a close. "However; I do have a favor to ask of you, my boy," said Simon.

"Yes," replied Albert. "What would that be?"

"If you happen to meet Wat Tyler, would you inform me? I would like to meet and talk with him about his tiling work."

Albert knew immediately what the archbishop's intentions were, but he agreed to the request. "Oh yes, Your Eminence. I will do that right away." He lied as he turned to leave.

He walked home wondering if he would be followed and how he would warn Wat. Not knowing that the archbishop wanted him for questioning, Wat had taken a job working on a house that was located only a short distance from the rectory. Albert was aware of this, and after looking around carefully, he headed toward the work site. When he arrived, he found the job had been completed, and Wat and his family had moved on.

He turned and walked back toward home, concerned that Wat and his family were no longer working in the area. If they were, Elizabeth would come by at night to visit Albert. They would meet secretly in his barn, and he would have the chance to get word to Wat without having to actually meet with him, which could be dangerous at the moment. But if she didn't show, he didn't know what he would do. He prayed she would come if not tonight, then soon, and before the archbishop had a chance to get to Wat first.

As he did every evening, Albert made an excuse to work in the barn after having supper with his parents who would retreat to the living room. There they would sit next to the large stone hearth where Sara would work on her embroidery and John on his books. It would not be long before the two would retire for the night, leaving Albert to his own devices. Neither knew of his secret meetings with the pretty, little peasant girl and the romance and intrigue they were so deeply involved in.

Soon, there was a gentle tap on the barn door that signaled Elizabeth's arrival. As she opened the door, the sight of her made Albert sigh with relief. The moment their eyes met, she knew something was wrong. "Are you not glad to see me?" she asked.

Albert took her in his arms and kissed her. "If not for seeing you, love, my life would be meaningless." He paused, looking at her with sad eyes.

"Why do you look at me in that way?" she asked.

"The archbishop is looking for your brother. He says it is about business, but I know it's more about Brother William. Although he has agreed to release the brother, he is hoping that it will lead to finding out more about his following. I fear that he plans to arrest him again along with Wat and everyone associated with him."

"Well, we have been working within a short distance, and Simon's men have not approached. Perhaps, he really wants to speak with him for business purposes," said Elizabeth. "And since your family had our family work for you, it would make sense to send a message through you."

"Why didn't he ask my father for that information? Wouldn't he be more likely?"

"Yes, I suppose so," she replied. "What do you think we should do?"

"Where are you planning to work?" he asked.

"New Braintree."

"No," Albert said. "Don't go there. It would be too easy for Simon to find him there. My suggestion is to go to London. There are many more people, which would provide more shelter." He paused for a moment and looked at her.

Without a word spoken, she knew that going to London would mean she and her family would have to go into hiding. She also knew it would be a very long time before she and her Albert could be together again. For now, they tried to make the best of this meeting. As they lay in each other's arms, they spoke of happier times when they would be forever joined in marriage.

Soon, Elizabeth had to leave. Albert held her in his arms as they stood at the door. He stepped out first to make sure there was no one about. He looked around and turned to her for one last kiss. She took her leave with bowed head and tears in her eyes.

As she walked back to her family's hovel, she thought of the impossibility of it all. *How would I ever be allowed to marry him?* she thought. *And now my brother is a wanted man.* There was one good thing about it; their beloved Brother William would be spared, all because of her Albert's quick wit and bravery. She hurried on to deliver the news to Wat and their father.

When Elizabeth told Wat, he felt he was lucky to have escaped apprehension and prepared immediately to leave for London before sun up.

For John and Albert, there was quite another scenario. Albert was recalled by the archbishop and questioned once again. "Eminence, I have neither seen nor heard from Wat Tyler," he claimed. But Simon knew differently.

"Well, my boy," said Simon. "It seems that what you tell me is not altogether true. I know that you have not actually met with him, but I do know that you are friends and that you are in love with the beautiful Elizabeth. Is that not correct?" Before Albert could answer he went on. "You see, I have ways of finding out about everyone. We questioned your Brother William. He had no choice but to comply," he said with a wide grin.

Albert clinched his fists as he felt the anger rise to boiling point. *The bastard has betrayed me!* he thought. Simon never intended to drop the charges against Brother William! Instead, he had him tortured without mercy.

Albert stood quietly, seething as Simon made other accusations. "Does your father know of your plans to marry the sister of an outlaw and a peasant as well?" he asked.

"My father has nothing to do with this!" said Albert. "When he came to you before, it was on my behalf. He never knew of my association with the Tylers or

Brother William. He is most innocent, and there is no need to implicate him."

"I admire your willingness to protect your father, my boy, but I do believe he is already implicated. After all, you were the one who implicated him; is that not correct?" he said as he rang his little bell for his assistant. "Go and fetch John Deaconson," he commanded.

A short time later, John appeared. The archbishop summarized the discussion he had had with Albert, including his intention to marry Elizabeth.

John looked at his son in surprise. He was just now realizing how deeply Albert was involved with this gang of rebels. "Is this true?" he asked.

"Yes, sir," said Albert with his head bowed.

"Why didn't you tell me this before, son?" his father demanded.

Albert looked at his father without answering.

John turned and looked at Simon. "Forgive me, Your Eminence, I had no idea the boy was so wayward."

Simon excused Albert to the other room to await his father.

He invited John to sit, and they discussed the issues at length. "Giovanni," he said in a more amiable tone. "We have been friends for many years. You have proven yourself to be most trustworthy, again and again. I would not want you or your family to come to any harm, but Albert's offence against the church is quite serious."

John's voice cracked as he spoke. "Excellence, my son is young and somewhat naïve; he has been led astray."

"Yes," Simon agreed. "He has been led astray. And

you had no inkling of his intention to marry this peasant girl?" he asked.

"Certainly not, sir, only casual talk about her brother. I am quite shocked and dismayed by the whole matter," replied John.

"Yes, I expect you would be," said Simon. "Well then, Giovanni, I have a way to settle this whole affair," he said with his arms outstretched in a holy manner. John listened intently as the archbishop divulged his plan.

"Your son has proven himself in battle during that skirmish at Peterborough, has he not?"

There was a short hesitation in John's answer as he tried to figure out where Simon's question was leading. "Yes," he replied. "In my opinion he was exemplary. He saved my life that day."

"Yes, so I heard. He is a remarkable young man. That is why I would make the proposition for him to be sent to the estate of a nobleman where he would be trained in the ways of chivalry and knighthood. John couldn't believe his ears, and for a few moments, he just stared at the archbishop.

"Well?" asked Simon. "What do you say to that?"

John stood up and reached out his hand. "I would be very much in agreement, Excellency, and I thank you. But I must ask, how would that be possible? He is already past the age of becoming a page."

Simon let out a loud guffaw. "There is nothing that the Archbishop of Canterbury cannot do, my friend," he boasted. "Whether a serf, an innkeeper, too young, or too old, I have the means to perform miracles. I can create a knight out of a straw man if I wish to," he continued arrogantly.

John grew thoughtful for a moment.

"What is it?" asked Simon.

"Well, I was thinking of how his mother would accept this plan. I believe she was as sure as I was that he would be following me into the merchant business," said John.

"Are you not the keeper of your household?" Simon asked. "It is your decision, not hers. Besides, I think she would prefer to have him become a knight than a convicted felon. Would she not?"

"Yes, of course," said John.

"This is in the best interests of your son, John, and you must convince your wife that it is the only way! The matter is settled," said Simon. "I suggest you return home and inform Sara of the planned departure. I will be leaving for Canterbury within the next few days. On the way, your son and I will have an audience with Lord Stafford in London. He will remain there until he is called into knighthood."

"Yes, sir," said John. "And thank you."

"I'm sure this will end your problems, my friend. He will soon forget this peasant girl and her wayward brother. As for that scoundrel William, he will certainly be burned at the stake and forgotten within a fortnight. Off with you then, Giovanni, and have your son report to me in the morning with his bags packed."

"Yes, sir," said John. "And God be with you." He left the archbishop's chamber and met Albert as a priest led him back to his father.

On the walk home, John explained that he would not be arrested.

Albert was elated but was afraid to ask how his father had changed Simon's mind.

John delayed telling Albert of the plans for knighthood as he wanted to tell his mother first. He felt saddened that his son was about to be taken from him and that all of his plans for Albert's future were going to be changed. He comforted himself with the thought that he was doing his best to preserve Albert's well-being. He knew how ruthless Simon could be even if it meant taking the life of a close friend. It wouldn't matter that John had saved his life many times in the past. If there were anyone who challenged his authority, he would immediately disappear.

He wondered how his family would accept the news. He knew Sara would be upset, but Albert, on the other hand, might be excited about becoming a knight. After all, if it were good for him, it would be good for Albert too.

Upon arriving home, he thought about how he would explain. The moment he walked in, Sara asked about his meeting with Simon. "We will discuss it together, at supper," he said. "But I will tell you that Albert will not be arrested."

Sara gave a sigh of relief and went about preparing the evening meal. When they were all around the table, John explained that Albert was to leave the next day, and Sara would have to help him pack his things for the journey.

"How long will he be gone," she sobbed.

"Indefinitely. Please don't cry so," John said as he stood to put his arms around her.

Albert looked at his parents and thought about Elizabeth. He knew he would sourly miss his parents, but in London he would be close to Elizabeth; and the thought of becoming a knight was very exciting.

He stood and tried to comfort his mother. "You'll be proud of me when I'm a knight, Mother," he said. But the sound of his boyish voice and the innocence of his words only made her cry harder.

She looked up into his handsome, young face, stood, and took him in her arms. "I must pack your things," she said, collecting herself. She turned and walked briskly up the stairs to Albert's room and began the task.

The next morning, they said their tearful good-byes as John and Sara delivered their only child to All Saints Church. After a last hug and tearful kiss, he was gone for who knew how long.

The archbishop's guards appeared at the rectory door to greet Albert. He turned to look back at the two people who been by his side forever and wondered what life would be like without them. He chocked back the tears and stood tall. He was determined to make them proud. The guards led him away to a private room and a new life. In the sparsely furnished room, Albert sat alone with his thoughts. The day's dampness and his nervousness made him shiver as he sat on the hard cot awaiting the archbishop.

He looked up at the window where the wooden shutter let slivers of light through the cracks. He stared at the light, momentarily mesmerized, and daydreamed of Elizabeth, Wat, Brother William, and his parents.

Soon the sounds from outside would bring him back to reality. Heavy shuffling of feet, muffled voices, and the town crier's bell could be heard with a faint cry of the news being bellowed throughout the village.

It was late in the day, and he had not eaten since the morning. His stomach was in protest as it gurgled and rumbled in want of food. He stood up walked to the door and found it to be locked. He shook it hard in anger.

Day melted into evening, and darkness came upon him. The only sound now was vespers. His hunger grew, and he began pounding on the door. Finally, lying down he fell into a restless sleep.

The morning brought a guard's heavy hands roughly shaking him awake. Food and a candle for light were brought in for the first time since he arrived. Without a word, the guard laid the tray on his cot beside him and left. Albert put his fingers into the rough porridge and filled his mouth. His teeth began to tingle, and chills ran down his spine as he chewed the gritty substance. He dropped the empty bowl and grabbed the beaker of beer, putting it to his lips and drinking heavily to wash down the horrid gruel. The rancid taste of the beer made him spit it out about the room. The atrocious brew tasted as if it had been expelled from the archbishop's bladder. He threw the beaker to the floor.

"This is how he treats the son of a friend?" he asked himself. "My God, what does he do to his enemies?" It would not be long before Albert would have his answer.

Soon the guard appeared again and led Albert outside to the village square. There were a good many people gathered for the spectacle that was planned. Albert looked about and wondered what was going on. He saw many familiar faces of those whom he knew through his parents. Then he noticed the stake surrounded by faggots and knew what was to take place shortly. He wondered who the unfortunate and most likely innocent victim would be. Finally, the archbishop appeared with his entourage of guards. The village priest along with another servant brought his chair, and Simon Sudbury took his place with Albert standing to his right with his bodyguard.

They stood in a semicircle so that Simon could watch Albert's every move during the execution.

Albert's legs grew weak as he watched the guards bringing the prisoner. "Oh, God, no," he whispered. As his knees began to buckle under, the guard grabbed his arm and steadied him. The village priest, who was standing to Simon's left, reached over to catch Albert's other arm.

"Come, Albert," he said sympathetically. "Hold firm, my son."

Chapter Ten

Albert watched helplessly as Brother William, weighted down with chains, was led by a procession of guards. The bloodthirsty, so-called pious villagers became deathly quiet as they watched the heavily shackled, ragged heretic being led to the hastily assembled execution podium. In his bloodied hand, he held two sticks formed into a cross. His face was a mask of bewilderment and shock much to the archbishop's dismay as he was hoping to hear William beg for mercy and prove to the public his true cowardice. But the torturers did their job too well, for all that was left to the execution flames was the shell of a man.

It seemed to Albert that through the mercy of the Almighty, William's soul was already in heaven. He hoped it would be quick as he said a silent prayer.

William stood before the archbishop as he read the charges. "And may God have mercy on your soul," Simon concluded. He asked William if he had any last words. In a brief coherent moment, William raised his head and gave Simon a look that made him shiver.

"May God have mercy on *your* soul," he said quietly.

Simon, visibly shaken, watched as they led William off to his destiny. The order was given, and the faggots were lit. The lusty crowd looked on, most of them making the sign of the cross and some trying to cover their eyes. But morbid curiosity overcame good sense, and they watched, licking their lips in holy ecstasy. "The Lord's work is done," they cried.

The untamed flame rose under the gentle breeze, and within an instant, dear William's body was set ablaze. Not a whimper left his lips as the dried wood crackled and popped, and the roaring fire consumed him.

Albert's eyes filled up with tears as the life drained from William's body, and he cried openly as he thought about his failure to save his dear friend's life. He remembered all the sermons, the good advice, the friendship, and love that had grown between them.

As Simon looked on, the blackened face peeled away from the skeletal frame. He watched in disgust and fascination. Finally, he was able to look away and glanced at Albert where he found a small measure of satisfaction. Soon, the fire burned down, and the spectators all but disappeared.

The archbishop and his entourage remained until the fire had breathed its last and all that was left was smoke, ashes, and bone. It was late in the afternoon when they prepared to leave.

Simon gestured for the priest to lead Albert to stand

before him. He stood with his head down, still weeping quietly as Simon spoke.

"Look at me, boy!"

Albert looked at Simon.

"This is the last you will see of Sudbury," he said sternly. "I hope that I have driven the evil of this place out of your soul forever."

Albert took a deep breath of the fetid air, and the smell of the burnt flesh made him vomit at Simon's feet, splattering both their shoes and Simon's hem. He fell to his knees as his body shook violently.

Simon looked down at him in disgust and ordered two guards to take him away. Still sitting in his gothic throne, he spoke with a sense of accomplishment to the village priest, Father Henry, who had begun wiping the vomit from the archbishop's red and gold velvet shoes. "I believe I've broken the lad's spirit sufficiently. Now, we'll see how easy it is to turn this child into a brave and strong knight."

Albert was brought back to his room where he sat on his cot with his head in his hands. He was mentally and physically drained. In his mind, he witnessed the execution over and over. Finally, out of sheer exhaustion, he fell into a deep sleep.

The morning brought hunger, an aching body, and depression. He heard the door open and sprung to a sitting position, which made his head swim and his stomach lurch. Father Henry stood with a tray of food. "Your breakfast, sir," he said in a surly voice.

Albert took an immediate disliking to the man for reasons he could not put his finger on. Father Henry was small in stature with a bald head and a full beard that obscured his facial features. The hair that he did have on his head grew down to his shoulders and looked as though he had never in his life groomed it. Albert felt he could not trust this man, and his instincts were correct.

Father Henry was a contradictory man who knew little about the life of Christ and much about the madam who owned the local brothel. He fervently preached following the commandments to his parishioners, but he seldom followed them himself. He spoke of heaven and never believed in anything higher than the roof above his head. The villagers were well aware of his vices, especially his flagrant womanizing; however, they never expressed their feelings but kept a close eye on their wives and daughters whenever he was around.

The church hierarchy was well aware of the all of the illicit activities of some of their clergymen, including Father Henry, but because of the Black Death, the wars, and the conversion of many, there was a shortage of clergymen; therefore, the church turned a blind eye to the matter.

"You would be wise to accept your fate, sir," he said as he turned to leave. "You would not want to disgrace your family; would you, my boy?"

Albert didn't answer. He just stared down at his food for a moment.

"God be with you, son," Father Henry said.

Albert looked up, surprised at the sudden softening in the priest's voice.

"Thank you, Father," he said respectfully.

Albert sat quietly for a moment, thinking about what was to come and what had taken place the day before. His thoughts of Brother William saddened him beyond everything else. And he worried about his other friends. *What will become of Wat Tyler?* he thought. And would he ever see Elizabeth again?

The only good thing about going to London was the possibility of seeing her. He thought about escaping after his arrival there, but he quickly put it out of his mind. He knew if he did, he would bring dishonor to his mother and father, and anyway, he would not want to have to be on the run for the rest of his life. He decided the best thing to do was to follow his father's and the priest's advice.

The archbishop's guard appeared as he sat deep in thought, informing him that it was time to leave. They led him down to the front of the church where Simon, his servants, and guard awaited his arrival. The servants loaded the baggage onto the coach's roof and climbed onto the back as Albert, Simon, and the guard seated themselves inside the coach. Theirs would be a most comfortable ride with many cushions and blankets to keep them warm.

Soon they were on their way. Albert poked his head out the window and watched as the village of his youth faded away.

The archbishop's entourage arrived in London a few days later, and Albert was hurriedly whisked off to the estate of Lord Hugh Stafford where he would embark upon a brand new chapter in his life.

In order to attain knighthood, a man would have

to be born into it. His lineage had to be traced back at least two generations, and he would have to born of a noblewoman as well. His family would have to be wealthy enough to provide him with a horse, armor, weapons, and other necessities. He would be sent to live with a nobleman or former knight and become his page.

Albert fit very few of the requirements of becoming a knight. Most men started as young children at the age of seven, would serve their masters, and be tutored in all the aspects of nobility and chivalry. Albert was twice the age of the average page, and he was not born of noble birth; but his father was a knight before he came to England. And even though John was a foreigner, he could claim his knighthood in any other Christian country.

Also, in Albert's special case, he was the friend of a very powerful public figure. His bravery in saving his father's life at the Peterborough melee was a point in his favor as well, for Prince Edward himself had taken notice.

Lord Stafford's estate was a great, stone manor encompassed by a formidable stone wall. The grounds consisted of a front courtyard for receiving guests, a smaller but noble domicile that housed the lord's knights, and a stable for the horses that included an extension where the squires lived. The grounds surrounding these living quarters were designed exclusively for the training of the young squires in the art of war. For Albert, who was the lord's only page at this time, there was little interaction with other pages. He was kept busy with the various needs and requirements imposed by his master and mistress.

Under the watchful eyes of his tutors, he received training in manners, religion, and other aspects of courtly life. By rights, he should have been receiving instruction in the art of warfare as other squires, but his masters, in their attempt to cram six years of training into one, felt that it was important for him to learn the art of the social graces first as they were sure his ability in combat would come more naturally than other skills.

Every day brought many new challenges, and Albert worked from the time he awoke early in the morning until he fell into bed at night. Although exhausted at the end of the day, he lay in bed for a brief time every night and reflected on all that was happening in his life. His thoughts were filled with melancholy memories of his mother and father, Brother William, Wat Tyler, and most of all, Elizabeth.

So much time had gone by, and he realized it had been nearly a year since he'd seen her last. He hoped that she hadn't changed her mind about him and found someone who was more available to her. He knew she was maturing quickly, and he remembered the way other boys and even older men looked at her. These thoughts made him fearful and angry, and he tossed and turned before he would finally fall asleep at night.

John and Sara remained in Sudbury and waited to hear from Albert. Sara missed her son terribly and still felt depressed over his leaving. However, hard work and a busy schedule kept her sad feelings at bay. She was now busier than ever as she had taken over her son's job as apprentice as well as his household chores. John was also very much aware of his son's absence, but he felt the rigorous training he was receiving toward knighthood was what the boy needed most. There, he would learn discipline and self-respect. And although John was always proud of his boy, he could now respect him as a man.

Thomas Hawkins' wife Anne had again married—this time to another wool merchant whom John had become quite fond of and taken on as an associate. Peter Hawkins had already become a priest and was rising steadily in the Benedictine monastery. Margery's betrothal to Albert was annulled at the request of both families much to her disappointment. She had always loved Albert and looked forward to marrying him; however, it was not meant to be. She cried for a while and decided (with a bit of prompting from her mother) to enter the priory of St. Mary Avery in London.

The Tylers remained in London where the work was plentiful. London was growing bigger by the day, and building was widespread. The archbishop's search for Wat had been abandon and eventually forgotten. After all, what harm could a lowly tradesman do to the Archbishop of Canterbury?

The news of Brother William reached Wat and made him even more determined in his quest for change. Over the next several months, the family worked on many of the homes in and around the London area.

On one fateful day, they had started a new job. They had constructed scaffolding, and Peter climbed up to the roof as Wat gathered material to be used for its construction. On his way up the ladder, one of the supports gave way, and the whole scaffolding collapsed to the ground with Peter landing among the debris. Wat rushed to his father and lifted the heavy boards and posts off him. They had had accidents like this before, but somehow even before Wat had gotten to his father, he knew that they were not so lucky this time.

Elizabeth was inconsolable at her father's passing, and Wat spent most of his time drinking at public houses and getting into fights. Finally, she had had enough, and they both decided it would be best for her to enter a convent where she spent her days praying and her nights dreaming of Albert. Her sadness was great as she had lost her beloved father, and Wat and Albert were no longer a part of her life. She had all but given up hope that she would ever find happiness. With only her prayers to comfort her, she resigned herself to the service of God and her new life.

Wat remained in London, working, drinking, and brawling. Soon his drinking began affecting his work habits, and he was spending more and more time in the many London bordellos. Without working regularly and spending his money on liquor and women, it wasn't long before he was penniless and took to the streets.

Hearing of a proclamation to recruit soldiers for the French wars and considering his state of affairs, he decided to join the cause, despite his distaste for the nobles, and shortly afterward, he left London to serve in a force led by Sir John Gaunt. Soon he found himself involved in a massive raid in France, beginning in Calais and ending at Bordeaux.

The campaign accomplished very little and cost a fortune in weaponry, equipment, and livestock, as well as men's lives. The French used the strategy of withdrawal into fortified towns, which prevented the English from invading and ravaging. It was a technique that wore down the English forces. The struggle to take the towns without engaging the French left the English exhausted, and the lack of provisions brought them to the brink of starvation. At the conclusion of the raid at Boulogne, Gaunt was forced to bring his army home—the mission a complete failure.

Wat remained in Gascony for a time. He was a soldier in one of the few English levy towns left in France. He became a skilled infantryman and organizer—abilities that would prove to serve him well.

News from home reached Albert through word of mouth via friars traveling to Canterbury, who would keep him informed fairly regularly. Although he was happy to hear about his parents, he was saddened by the lack of news about Elizabeth and Wat. He wondered what had become of his friends and if Elizabeth still thought of him. Did she still love him? Was she well? These thoughts always disturbed him and kept him wide-eyed at night in spite of his exhaustion. He had not heard of Peter's death and had no way of knowing that she and her brother had parted company.

His life as a page was drawing to an end, and he was about to become a squire. As he was prepared for that day, he was also to be on hand to witness the knighting of John Audrey, a squire to Sir William Warde. He was twenty-one years old and one of the oldest squires in Lord Stafford's household. Although he fought bravely in France with Sir William and was considered to be an excellent squire, there was some reason why he was not knighted on the field of battle as all exceptional squires were. Whatever the reason, he was to be knighted today at the palace of Sir John Gaunt, at which time Albert would assume his duties as a new squire.

The knighthood rituals began the night before with a purification bath followed by the intended knight praying before the altar with his armor at his side. In the morning, he was led to the courtyard of the lord in a procession of knights and ladies.

He was then dressed in his armor one piece at a time, a sword girdled about his waist, and spurs attached to his feet. Then he knelt for the accolade, which was preformed by Sir John Gaunt. As he placed the flat side of the blade of a sword gently on one of the knight's shoulders and then the other, he recited the verse. "In the name of God, St. Michael, and St. George, I dub thee knight; be brave and loyal."

After the ceremonies, the new Sir John rode off to begin his service to the household of William Bohun, Earl of Essex. Albert would replace him as squire to Sir William and begin his second phase of training toward knighthood.

Whilst in training, he was quartered with three other squires. Their quarters consisted of a stone barrack that abutted the stable. Spartan conditions prevailed with cots of straw and reeds covering the floor which needed to be replaced daily. Orderliness was a priority, and purity and chivalry, although questionable in some squires, were foremost. A constant watch over the squires' behavior was provided by the crucifix that hung above the door. Most were aware and followed not so much out of fear but out of respect; however, there were some who were especially defiant and would be able to get away with their misdeeds only for a short time before Lord Stafford caught up with him. And sometimes he would overlook the transgression with a quick act of contrition from a favored squire.

All of those quartered with Albert were of noble birth. One of them was Squire Thomas Montacute, who was a relative of the Earl of Salisbury who was a member of King Edward's inner circle. Squire Thomas was a lad of fine manners, deep religious conviction, and strong sense of loyalty. He was tall, lean, and exceptionally strong. He kept to himself, mostly, so no one with exception of the lord really knew about him or his family. His ruddy complexion gave him the appearance of more ruffian than mild-mannered squire.

Another was Squire Gilles Marshall from Plimstead whose family was the illustrious Norman English Fitzgilberts. The first Marshall was William, who was a great tournament warrior—a fact that Gilles would not let any of the other squires forget. He was tall and thin and not one of Albert's favorite people. He found Gilles to be of a haughty personality, critical, and short of temper.

Then there was Squire Henry Bury whose grandfather was the tutor to Prince Edward and who hailed from London. He was of medium height with a rounded physique. A crop of thick, black hair and an infectious smile added to his jovial appearance. His personality was one of fun and games, and when he was present, everyone shared in his good spirits. Compared to the rest of the squires with their formal manners, including Albert, he seemed the least likely candidate for knighthood.

Each squire was assigned to a household knight. Thomas was the squire assigned to Sir George Irland, a typical Arthurian knight, good-tempered, and kind to all, especially the poor and unfortunate. He walked with a pronounced limp due to a wagon accident, which left one leg shorter than the other. Also, he bore a strong resemblance to Richard Coredeleon.

Gilles was assigned to Sir Godfrey, a fine and serious soldier. He was valiant in arms and present at the battle of Poitiers, where Prince Edward captured King John of France. His face had the marking of a true warrior, and though an older man, plenty of fight still remained in him. Henry was assigned to Sir Robert DeNortone, a rather bland knight with ample fighting ability, but he had little use for the pomp and flare. He spoke little and was very pious and stern. His pale complexion and slight build was more befitting a priest than a knight.

Squire Albert Deaconson was assigned to Sir William Warde, a knight errant. He was a true warrior by all standards, veteran of the French wars and the winner of many a tournament. His build was of medium stature, and he had the courage of a lion. His face bore a severe scar over his left eye, which drastically affected his vision.

The training of the squires was rigorous with a great deal of time spent learning the techniques of hunting, which were essential in certain types of battle. Once, while hunting wild boar, Gilles revealed a particularly nasty side to his personality. He had let his arrow wound an animal, and instead of making a clean kill, he stood over the beast, watching it writhe in pain. His face was red, he was breathing hard, and it seemed to Albert that he was enjoying the suffering. Albert walked up to the dying boar and with sword drawn mercifully ended its life. "That was my kill, sir!" Gilles yelled, outraged.

"What in hell do you think you are doing?" Albert screamed.

"Go back to your sheep shearing, wool merchant!" Gilles retorted.

"What cowardice, the likes of which I have never seen before!" Albert yelled.

"I'll show you who's a coward, you peasant," Gilles replied.

"Come over here, and show me then," Albert challenged.

Squires Henry and Thomas stepped in before it could come to blows much to Albert's frustration and Gilles' relief.

"What's going on?" asked Thomas.

Albert began to explain. "He wounded the animal and took his time making the clean kill."

"That's not at all what happened," Gilles chided. "This country yokel stole my kill!"

Albert's face flushed red, and his eyes flashed. Henry stood between them, facing Albert.

A smile crossed his face as he placed his hand on Albert's chest. "We are all brothers," he said softly. "We have trained together, and one day we will fight in battle together. We will have to depend on one another. It would not be a good thing to become enemies, my friends. So put the disagreement aside, and shake hands."

Henry stood back, and Albert reluctantly held out his hand but was immediately snubbed. Again his anger soared.

"Squire Gilles!" Henry demanded.

Gilles took Albert's hand a bit too roughly and shook it. They glared at each other and turned away.

"Fine, the matter's settled then," said Thomas as the two walked away.

The matter is far from settled! Albert thought as he knew there would many more encounters with the most arrogant Gilles.

Chapter Eleven

In the year of our Lord, 1376, a terrible tragedy befell England. Prince Edward, who had been ill for quite some time, passed quietly on the morning of June 8, Trinity Sunday, from a disease contracted during his Spanish campaign. A true warrior and victorious leader at the battles of Crecy, Portiers, Nageria, and Lenogs, he was compared to Alexander the Great. And like Alexander, he would never attack a people whom he did not conquer nor besiege a city he did not take.

The funeral procession included Lord Stafford's knights and their squires. In the cool morning air, the cortege made its way from London to Canterbury where they would lay him to rest in Trinity Chapel alongside St. Thomas á Becket. It was the first time Albert had ever been a part a royal event, which brought nobles from near and far. Never had he witnessed such glorious formation and pageantry after which an elegant sermon was delivered by Thomas Briton, Bishop of

Rochester. Everyone present listened intently to the reflection on the glorious life of the prince and on his most perfect example of all that a knight should be. The presentation struck a cord within Albert's heart, inspiring him to work toward matching such standards as the prince in his pursuit for knighthood.

After the funeral service ended, Lord Stafford and his knights and squires remained in Canterbury two more days to rest for the coming one-and-a-half day journey. They stayed at the palace of John Gaunt where Lord Stafford would spend his time discussing foreign affairs with other members of the nobility before leaving for his estate.

On their way back, they passed the priory of St. Mary Avery as they had done on many other occasions, but this time they observed a most welcoming sight. There, picking flowers with some of the sisters was a most beautiful young woman. She raised her head as the entourage was passing by. All of the knights were craning their necks around to gaze at her. The nuns began to giggle as they passed clumsily by, but the young woman just watched. The young men made her think of her own lost love. *He would be about their ages*, she thought sadly.

The knights were followed by their squires in the rear. Gilles was the first one to notice her. He gave a smile, which she politely returned. "Did you take note of the one fair maiden?" he called out.

The rest turned to look, catching sight only of an elderly nun. Apparently, the young woman had already entered the back door of the convent, leaving the mother superior outside when the others took notice. They all laughed loudly as they jeered and mocked Gilles who sat on his horse red-faced and trying to explain.

For the remainder of the journey, the squires thought about the young woman and began to talk of one day meeting a lovely maiden.

"The only ladies in my life are my mother and Lady Stafford," said Henry.

A roar of laughter rose up from the squires.

"What are you all laughing at?" Henry said with a smirk. "After all, when would I have a chance to find a lady love? I was sent from my home at age seven to become a page as you all were," he said.

"Not all of us," Gilles interrupted. "What about you, Albert?" he asked. "You joined us only recently and well over the age of seven."

They all looked at Albert. "What say you to that, friend?" called Henry.

"'Tis true," Albert replied, his face reddening. Suddenly, the group got quiet as Albert lowered his head. "She was a lovely little peasant maiden," he continued. "I was most taken with her sweet ways and lovely face."

"A peasant?" Gilles exclaimed, holding his nose. Albert glared at him, wanting to hit him hard in the face.

"What of it?" said Henry. "Who among us can say the same? Alas, we have no one."

Everyone except Gilles agreed. "Well, a peasant is hardly a lady," he said. "More an animal than a girl," he mumbled lower but not low enough.

Albert turned toward Gilles in a flash. "Hold your

tongue, squire, lest you would have my sword remove it!" he yelled.

Gilles rode up to face Albert, bringing his horse close enough so that their hooves nearly touched one another's. Thomas was the one closest to them and nudged his horse between the two.

"Is there a problem back there?" called Sir William as he turned his horse toward the rear.

"Not at all, sir," Thomas called back respectfully. The interruption was enough to quell the tempers of the two squires if only for the moment.

Soon after they returned to the estate, the squires were allowed take leave of their duties and go into the city. On their way, they again passed the St. Mary's Priory where Gilles kept a keen eye out for the young beauty that he had seen there the day before. He caught a glimpse of her standing behind the gate.

"There she is!" he exclaimed. Henry looked over as indicated.

"She is a lovely little thing, isn't she?" said Henry with a knowing grin. Following behind a ways down the road were Albert and Thomas, but they didn't see the girl in the priory courtyard. By the time they had arrived there, she was gone.

They rode into London proper from Bridge St. to Lombard and onto West Cheap where they parted company. Gilles and Henry were off to a night of drinking and other debauchery, which were forbidden but only if they were found out. Albert had other plans. He remembered that Elizabeth and her family were living somewhere in the area, but he didn't know exactly where.

"This may seem like a foolish waste of time," he said to Thomas. "But I would like to use this time to search for my maiden. There's a possibility that her family still resides in London, and I must try to find her."

"London is a very big place," said Thomas. "You may well use all of your free-time looking, my friend."

"Yes, well, I'll take my chances," he said, turning his horse. "What about you?"

"I'm off to St. Paul's," replied Thomas. "I feel a need for prayer and reflection."

Albert smiled. "You remind me of the Knights Templar," he said.

"Oh, and how is that?" replied Thomas, smiling back.

"Well, you know of the Knights Templar, don't you?" said Albert.

"Yes, of course. They were the warrior priests of the Crusades, and I shall take that as a compliment," said Thomas.

"If it pleases you, I could accompany you to St. Paul's," said Albert.

"And I could help you look for your lady on the way," Thomas replied.

Albert thought it a bit odd that Thomas would choose to pray rather than enjoy his time away from duties, but at the same time, he respected Thomas for his self-control and devotion to God. His quiet manner and kind heart made Albert think of Brother William. Although there was very little physical resemblance, there was that same look of understanding and compassion in Thomas' eyes as Albert had seen in William's.

They continued riding on through the filthy streets

of London, keeping a look out at any house or building that was having its roof tiled. The squalor was horrible, the likes of which Albert had never seen before. The streets were littered with garbage and human waste, along with a few dead animals here and there. They passed many people, some lying sleeping, or maybe dead from the smell of them on the side of the road. Some called out their begging pleas.

"Would ya have a coin for the poor, sir?" said a ragged woman as she stepped toward Albert's horse.

He could smell her rancid breath even before she opened her mouth to speak. One eye appeared to look toward Thomas, and the other looked straight at him. Albert felt unnerved by his encounter with her, but at the same time, he felt a profound sense of pity, which turned to confusion as they continued to ride past her.

"You bastards!" she screamed. "Go back to your castles and your well-dressed whores then, and may God damn ya both to hell!"

Albert turned to look as she spit on the ground after them. He turned back and looked at his friend; his eyes filled with questions.

"Just go about your way," said Thomas. "There would be no good reason for giving anything to her. She would more likely drink it away if you did anyway."

The incident brought back memories to Albert of his father's words. "It's the way of the world," he said. "And we cannot change the ways of the world." But what had happened to him? Then, he was convinced he could change the world, and he wanted to help bring about that change. Had he abandon his principles and embraced the ideals he wanted to change? It was all so confusing.

He glanced over at Thomas as they rode. He seemed to be unaffected by the encounter. He looked up at Albert.

"Is there something on your mind?" he said, smiling.

Albert began to tell his friend about his past and how he ended up there. He told him about Brother William and his execution, all about his feelings concerning the church and the nobility, and how he became involved with Wat and his sister. He wasn't sure how Thomas would accept him after this revelation. After all, Thomas was devoutly passionate about his faith, but he listened quietly until Albert had finished. He looked up at Thomas almost fearing what he would say. Thomas reined his horse to a stop.

"Albert," Thomas began. "Please take no offence in what I'm about to tell you. With all due respect, my friend, I think your attitude about the church may be wrong. I believe you are feeling as if you have betrayed your friends and their cause by not being able to save Brother William, but let me tell you that there was nothing that could be done about the good brother. You were dealing with those who have the power to do whatever they please, but that doesn't mean that all the clergy is evil and that all the peasants are saintly. There are many, rich or poor, that would sell their soles to the devil; the only difference between these scoundrels is wealth. Some scoundrels hold positions of power and others do not, but they are all scoundrels. Then, there are those who never forget that they are human beings and turn only to God for power. Those are the people you can trust."

Albert said not a word and listened intently as Thomas continued. "I can well understand why you would take the side of peasants. The injustices done to them are obvious. There are certain members of the nobility and the church who are guilty of living frivolous lives and overtaxing hardworking folks, but that isn't the worst of it. These folks never see any material gains for themselves; they only see themselves working harder and the nobles getting wealthier. And, yes, the church has its share of hypocrites.

"Take John Wycliffe, for example. He has many good ideas, but are his intentions really good? He preaches that the clergy should revert back to the ways of Christ and his apostles and honor the vow of poverty, yet he lives a life of comfort and ease. So you see that sometimes it is hard to distinguish between those who are sincere and those who only talk a good deal. The only way to know the difference between them is to listen carefully to their words and watch their actions even more carefully. Also, I would like to make one last point, never judge people as a group such as peasant, priest, prostitute, soldier, or nobleman. You must take each individual and find his true spirit. The goodness or the evil within will reveal itself at one time or another."

Albert thought deeply about Thomas' words. He looked up at him, and they smiled at one another as they snapped the reins that started their horses forward.

"Enough of the preaching for one day," said Thomas as they continued their search.

The terrible filth seemed to abate as they rode down Bread Street toward the Thames. They approached the tannery, which was under roof construction, and stopped to look for the workmen. They dismounted and trudged carefully through the damp mud to the scaffolding. They could see a workman kneeling at the top and a laborer on the ground holding a rope attached to a pulley filled with tiles.

"Who is the master of this project?" Thomas asked.

"He's on the roof, sir," he replied.

"Would you give a call to him?"

The laborer's call was echoed until it reached the master workman. Shortly, a figure appeared at the edge of the roof and looked down curiously at them. As soon as he recognized the colors of their clothing as squires, he made his way down the ladder. He turned with a look of concern.

"How can I be of service, squires?" he said respectfully.

"Do you know or have you heard of Wat, the Tyler from Colchester?" Albert asked.

The man wiped his sweaty brow with his sleeve. "Oh, yes, sir, I do know of him as everyone in my trade does," he said with a wide grin. "Many a drunken eves were squandered with that gent. Would you excuse me, sir?"

"Yes, certainly," Albert replied. The man turned and quickly walked toward the corner of the building where he unceremoniously relieved himself and just as quickly walked back as he buttoned up his trousers.

"You'll pardon, sirs, but I was about to burst," he

chuckled. "Yes, as I was saying, Mr. Tyler and I had many a rowdy moment. He shook his head, sadly. "It's too bad," he said as his voice trailed off.

"What do you mean?" Albert asked with a look of concern.

"Oh no, sir, I didn't mean to mislead you into thinking something bad had befallen your friend. No, it's just that he joined the service of the king, and the last I heard, he was sent on the last excursion to France with John Gaunt."

Albert couldn't believe what he was hearing. *Wat, in the service of the king?* he thought. "What of his sister and father?" he asked.

"His father, poor devil, met with a fatal accident. He was on scaffolding that collapsed, and he died."

"I'm sorry to hear that," Albert said sadly.

"As for Wat's sister, she and Wat parted ways shortly thereafter. A beauty, she was! A man could get lost in his own wishful dreaming," he said wistfully. "Though, I'm afraid I don't know of her whereabouts," he said, coming back to his senses. "All the times we spent drinking together, he never once mentioned her. I suppose he wanted to protect her as older brothers sometimes do."

At that moment, a tile fell from the scaffolding and crashed to ground barely missing the master. "You foolish bastard!" he yelled up at the laborer who quickly apologized. He turned his attention back toward the squires. "I hope that I have been helpful in your quest for your friends, sir," he said. "Now I must get back to work before one of these idiots drops another tile and does not miss my head this time."

"Many thanks to you, friend," Albert said.

"God go with you, sirs," said the workman as he bowed his head.

The squires turned and mounted their horses. "Well, my friend," said Thomas. "At least, now you know where Wat is and what's become of his father."

"I'm grateful for the information, but I would like to know where to find Elizabeth."

Thomas paused and looked at Albert. He could see the concern in his eyes. "Well, you will find her; I am sure," he said, trying to comfort his friend.

"Yes, but for now, Thomas, I'll ride with you to St. Paul's."

"I don't think I will visit St. Paul's," said Thomas. "I've changed my mind and would prefer St. Mary's de Bothaw on West Cheap St. I went there many times as a page in the household of Lady Stafford," he said. "It's a peaceful place where a man can reflect quietly on life's trials and triumphs."

They arrived at the church and entered the darkened, empty chapel. The smell of incense and burning candles permeated the air. They walked up to the modestly decorated altar and knelt down. Thomas blessed himself, and Albert followed suit. Soon, a wonderfully calmed feeling came over both of them. Here, in this refuge, Albert found peace, and he could put his life into perspective. His mind drifted away for what seemed an instant only to be brought back abruptly by Thomas' firm hand on his shoulder.

"Are you ready to leave?" he asked.

"Yes," said Albert surprised that time had gone by so quickly. "I was lost in thought," he said.

"Yes, that is quite easy to do. That is why I'm so fond St. Mary's," said Thomas.

They rode back to the manor quietly, each in his own thoughts. There, they found Henry and Gilles passed out in a drunken stupor on their respective cots. The stench of vomit and body odor was overwhelming, and both put their hands over their mouths and noses. Thomas shook the two roughly.

"What do you think you are doing?" he bellowed.

Henry and Gilles were awake immediately and stumbled to their feet.

"Get yourselves together and clean up this mess!" Thomas demanded. They jumped to the task without a complaint as they greatly respected Thomas and thought of his word as law.

Chapter Twelve

The rigors of training resumed the following day as the knights and squires prepared for the battle that they would soon be facing. For now, the war in France was at a stalemate with the English withdrawing to their fortresses and the French controlling the interior countryside. However, the year of 1377 brought misfortune to English arms with the passing of the great Edward III and the crowning of the boy, King Richard II. A call for more troops would be necessary as the French would now see an opportunity to drive the English from their land altogether.

For the squires, it was arduous training in horsemanship and weaponry. Testing each other's prowess with mock battles was daily routine. Thomas bested all others with his skill and power of arms, driving the other squires to the ground with the fierce swipe of his doubled-edged sword. Albert was most persistent, for as many times as Thomas had beaten him, he would return more determined than before. This was a trait that drew enormous respect from Thomas, and their friendship grew stronger over time.

Henry was forever the fun lover; whether engaged in combat or hunting, the smile was always etched on his jolly face. Happiness beamed from inside Henry, and it was contagious to most people, with the exception of Gilles whose temperament was often unpredictable. He was always bragging but had nothing to prove his claims of superiority. His military power could scarcely compare to that of his famous ancestor, and his animosity toward Albert stemmed from the losses he suffered at the hand of Albert's skill and strength whenever Gilles sparred with him.

The two seldom spoke except when necessary, and try as he might, even Henry could not bridge the path of friendship between them. Albert thought Gilles was irresponsible and careless, and he hated the way he was always preoccupied with the opposite sex. He continuously bragged about his so-called conquests when Albert, as well as everyone else, knew of his habit of embellishing his tales of womanizing.

To Albert his stories were crass, disgusting, and mostly untrue. In truth, his success with women was sourly lacking to say the least, and Albert always chuckled to himself when he caught the look of a young woman's face when Gilles flirted with her. Usually she would appear very disgusted and a little fearful. Albert could not have known of Gilles' secret admiration for the lovely maiden who lived at the convent. Every time he passed by, Gilles' eyes searched the convent garden and courtyard to catch a glimpse or perhaps make her acquaintance.

He had the opportunity on the day that he was sent to the priory by Sir Godfrey who had developed a severe toothache. He was selected to go there to obtain medicine that would alleviate his knight's pain. He reached the priory to find the girl in the garden. At first she didn't hear his approach and continued collecting herbs. He stood watching her for a moment.

"Dear lady," he called.

Elizabeth stood and turned.

Looking at her was gratifying, and Gilles caught his breath. "Finally," he said, "I have been given the privilege to make your acquaintance! Please let me introduce myself. I am Gilles, a squire from the house of Lord Stafford, and you are … ?" he asked with an exaggerated air of elegance.

"Elizabeth Tyler," she answered.

"You are quite the fair lady," he said. "I must say I've been admiring you from afar. I hope you don't think me to be presumptuous, but I could no longer keep my thoughts to myself."

"To the contrary, sir, I am quite flattered," she said, lowering her eyes to hide her embarrassment.

"Tell me, dear lady, do you live here in the convent?"

"Yes, sir, but I'm not of the nobility and not entitled to ladyship. I came to live here after my father died."

"I see," said Gilles. "Well, gentle woman, you may not be of noble birth, but your beauty surpasses that of any lady."

Elizabeth smiled and lowered her head.

"Tell me, dear maiden, where are you from?" he asked.

Before she could answer, a loud voice beckoned her. "Elizabeth!"

She looked up immediately.

"Who is that with you, and what is he doing here?" asked the prioress as she walked toward the two. "Forgive me, sir, please state your business," the prioress demanded.

Gilles explained that he had been sent by Sir Godfrey for medical advice.

"What the gentleman needs is pellitory. Elizabeth will cut you some," she said.

"Yes, Sister," said Elizabeth.

She stooped down to cut the herb. As she handed it to Gilles, he paused. When she looked up, he was gazing into her eyes. She handed him the herb and looked away quickly for it was at that moment that she knew his intentions, and it made her a little nervous. She was afraid that she might have given him the impression that she too was interested, but she was just being polite and didn't really have any feelings for him at all.

"Thank you, my lady," he said softly.

"Come along, Elizabeth," said the prioress as she walked back toward the convent door.

Elizabeth followed, but before she could leave, Gilles asked if he could visit again.

"I'm sorry, sir, but that would not be possible," she said. "You see, I am a novice here and soon to take my vows, and then I will become one of the Grey Sisters."

"I see," he said sadly. "But why would a beauty such as you want to forgo the wonders and pleasures of the world and possibly marriage to someone who could provide for you and love you?" he asked, smiling.

She looked into his eyes without shame. "Sir, the convent life is for those who want to devote themselves to God. Come, follow me through the garden, and I will explain. But we must look as though we are still choosing herbs as the prioress will call me in if she thinks we are just talking. You see, talking to strangers is only allowed when it pertains to the business of healing."

Without going into great detail about personal matters, Elizabeth explained her past life to the squire, which included the story of the young man she had loved and lost. She did not really believe it was any of his concern, but explaining would satisfy him enough so that he would not pursue her any longer. She did not want to lead him down the wrong road where he would believe she was interested in his attention.

"Ahh," he sighed. "I knew that you could not have come to this place without some young man falling in love with you, but I wonder how he could ever bring himself to leave your side. What was his name?" he asked.

Before she could answer, she was called back by an impatient prioress.

"Yes, I'm coming," called Elizabeth. "I must go, sir, forgive me."

"Yes, of course," he answered as she hurried toward the door.

Chapter Thirteen

Two years passed, and England's possessions in France were reduced to the southwest corner and the city port of Calais. Her commanders, lacking in leadership abilities, were leaving English homeland ports vulnerable to attacks by French fleets. However, life went on, and the nobility still enjoyed their tournaments.

King Richard held his at Cheapside, London in the shadow of St. Paul's Cathedral. Knights and their squires from as far away as Germany attended. Contenders arrived days in advance. From Lord Stafford's household, the ride was short. The retinue left the manor early, marching out over London Bridge to a beautiful sunrise which gave an idyllic view to the Thames with its water reflecting the sun's rays and masking the true nature of the grime and filth of the river. All of London and other towns and villages along the Thames used it as a dumping ground, and as you got close to its shores, you could smell the rancid stench of human waste and dead animals. But on this morning, it was as lovely as a shimmering pond in the garden of Eden.

By the time they reached Cheapside, Apollo's chariot had ridden across the sky and cast its heavenly rays on every lady's necklace and knight's amour, causing a blinding effect on the crowd. The masses of multicolored tents with their various coats of arms informed all of the glorious family histories of stout veterans and hardy newcomers. The gods of Olympus would look down with envy at the magnificent spectacle.

A pavilion had been prepared and set at the end of the field for Lord Stafford's retinue. The stands were hastily built, wooden productions that were decorated in fine cloths and many banners. Most of the banners were decorated with the king's arms, but there were many that bore the arms of other domains. The king and his ministers took center stage while lords and ladies were seated to the left and right of him.

The trumpet sounded the opening of the tournament, and the there was a short speech given by His Majesty. The competition began with the main event of jousting, and in which Lord Stafford's knights participated. Albert assisted Sir William with his field armor, as did the other squires with their knights. They wore plate armor, which was being reintroduced in current warfare. Originally, this was used by the barbarian tribes a thousand years earlier; its reappearance was initiated by the improvement of the crossbow weaponry, which could penetrate chain mail armor. They also wore surcoats that contained the arms of Lord Stafford.

It was not long before the contest began with the first eight combatants entering the field from opposite ends of the grounds and the last of the (lists) enclosures were cleared.

"God be with you, sir," the squires called to their knights as they proceeded onto the field.

They rode onto a defined area where they would defend a designated piece of land. The opposing French knights rode in at a gallop, anxious to engage. These French knights were captives of England and held for ransom. Since their ransom had not yet been paid, they were allowed to participate in this event.

The crashing of heavy metal rang throughout. In this opening salvo, Sir Robert's broadsword did the most damage as it made contact with an opponent's helmet, dazing him. His arms fell to his sides, dropping his shield and lance to the ground. A great cheer rose up from the crowd only to be silenced moments later by the unhorsing of Sir Godfrey by a French lance. Sir William quickly rode to his defense, only to suffer the same fate.

Albert and Thomas looked at one another in horror. "I have never seen Sir William unhorsed in all the tournaments we have participated in before," he said.

Sir Robert and Sir George immediately rode to the defense of their comrades. The English knights on the ground prepared themselves for their opponent's onslaught, but the French had decided instead to try to unhorse the remaining two English knights. They rushed to attack Sir George and Sir Robert.

With devastating force, the five collided, and within moments, all were unhorsed. One of the Frenchmen's horses lay dead and the other two scattered. Sir Robert's leg was bleeding as he, and the others on the ground tried to regain their footing. Sirs William and Godfrey joined the melee as the ground combat began with a clashing of steel. Blow and counter blow were being thrown in a wild frenzy as the crowd roared with excitement. The weighted assaults shook their bodies furiously as teeth cracked and blood spewed from wounds.

The English now chose to take a defensive posture to save strength until their opponents' might began to wane. Seizing the opportunity, Sir William gave the command, and within moments the French were mercilessly driven to the ground. Cheers rang out as the squires ran onto the field to give aid to their knights. And the French, wounded and exhausted, limped or were carried off the battleground in humiliation.

Albert ran to Sir William, who was leaning on his sword, and helped him remove his battered helmet. As the helmet came off, Albert winced when he saw the swollen area of William's head where he took many blows from a French sword. A large gash on his hand dripped blood onto the already soaked ground. Albert draped the other hand over his shoulder to help his knight walk off the field, all the while praising his performance in the battle.

As they walked, Albert noticed Henry struggling to lift his knight. "Will you need a litter?" he asked.

"Yes, Albert, and thank you," he replied.

"I will send one momentarily, sir," said Albert.

Once he had gotten Sir William to the pavilion where he could be looked after, he then ran back to the field with the litter, and he and Henry lifted Sir Robert onto it. As they did, Sir Robert cried out in pain. He seemed more angry than hurt as he yelled obscenities, cursing the French. They delivered him to the physician, and Henry knelt down beside his knight, wiping his face and trying to make him feel comfortable.

"Call the squires to me," said Sir William.

"Yes, sir," Albert replied and helped him to his feet. He returned quickly with the other squires and stood before Sir William.

"I want you to go to the defeated French and collect the spoils of this well-earned victory," he commanded.

Soon the squires returned with all the French armor and horses. Since Sir William was the spokesman for the other knights, he took charge of the rewards.

"This day was a great day, gentlemen," he boasted. "For it has shown the French that England's prowess in battle has not lost its luster!"

"Here! Here!" everyone cheered.

"In agreement with my fellow knights, we now present these spoils to our squires along with our deepest gratitude," he continued, pointing to the seized items. As he spoke, the squires served wine, and they all raised their goblets toward him.

"To our brave, victorious, and generous knights!" said Albert. A loud cheer followed, and they all drank up.

The rest of the day was spent eating and drinking for all except Sir Robert, who was still recovering from his wounds. Henry, his squire, did participate but at the same time kept a watchful eye on his knight. Soon Lord Stafford arrived to take part in the festivities and to thank his retainers for a job well done. This victory meant that his household would receive recognition at court for their accomplishments and be paid handsomely by the king.

The next day a cart was procured by the squires at Black Friars Convent. “Yes, sirs, and by all means, you may certainly borrow our cart,” said the gray-haired friar. “Sir Robert is a fine man and a brave knight. He has always been very generous to our convent, and we would gladly lend a hand toward his recovery. Will he be brought here for medical attention?” he asked.

“No, but many thanks for the cart and your offer of help, Father, but we will be transporting him directly to the manor,” said Henry.

Later, they arrived back at the pavilion and prepared to leave for the manor as Lord Stafford arrived.

“Sir William,” he said. “I have a request from the king. He is in need of knights and soldiers at the coast.”

“I have heard of no impending danger at the coast, my lord,” replied William, looking concerned.

“Yes, sir, there is now. The French and her allies are destroying our coastal towns,” Lord Stafford explained. “We have two days to prepare before departure.”

“Yes, my lord, right away,” replied William. “We shall be ready.”

Everyone was pleased with the news except Henry. He knew he would not march with the others, as he had to remain with Sir Robert until his recovery.

The squires and knights rode home in good humor. Henry had little to say and that ever-present smile on his face had disappeared. They finally arrived at the manor and carried Sir Robert to his bed. His wound had been left uncovered and had stopped bleeding, but it was extremely moist. He was conscious and was massaging the area around the wound with his hand, indicating that he was in a great deal of pain.

They decided that they should send for a sister to care for him for a few days. When asked for a volunteer, Gilles was the first. He had been thinking about the lovely maiden he met the last time he visited the convent and hoped he would see her again. On his way, his thoughts wondered to romantic lands as he dreamed of her angelic face and young, slender body. He envisioned himself making sweet love to her, and the image made him feel flushed. He took a deep breath and sighed wistfully. He finally arrived, but to his disappoint Elizabeth was nowhere in sight. He quickly dismounted and walked to the door.

When he was admitted, he reported his mission to the prioress. "We will need someone to provide medical attention to Sir Robert at Stafford Manor," he said.

After some hesitation, the prioress gave a lecture on the horrors the tournament, which the church had strictly forbidden and tried for many years to have banned. The clergy claimed it caused undo violence and bloodshed. It was also frowned upon by secular authorities, who claimed it could become a prelude to revolt. There were those, however, who claimed the practice was a way to keep knights sharp for battle.

After the lecture, to which Gilles paid little attention, she agreed to send someone. She called to her assistant, who sat nearby. "Please fetch Elizabeth, Sister," she ordered.

Gilles could not believe his luck, and he grinned

widely as he stood waiting. She entered the chambers quickly and favored Gilles with a smile.

"Yes, Mother Superior, you called for me?" she asked.

"Yes, my dear, you are to accompany Squire Gilles, here, to the Stafford Manor," replied the prioress, "where you will tend a wounded knight." She then turned to Gilles, "Squire, give Elizabeth a description of your knight's wounds so that she may bring the necessary medicines."

"Very well," he said. "He has a long, deep gash on his thigh, and we fear it may become infected."

Elizabeth and Gilles both nodded politely to the prioress and her assistant and left the chambers. They went directly outside to the garden where Elizabeth collected the appropriate herbs to make salves and teas for healing. She tucked them into the small pull string bag she had hanging from the sash of her frock. She went inside to collect medical instruments that she would need, and soon they were on their way.

As they rode, Gilles asked how a novice in servitude acquired knowledge in the practice of medicine.

"Well," she said thoughtfully. "I learned some while working with my brother and father as they worked with tiles and would often be in need of someone to tend minor wounds and bruises. However, I received more formal training from the good sisters of the convent. They told me that I had an aptitude for medicine," she said, shrugging modestly.

When they arrived at the manor, Gilles dismounted and helped Elizabeth from her horse. Together they walked to Sir Robert's quarters where Henry stood watch over his knight. She entered the room and looked over at the patient and up at Henry. He nodded and smiled at her as Gilles made their introductions, and Elizabeth went directly to work.

She lifted the bandage that covered the wound and then looked at Robert's face. His gray complexion and red-rimmed eyes worried her. She knew that infection had begun to set in. She placed her hand gently on his forehead, which was warm to the touch.

"Gentlemen," she announced. "Sir Robert has a slight fever, which indicates his wound is becoming septic." She ordered a bath to soak the wound, and Henry sent Gilles for two more squires to help lift Sir Robert. He returned shortly with Albert and Thomas.

As they entered the room, Albert stopped dead in his tracks. Even though her back was to him, he knew it was her.

"Elizabeth!" he said in surprise.

She turned around, immediately recognizing his voice, and looked at him in disbelief.

"Albert," she whispered. "My God, I didn't know that you were here," she said as she walked toward him. He opened his arms, and she fell into them.

Everyone stood stunned at the display of affection between them. Gilles stood, looking puzzled and angry. Sir William regained his composure and cleared his throat impatiently.

"We really must tend to Sir Robert, miss," he said, looking at Elizabeth.

"Yes, of course, sir. I'm very sorry," said Albert.

"Yes, sir," Elizabeth said, looking embarrassed. She

hoped that he would not tell what he saw to the mother superior.

Servants from the kitchen carried buckets of heated water to Sir Robert's room to fill the tub. Afterward they helped lift him from his bed and lower him into the bath. Elizabeth instructed Henry to sprinkle a good amount of herbs into the water. She sprinkled the remaining contents of her sack into a bowl of hot water and mixed it up into a plaster. Soon he was lowered back into his bed, and Elizabeth dressed his wound.

As the others watched her perform her healing powers, Thomas placed a hand on Albert's shoulder. "God is good," he whispered. "For you did not have to find her; after all, she found you."

Albert smiled and nodded in agreement.

"Now, Sir Robert," she said in a motherly voice. "Make sure you do not remove these bandages or touch the wound. It may itch somewhat, but please resist the urge to scratch. It is quite deep and will take some time to heal. I have applied a mixture of betony and other herbs into the plaster."

She turned to Henry. "Be sure to change the bandages every few days. There is the remaining plaster," she said, pointing to the bowl. "You must wash the wound, put on a small amount of the plaster, and replace the dressings with clean bandages."

"Yes, miss, and thank you," he said, bowing his head.

After Elizabeth's gentle ministration, Robert seemed more comfortable, and he began to fall into a peaceful sleep. She felt his head one more time and noted that the fever had subsided.

Satisfied with Robert's condition, everyone, except Henry, began to leave the room. Albert and Elizabeth were the last to leave. He held the door for her to pass and closed it quietly behind him. Gilles watched them pass, steamed with envy and resentment. They walked out into the night air talking about the past and the time they were apart. She told him what had transpired between her and her brother. He told her how he had learned of her father's death and how it had saddened him.

"Why did you not tell me where you were going?" she asked.

"I didn't have enough time to reach you. They were going to imprison me for my association with Brother William," he said. "It was by chance that I was sent to Stafford Manor."

"Oh," she said softly. "I assumed with your father's association with Simon that you would be cleared of any charges, and I thought that you were angry with me because of your trouble."

"Angry with *you*?" he said, surprised. "How could I ever be angry with you?"

She looked at him and smiled.

"Still, Albert, I am sorry for what you must have gone through at the hands of that scoundrel," she said as she stopped to face him. "A great deal of time has passed since we were together. We are not the same people as when we were younger. I can see that you have been swept up by knighthood, and I have had a change of heart and chosen the religious life," she said, lowering her head. "I turned to the priory when the three most important people in my life were taken away. I had hoped my brother would stay in London, but much to my surprise, he chose to join John Gaunt's expedition in France. He left while we both were still grieving my father's death. I have not heard from him and know not how he is faring. It worries me greatly," she continued, her voice quivering. "I gave little hope that I would ever see you again," she sobbed as the tears started to fall. "But I thought of you every day. I ... "

Albert, moved by her story, lifted her face and looked into her eyes. He reached for her hand and brought it to his lips. As he did, he noticed that she still wore the ring he gave to her so long ago.

"You still wear the ring," he said.

"Yes," she replied, looking down. "I have not taken it off since you gave it to me, even when the prioress demanded I do so. She said that I should dispose of all reminders of my past life and for the most part I did, but I knew throwing the ring away would never wipe your memory from my heart."

"She never questioned why you continued to wear it?" he asked.

"Yes, she did," she replied. "But she changed her mind when I told her I wore it to remind me to follow God's law, and in many ways, it helped me to do that. I don't like to lie, but I felt that what I told her was partly true. However, you were always in my heart."

As he looked down into her innocent green eyes, his smile faded.

"What troubles you, my love?" she asked, putting her hand to his cheek.

"We are planning to leave for the coast soon. We must protect our shores from the French, but I will return before long," he promised. "I still love you very much and want us to be together thereafter," he said.

She smiled and embraced him, overjoyed that he still cared.

They continued walking and looking dreamily up into the night sky. They witnessed a shooting star gliding through the heavens. "Did you see that?" Albert said.

"Yes, it was beautiful," she replied.

"It is a sign of good fortune," he said. "I believe that soon happiness will be ours."

"Oh yes!" she agreed.

Albert escorted Elizabeth back to the priory. As they both said their farewells, their spirits soared when their lips met, for they both felt a long, difficult journey was over and there was a new beginning on the horizon.

Chapter Fourteen

The next morning everyone at Stafford Manor was preparing for the journey to the coast. The knights and their squires gathered at Sir William's request.

"The French and Castilians have burned much of the city of Gravesend," he declared. "We are to muster with forces from the south to prevent a full-scale invasion of England. We are ordered to Gravesend where we will join Lord Buckingham's forces," he continued. "There, we will board transport, sail to Calais, and commence a massive raid into the French countryside."

Before long, the company began their march to defend their beloved England. Albert rode without a word. His mind was occupied with mixture of fear and pride, and his heart was filled with love for the sweet-faced, little peasant girl he was leaving behind. He rode in silence until Thomas brushed his horse alongside him. He leaned forward and tapped Albert on his shoulder.

"Cheer up, friend," he said, smiling. "Everything will be fine."

Albert looked up. "Yes, of course," he said half-heartedly. He looked to the other side of him where Gilles was catching up. Gilles looked back with resentment as he passed, but there were no angry words exchanged.

At Stafford Manor, Sir Robert yelled for Henry. Henry came immediately into the room to find him standing and trying to remove his nightshirt.

"What are you doing, sir? he yelled. "You must get back into your bed this minute, or I shall go and fetch Miss Elizabeth," he threatened.

"Yes, that is exactly what I want you to do. I feel well enough to go on that mission to Gravesend," he said. "But I would like to consult Elizabeth first."

"Yes, sir," said Henry. "But I must ask you to at least to sit while I go to get her."

"Just go!" demanded Sir Robert.

"Yes, of course, sir," Henry said as he left the room.

He arrived at the priory to find Elizabeth working in the garden. She stood as he approached and hoped he would tell her that Albert had not gone to Gravesend.

"Can I be of assistance?" she asked.

"Yes, miss," he answered. "Sir Robert has requested your consult. If it is convenient, he would like you to pay him a visit."

"Yes, of course, sir. Is there anything wrong?" she asked.

"No, he is doing quite well and wants to know if he can return to active duty," he answered.

"I will go and see him, but I sincerely doubt his

wound is healed enough for travel much less to partake in battle," she said.

The two walked to the barn and saddled her horse. "Has Sir William's party left for Gravesend?" she asked, hoping she would get a chance to say a last good-bye to Albert.

"Oh yes," he said, "early this morning."

"Oh," she sighed.

"You need not worry about your gentleman," he said, trying to quell her fears. "He is quite skilled, and I'm sure he will return to you unscathed."

As they rode, it was not long before Henry made her smile with his usual good humor.

"Sir Robert, it is true that your wound is healing quite rapidly, but I must advise you that it would be very unwise to travel before it has completed the healing process. You should be resting, sir," said Elizabeth, "not prancing about the countryside."

"You will not allow me to do my duty and join my comrades then?" he asked.

"Sir," she said firmly. "I cannot stop you from doing anything, but riding and other vigorous activities could start the bleeding and reopen the wound," she explained. "Consider what a hindrance that would be to your comrades not to mention the fact that it could very well be the death of you," she continued.

"Oh yes, you're quite right," he sighed as he lay back on his pillows.

The last of her speech was what convinced him. "Go Henry," he said, turning to his squire.

"Go, sir?" said Henry, looking puzzled.

"Yes, go and join the others at Gravesend," said Robert.

"What of your welfare, sir? I cannot leave you in your hour of need," Henry replied.

"I will have others in the household to look after me, and I feel strong enough to be up and about—it's best you go. I know that's what you really want. Is it not?"

Henry's face lit up. "Yes, sir, but are you sure you'll be fine?" he asked.

"Yes, yes of course," said Robert, waving his hand. "Go now, and God be with you."

"Thank you, sir," said Henry gratefully. "I will go, prepare for the journey, and leave in the morning, but I will come and check on you before I leave," he said. He turned to Elizabeth for approval.

She nodded to Henry and pointed a finger at Sir Robert. "I won't object to that as long as you remain indoors and do not overextend yourself, and I too will check on you periodically," she said with motherly authority.

"Yes, madam," said Sir Robert, smiling. "Go now!" he repeated. "And make sure our lovely lady arrives home safely."

"Yes, sir, and thank you again, sir," said Henry.

He escorted Elizabeth back to the priory, but before they parted, she had another errand for him to perform. "Please, Henry, take this ring to Gravesend with you and give it to Albert," she said as she pulled the ring from her finger. "He gave it to me long ago. Please tell him I'm giving it to him now in the hope that he will come home safely and give it back to me."

Henry smiled, bowed his head, and promised he would do what she asked.

"God's speed, Henry," she said as he mounted his horse.

"Thank you, miss," he said, and she watched as he rode out of sight.

Henry left for Gravesend the next morning. He rode hard most of the day until he realized he had lost his way. Soon, he came upon a band of traveling clergymen who pointed him in the right direction. The mishap made him lose time, and he would arrive at Gravesend very late. As he approached from a short distance away, he could see the town was in turmoil.

Earlier, skirmishes had broken out with foreign troops as they landed. They had looted and burned homes and businesses almost at will. The closer Henry rode toward the town, the sights of the melee were becoming clearer. He rode headlong into the fray, his sword raised above his head. The smoke and dust made it difficult to see and breath, but he kept his pace and rode through the debris-strewn streets. However, when he arrived, he made no contact with foreign troops or English troops for that matter. He looked around in bewilderment. There were no signs of life except a cry for help coming from a burning building. He jumped from his horse and rushed into the house. On the first floor, he found a young woman trapped beneath a pile of rubble.

He immediately started to remove the debris. Once freed, he asked her if she could stand up. As he reached for her hand, he heard a muffled sound coming from under the piles of plaster and wood. Henry reached under the debris to find a soot-covered infant kicking and screaming. He held the child close to him as he helped the woman to her feet. She stepped out the door, coughing and gulping frantically and trying to get fresh air into her smoke-filled lungs.

Henry handed her the infant and turned back to retrieve his sword.

She turned and looked back as a flaming beam came down, trapping him inside. "Oh God, no!" she cried. "Sir, can you hear me?" she screamed. She got no answer. She fell to her knees with the child in her arms and wept for the kind stranger who had just saved her and her baby from certain death.

The troupe of knights, waiting out the last pockets of enemy resistance, seemed to have the situation under control. As they rode through the smoke and dust looking for the wounded, they found the woman and her baby lying on the road in front of the burned-out building.

Sir William halted the troupe, and they all dismounted. Sir William and Sir George knelt down beside them. "Go and fetch some water," William commanded.

Sir George went behind the building where he found a well. He returned with a bucketful of water and held a cup to her lips, and the woman immediately regained consciousness. She pointed to the building.

"There is a squire in there," she sobbed. "I don't know whether he is dead or alive. He saved our lives!" she cried. "He saved our lives," she repeated in a whisper.

The others ran into the house. Inside they could barely see through the thick smoke. They rubbed their stinging eyes and their throats burned with fierce pain.

"He's there!" Albert yelled as he and Thomas made their way toward the man.

"We need some support here!" yelled Thomas.

Everyone rushed to the beam and started lifting until they could pull Henry free. Thomas and Albert grasped under each arm and carried him outside. They laid his charred and battered body on the ground. Albert tore off part of his tunic and dipped it in the bucket. He gently wiped Henry's face, but there was no response.

Sir William decided they would need a cart to transport the injured and sent two other knights and their squires off to look for one. They hadn't ridden far when they came upon a merchant family loading what belongings they were able to salvage after their home had been burnt to the ground. They stopped and looked up as the troupe approached. The merchant stepped up in front of his family protectively.

"I say there, my good man," Sir Godfrey called. "Would you please come forward so that I may speak to you?"

The merchant motioned to his family to stay back while he made his way through the piles of smoldering timbers and walked up to the knight's horse.

"Yes, sir," he said, looking up at Sir Godfrey expectantly.

"I must requisition your cart to transport a wounded comrade and a young mother and her child to a convent hospital," said the knight. "I am sorry for the inconvenience to your family, sir," he added.

"No inconvenience at all, sir," said the merchant. "Had it not been for good soldiers such as yourselves, we would have been much worse off than this," he continued as he pointed to his destroyed home.

"But you've lost your home, sir," said Sir Godfrey with a look of bewilderment.

"That is true, but we still have each other, you see, if your soldiers had not rescued us promptly, we surely would have been put to the sword," said the merchant, smiling. "Permit me to introduce myself; my name is Harold Williamson. May I ask what your name is, sir?"

"Yes, Sir Godfrey of Stafford Manor."

Harold bowed his head in respect. "Sir," he replied. He then turned and waved to his two grown sons and directed them to unload their cart, which the young men did without question.

"I am pleased to make your acquaintance," said Sir Godfrey as he turned to his troupe. "Squires Thomas and Albert, you will remain on guard so that no harm comes to this fine man's goods or family!"

"Yes, sir," they responded.

"Now, my good man," said Sir Godfrey, turning back to the merchant. "Would you be so kind as to transport our wounded to the nearest convent or hospital?"

"By all means, sir," Harold replied graciously.

The troupe gently loaded the injured onto the cart, and they were on their way with the cart leading and the escort following close behind.

After a while, they reached the convent of the

Cistercian monks. The merchant stopped the cart in the deserted courtyard. The place seemed to be abandoned. He jumped down from his seat with a long, wooden staff he retrieved from behind him. He walked to the door and gave a loud bang with his stick but got no response. He banged a little harder in a pattern that to Sir Godfrey sounded like a signal. "The good brothers must have been frightened by the violence," he said, turning to Sir Godfrey.

"Would they still be here?" asked Sir Godfrey.

"I'm sure they are," Harold replied.

The heavy gate finally swung open, and they were admitted inside by two monks who closed the gate behind them and replaced the large, wooden timber that bolted it securely. The merchant turned the wagon over to one smiling brother, whom he seemed to be acquainted with. They exchanged greetings, and Harold explained the situation. Afterward, he walked back toward Sir Godfrey and motioned the troupe to dismount.

"The good brothers want you to bring the wounded to the infirmary," he said.

Sir Godfrey, Sir William, and Sir George with the help of Gilles and Harold, ever so gently removed the wounded from the cart.

The baby, who had fallen asleep during the ride, was now awake and giving all present a full serenade. The brothers looked at one another in delight.

"There was not a thing wrong with that child," they all agreed with a chuckle.

After leaving the wounded in good hands, they were

escorted to the dining hall where they would partake of the evening meal.

Harold decided that he must get back to his family and went to retrieve his cart.

"Many thanks to you, Mr. Williamson," said Sir Godfrey, shaking his hand. He reached into his money purse and handed five grouts to the merchant who accepted the payment graciously. The others thanked him as well as he turned to leave. He gave a wave and wished them all good fortune as he left.

Albert and Thomas were sent back to their troupe. Sir William greeted them as they walked into the dining hall. "Did you encounter any problems in the town?" he asked.

"None, sir," Albert replied. "The French have abandoned the area, and things seem to be settling down. Many of the people are returning to what is left of their homes."

"How is Henry; has he regained his senses yet?" asked Thomas.

"I'm afraid not," replied Sir William. "And I fear we will have to leave for Dover before he can recover. I'm wondering why he came to join us when his Sir Robert was still infirm. He should be there taking care of him," he said, more to himself than anyone else.

The three sat quietly eating when Thomas noticed the small side door open, and a monk step through. He looked around the room until he spotted Albert and waved to get his attention.

"I think that monk by the door is signaling you," he said as he nudged Albert.

"Where?" Albert asked, looking around. By that time the monk had made his way toward the group.

"Squire Henry has regained his wits and is asking for a Squire Albert. Would that be you, sir?" he asked.

"'Tis me," said Albert as he stood.

"Please come this way," said the monk as he turned to walk back.

Albert looked at Thomas and Sir William and shrugged.

"Why would he want to talk to you?" asked Thomas.

"I don't know," Albert replied as the three of them stood and followed the monk out the door. "Is he in his right mind?" he asked as they walked.

"Oh yes, he seems quite lucid, and his appetite is hardy," said the monk.

"How are the young woman and her infant?" asked Sir William.

"They are fine too, sir," he replied.

Henry was sitting up and eating his dinner when they came in. "I suppose you are wondering what I'm doing here," he said to Sir William.

"Yes, that question had crossed my mind," Sir William said with a frown.

"Well, sir," Henry began. "I was given leave by Sir Robert, who has recovered enough to take care of himself, and Elizabeth promised to make sure he would do what he should to get well."

"I see," said Sir William. "Well, why were you asking for Squire Albert then?" he asked.

Henry explained about the message Elizabeth had given him to relay to Albert. Albert flushed with embarrassment as the others chuckled.

"Sir, if I may, I would like to speak to Squire Albert in private," said Henry.

"Of course," replied Sir William with a smile as he and Thomas headed for the door.

Henry reached into his pocket and handed Albert the ring. He looked at it in bewilderment.

"She asked me to give this to you," Henry said.

Albert's eyes began to fill. "Why?" he asked. "Has she found another?"

"Oh no, not at all," replied Henry. "She said you must come home after your battles and return it to its rightful place on her finger. For luck, you see," he said, smiling.

"Yes, I see," Albert replied in a relieved voice. He took the ring in his hand and looked at it longingly; he then raised it to his lips before putting it into his satchel.

"Do you think I will be able to accompany you to France?" asked Henry.

Albert looked up at the monk who was sitting in the corner of the room. The monk shook his head slowly and mouthed the word *no*.

"I fear not, sir," Albert replied.

Henry lowered his head sadly.

"Don't fret, my friend; you will have plenty of other opportunities when you are better," said Albert, placing a hand on his friend's shoulder. "I want to thank you too, my friend, for delivering the ring to me. I can't say how much that means to Elizabeth and me," he said. "And if you should see her before my return, give her my love."

"I pray for your safe return, Albert," Henry replied."

"Thank you again and good night," said Albert as he walked toward the door.

It was late in the evening, and the troupe remained at the convent for the night. They all awoke to a cloudy, gray day but enjoyed a hearty breakfast before bidding farewell to the good brothers and Henry. The large, wooden timber that protected the convent was lifted, and the gates of the now secured courtyard were pushed open by two stalwart monks.

"Good-bye to you all, and thank you for your hospitality and kindness," said Sir William as he shook the hands of the monks.

"May God go with you, sir, and with your knights and squires," one monk replied.

As the troupe passed through the gate, the monks bowed their head and blessed them all as they left. When the last horse hoof crossed the threshold, there was a loud thud from the large gate closing behind them, locking out the sins and violence of the outside world.

The clouds hung heavy in the sky as the troupe made its way down the coast where the smell of charred wood from Gravesend began to fade away. Drizzle was overtaking the land, and the accumulating wetness was cascading down the plate armor and seeping into every void making the men wet and uncomfortable. As the day passed, the sun reappeared, making the air warmer than usual and causing bodies to sweat profusely.

"I feel as though I'm inside a caldron," Albert said, shifting about in his saddle, trying to remedy his discomfort. He had directed the comment to Thomas who was riding beside him, but Gilles was the one who responded.

"Should one as particular as you be going to fight the French?" he asked with a sarcastic smirk. "After all, French steel will be much more uncomfortable than a little sweat and grit," he continued.

Albert shot a look at Gilles, eyes glaring.

Sir George who was riding just ahead of the squires intervened. "What is the difficulty back there?" he asked with annoyance.

"Nothing, sir," called Albert. "Just nonsense," he said, looking at Gilles.

Thomas, hearing the exchange, pulled his horse between the two combatants and directed Gilles to ride behind them. Gilles obliged, but with his nose in the air.

"Albert, I know he tries your patience and can be quite annoying. However, when in battle, we will need one another and must put our petty differences aside," he said.

Albert nodded and rode the rest of the journey in relative peace. As always, he was grateful to Thomas for helping him to see things clearly.

Chapter Fifteen

The first night of the journey was spent in Canterbury where they ate and rested well before resuming their way to the seaport of Dover. They reached their destination about noon. The day was filled with sunshine and a light, easterly breeze, prime for sailing.

When Sir William and his troupe arrived at the wharf, they found it filled to capacity with knights and squires from all over southern England. As they mingled with the crowd, they learned that they would be sailing that day. According to one knight, they would leave as soon as the infantries from Kent and Cornwall arrived. With the news, Sir William dismissed the men to dine before they had to leave.

Albert remembered his last sea voyage and ate lightly. He advised some of his companions to do the same and recounted his experience aboard *The Christopher*. His story brought a roar of laughter and a volley of unkind remarks from Gilles, which were largely ignored.

Sir William agreed that it was wise to limit the amount they ate. "Squire Albert is quite right," he said. "It has been some time since we have sailed the channel, and I believe this will be a first sailing for some of you squires," he continued, looking straight at Gilles. "If the seas are rough, and the channel waters usually are, you may end up swabbing your meals off the deck."

After everyone had eaten, they left the inn, thinking of the coming voyage to Calais. They were still awaiting the two missing infantries when a squire from another troupe was eventually dispatched to scout their whereabouts. The day was passing quickly as all the troupes awaited their voyage. They were beginning to get weary, and some sat down on the cold, wet dock and watched as the twenty great and battletested, wooden cogs sat idle at their moorings and gently rocked side to side in a mesmerizing dance of anticipation. In the ships' staunch wooden sides were a multitude of arrows, some broken, giving testimony to their histories of battle.

Suddenly, the scout returned with a resounding holler, which brought immediate attention. He announced that the infantries were outside the town by a league. Soon the sound of the marching feet could be heard as the troupes entered the city. The men from Kent arrived in a mass of confusion. They looked like a large band of ruffians, which was not far from the truth. The troupe was made up of broken-faced laborers, outlaws, and cast-offs—the scum of southern England, looking as if they were just coming from battle rather than going to one. By the time the last troupe arrived, it was much too late to sail. They would leave the following morning.

They awoke to heavy rain and high seas, so the launch, again, was canceled. The day was spent with everyone taking leave, and there was much imbibing, dicing, and brawling, which were instigated by the motley group from the south. They had destroyed a tavern and beaten up a knight by the name of Sir Roger of Chester. Although the others were outraged by the soldiers' actions, they decided it best to stay out of their way and let them wear themselves out.

The morning came, finding a disgusting scene of humanity staggering around the site of the riot where many bodies lay sleeping off their drunken stupors with one or two who would never see the sun rise again. The knights descended upon this roguish crew to bring order and board them onto the ships. The living dragged themselves to their feet, leaving the dead to be disposed of by the townsfolk.

Finally, everyone was ready to board with the ruffians and troublemakers going first.

They were followed by the knights on horseback and their squires. Provisions and arms were already stowed on board from the day before. The voyage would begin with a splendid sunrise and favorable wind that was strong enough to propel the heavily laden ships. It also brought up the stench from rotting bodies and drunkenness that permeated the air. It was not long into the voyage before the seas began to swell, causing those who were still hung over to vomit all over one another.

Some of the half-drunk ruffians became angry with one another and began to fight about who vomited on whom. When the fight was quelled by a knight's sword, the instigators were tossed overboard. This measure was surely extreme, but necessary in order to preserve the safety and well-being of the rest of the crew. Fighting with your own was an act of treason and punishable by death. With the few troublemakers disposed of, the rest of journey was relatively peaceful.

Later that day, the flotilla reached Calais without incident. Unloading the ship of men and cargo would take a full day, and preparations for their mission would take another. The work would help the knights and squires keep the other men busy. The only trouble would be disciplining the rowdy rustics, which would be a priority for Lord Buckingham if he was to have a cohesive force. The answer to his dilemma would be forthcoming.

He was a veteran infantryman, living in Calais, who had been in France since the first raid by John of Gaunt. He had remained there and had begun to train other would-be infantrymen from various English-held provinces. He became widely popular with nobles and knights for his great command over the most difficult and unruly trainees and was now employed to discipline the rabble-rousers who had just arrived.

Many were impressed with his ability to bring order to this rag-tag group in such a short time. Within days, they were organized and ready to march even before Lord Buckingham had completed all of his preparations. With this major problem solved, the lord felt confident that this would be a successful expedition

On that late summer's morn in 1380, Lord Buckingham's force left Calais. Since the French had withdrawn into fortified towns, this army, as armies before them, could not rely on foraging. In some cases, however, not all of the towns and villages could be saved. One such town that would feel English wrath was a small hamlet called St. Omer.

The scouts were sent out first and then the foragers. Next would be the main army followed by the archers, infantry, and supply train. The knights and squires rode aloof with heads held high in a swaggering display, and bringing up the rear were the bowmen. As the knights and squires rode, many engaged in conversation.

"Such a pity," said Thomas, getting Albert's attention.

"Why is that?" asked Albert.

Thomas was looking at the wild, summer flowers that were in full bloom alongside the road. "Here we are marching along," he said turning to Albert, "the sky being as blue as I've ever seen it, flowers all around us in full regalia, armor gleaming in the sunlight, and we're off to war!"

"Well, yes," said Albert pensively.

"To hack, beat, and savage people we don't even know," said Thomas. "Where you now see a lovely, peaceful village, you will soon see nothing more than charred ruins on blood-soaked ground. Tell me, friend," continued Thomas, "is that all there is to war?"

"I don't know," replied Albert with a shrug. "You see, the only experience I've had was at Peterborough, and I must admit, I was frightened."

"Ha, that's not hard to understand," Gilles interrupted. "Cowards are always running scared!"

Albert turned slowly to look at him. "I said I was frightened," said Albert in a low menacing voice. "I didn't say I ran. And what about you?" he continued. "We have all seen how well you run away, but what do you know of war?"

The smirk on Gilles' face was quickly replaced with seething anger as everyone laughed uproariously at Albert's retaliation.

"Now, now," said Thomas, trying to cool the hostilities. "We will surely have plenty of opportunities to prove ourselves. Let's not waste our energy fighting amongst one another."

Albert, still seething, said nothing as Gilles motioned his horse forward and parted company.

Albert looked back at Thomas. "Thank you for staying my hand from beating his idiotic head in," he said.

"Calm yourself and think. You may have to depend on him in battle." Thomas replied.

Word came down through the ranks that the scouts and foragers had started the dismantling of St. Omer. Soon, all the troupes would be taking part in the eradication of the little village and its inhabitants. They arrived with the village in flames, and the orders were given to unleash the infantry. All hell broke loose as the soldiers and knights began the final sacking. Gilles, with sword drawn, rode straight into the fray, swinging at anything that crossed his path.

Albert and Thomas followed, but with more grace and caution. "Come on, lads! Let's destroy these French bastards!" yelled a voice from behind them as they rushed into the battle.

As they galloped through the village, they were witness to the slaughter. They soon became separated as each took part in defending themselves against the men of the village. No one was spared. Women, children, the old, and sickly were struck down without mercy.

There was a moment when Albert just stared in numb disbelief. He had always thought that war was suffered by men, not women and children. Why were they being slaughtered? What threat were they to the mighty sword? He wondered. He turned with his sword held high at the commotion behind him.

His eyes burned as he peered through the smoke and dust to make out the figure of Gilles coming down on the head of a young boy with his weapon. The blow cut deep, and blood spewed all over. The boy collapsed in a small heap of bloody rags.

Thomas caught up with Albert and told him to at least look as though he was involved. The encounter brought him to his senses, and he realized he was standing conspicuously at the edge of the melee, looking bewildered.

He picked up his sword again and began charging toward the battling crowd. Most of the Frenchmen lay dead on the blood-soaked ground, and Albert led his horse around each as if he were on an obstacle course.

Through the screams and yelling of the victims and the soldiers, he heard his name called and turned to see Gilles, again at work. This time he was holding something that was dripping blood and tossed it at Albert. He dropped his sword, and his hands shot out in reflex to catch the object. He looked down at it and retched when he realized he held the head of a hapless victim in his hands. He dropped it to the ground and looked at Gilles, who was laughing manically and swinging his sword in the air.

Albert was not sure if he had lost his mind or if he was just seeing another side to this cowardly villain. He noticed that the victim's body on the ground at Gilles' feet was dressed in a priest's frock, and he cautiously approached him. "You had better hide this," he said, nodding toward the body.

"Are you giving a threat?" asked Gilles angrily.

"No, it would be treasonous to threaten one of our own," he replied calmly. "I'm merely warning you that if Thomas sees this desecration, there is no telling what he might do."

"Oh, and who does he think he is, the Lord?" asked Gilles sarcastically. "And who the hell do you think you are!" he shouted as Albert mounted his horse and rode away.

Albert had a good mind to tell Thomas about the incident, but he decided not to for fear that he might do something to get himself into trouble.

Finally, the carnage ended. There was nothing left to burn and nobody left to be slaughtered and the army moved on. They settled for the night in a place they thought would be safe. Exhausted, Albert and Thomas rested with their backs against the stones of a nearby well and watched the night fall. Albert's mouth was dry from the dust and smoke he had been inhaling for most of the day. He raised his weary body up to the top of the well and lowered the bucket down into the dark shaft. It made a splash and thump as it hit shallow water and mud at the bottom. He walked over to a building that had been all but burned out and picked up a half-burnt timber that was still on fire. He wrapped a rag around it and blew on it until it flared up enough for him to use as a torch. He held it down into the deep dark shaft as far as his arm could reach.

At the bottom he could just barely see the bodies floating dead in the water. "Damn!" he cursed. "Is there nothing sacred?"

Gilles guffawed suddenly, startling Albert. He reacted by quickly drawing his sword and pointing it in Gilles' direction. Gilles jumped to his feet immediately. Thomas rose and stood between the two. He leaned toward Albert and grabbed his arm.

"Let it be," he said. "He isn't worth it."

Albert lowered his sword.

"Don't stop him!" snarled Gilles. "I can easily teach this sheepshearer a lesson he won't soon forget!"

Thomas glared at Gilles as he lowered Albert's arm. "Silence your mouth, sir!" he demanded. "Or I will surely not stop him from driving one through you when the next opportunity arises," he continued in a low angry voice.

Gilles lowered his head and put up his hands in retreat, but when Thomas turned, he gave Albert a glower, bringing a smirk to Albert's face.

Suddenly, a call came out of the darkness, interrupting the tension, and the three were able to barely see the figure walking toward them. As he got closer, they could make out the facial features of Sir George.

"What is the trouble here?" he asked looking to Thomas. "I heard yelling, sir. Is there anything wrong?"

"No, sir," Thomas replied confidently. "Albert, here, was cursing the well's being dry is all, sir," he explained.

"Is that all?" said Sir George. "There is a small stream behind the church," he said, pointing in that direction.

The squires mounted their horses and headed toward the church. Thomas led the way with Gilles behind him and, finally, Albert, who inspected the back of Gilles' horse to make sure he had not taken the head of the priest with him as he didn't want Thomas to see it. There was enough trouble already; there would be no purpose in having more. He didn't see it anywhere on Gilles' horse and felt a little more at ease.

They continued on along the main street until they came upon the burned-out church, the fire still burning and finishing its work of destruction and then on to the rear of the building where they could hear the slow trickle of water. They first led their horses to drink and then got down on their knees to share in the refreshment.

"Great day!" exclaimed Gilles as he splashed water on his face. "Those French bastards will feel the wrath of English steel again tomorrow!" he said with a gloating smirk. He was looking at Albert, who didn't look back and just kept silent as Gilles ranted his nonsense.

Albert knew in his heart that this day was not filled with honor, for it was the slaughtering of innocence and nothing more. And he was repulsed and saddened by it. At the same time, he knew he was very much a part of it, and he realized it would be repeated again and again. In his mind, he would have to forgive Gilles and the others, including himself, for that violence. After all, this was war. Albert and Thomas continued listening in silence to Gilles' arrogant bragging about the conquest of the little village.

"Remember, Gilles," said Thomas finally. "This was a defenseless village."

"Still," said Gilles, "it was an invigorating experience that could prepare us for what is to come."

"Perhaps," said Thomas.

"But coming up against a trained soldier is a far cry from slaying little boys and old men," Albert interrupted.

"And how many men did you slay?" asked Gilles sarcastically.

"Not a one," Albert replied.

"Ha! Just what I would expect from a wool monger!" said Gilles. "If you can't beat a man without a weapon, what will you do against one who has one?" he asked.

"When that time comes, I will do what needs to be done," answered Albert.

"Why have you not asked me that same question?" Thomas asked.

"I know you are not like him!" Gilles replied.

"But I have not harmed a soul today, Gilles," said Thomas.

Gilles stood and looked down at Thomas in surprised anger. "I would not have believed that if I hadn't heard it from your own mouth!" he said as he mounted his horse and started back to the encampment.

"You know, he is right, Albert. This is war, and it's what has to be done."

Albert just nodded and mounted his horse, as did Thomas, and they headed back to the encampment.

Once settled and ready for sleep, Albert took out Elizabeth's ring and held it up in front of his eyes.

"What is it?" asked Thomas.

"It's the ring I gave to a lovely maiden once long ago," replied Albert wistfully.

"It's probably stolen from some peasant," said Gilles.

"Hold your tongue, man!" yelled Thomas.

Albert ignored the comment as he did most of what Gilles said and continued, looking at the ring and dreaming of Elizabeth.

Chapter Sixteen

The next morning, the squires rose early to groom and feed the horses before the day's advance began. On the march there were scanty French forces dogging the English, using quick strike tactics and then disappearing. The process did little to impede the march until they began to enter a forested area that shadowed the major town of Rheims. A French force lay in ambush as Lord Buckingham, and the bulk of the army marched in. From behind trees, rocks, and bush, crossbow missiles were launched with deadly accuracy. The center of the army caught full brunt, cutting it in two.

The knights and squires were caught in the front while the rustic soldiers were in the rear. Lord Buckingham gave the order to dismount, for the bush to each side was too thick for cavalry advances. He then let out a battle cry, initiating the knights and squires to advance. Sir William, evoking St. Michael, drew his sword and in a burst of vain glory attacked the cross-bowmen with a sustained fury.

Albert followed him with some reservations. Although fearful, his heart still beat courageously, and he moved forward until a crossbow bolt struck him in the chest. The force knocked him off his horse and tore his surcoat, but it was a glancing blow. Aside from the dent in his plate armor and a large bruise on his chest, he was unharmed. The blow wounded his pride more than his body, and he was on his feet in a flash, charging the French positions, this time with undaunted courage. As bolts whizzed by, he could see their toll amongst the squires and infantry; some of whom were wearing chain mail armor.

Finally reaching the French positions, his broad-sword dictated the battle, crashing down on the Frenchmen with an ever-telling blow. Turning left, he saw his comrades delivering their deathly onslaughts. Turning right, he saw Thomas cutting a human path with his battle-ax, swinging his weapon as the house-carls did in the times of King Harold. A smile crossed his face as he brought his sword down on another foe. *This is what war is,* thought Albert, *not the slaughter of defenseless women and children*. He now fought fearlessly and felt justified in his beliefs.

There were bodies to his left and right as he pressed forward, heading deeper into the forest. The English seemed to be gaining the upper hand as he looked ahead to see Thomas running as surefooted as a mountain goat, traversing all obstacles and pursuing his enemy. The French were on the run! But where was Gilles? *Could he be dead?* he wondered. He continued to give chase, trying to reach Thomas up ahead. As he did, his eyes caught sight of what looked like the sun's rays reflecting off armor or a helmet off in the distance.

He began to race toward it, worried that it might be a fallen comrade. As he came closer, he could make out that it was a squire laying curled up and shivering uncontrollably. His forearms covered his face, but Albert knew it was Gilles. He knelt down, locked his arm on Gilles, and raised him to his feet.

Gilles still shivered and sobbed.

"Gilles! Gilles!" Albert yelled. "Pull yourself together, man!" He shook Gilles with all his might but with no response. He was babbling and sobbing like a frightened baby. Albert slapped him hard in the face, almost knocking him off his feet and finally getting his attention. Gilles just stared at Albert in stunned silence and collapsed to the ground.

"What in God's name has come over you?" Albert demanded.

At that moment, a crossbow bolt whizzed past them, followed by another, grazing Albert's face and throwing him to the ground. He held his hand up to his cheek and tried to stem the bleeding. He looked over at Gilles whose swollen nose was trickling blood. He raised himself and ordered Gilles to do the same, but he just stared in wide-eyed hysteria.

"Christ, have mercy! We are going to be slaughtered here. Get up!" Still, Gilles remained on the ground. "By God, if I'm going to die this day, it will be like an Englishman, for my country!" he yelled. "Not for a sniveling coward such as you! Get on your feet!" he demanded as he drew his sword.

Finally, Gilles rose slowly to his feet. Albert turned again and charged past him, letting out a fierce battle cry with his eyes fixed on the enemy. He noticed with astonishment that they were turning to run. *Surely, it could not have been my battle cry!* he thought as his pace slowed. He turned around to see that the rustics were charging headlong toward him and the enemy. Again, he began running. As he reached the enemy position, one crossbowman turned to fire his weapon at him but to no avail, for Albert's heavy broadsword came down on the Frenchman, missing his body but coming down on his hand, crushing fingers. The man dropped the crossbow and fell to the ground, writhing in agony.

From the rear assault, the rustics cut a swath through whatever lay in their path—foliage or Frenchmen. However, they too left the forest floor littered with dead and dying of their own. The victors tended their wounded while the defeated French—some barely alive—lay in pools of blood, looking at their own body parts lying separated only a few feet away.

The fresh forest air was fouled by the stench of death. The blood had coagulated on Albert's face as he dropped back his pace and walked to where Gilles sat upright against an ash tree, his feet straddling the roots. His shivering had subsided for he knew the battle was over, and he got on one knee and peered through the brush at Albert and the rustics who followed close behind. This time, he was on his feet before Albert reached him.

"Squire!" yelled a rustic. "You are quite far from your fellows."

"Yes," replied Albert. "We became separated during the battle. If you had not been following me, we would have been killed, sir," he said. "My utmost gratitude to you and your men," he continued, glancing over at Gilles, who was standing with his head down. He looked back at Albert with a sheepish grin that angered and disgusted him, but he said nothing for the moment. "Are you leading the infantry?" Albert asked.

"No, sir, I'm afraid our leader is lying yonder with a nasty wound," he said, pointing.

Albert and Gilles walked in the direction indicated. Stepping over corpses and through the blood-soaked scrub, they made their way to where the infantry commander was lying. When they reached him, he was lying on his side and being tended by several of his own men who were more arguing over how to remove the bolt that was stuck in the man's arm than actually treating him. Finally, they slowly turned the man onto his back. Two of the attendants held him down, and a third readied himself to remove the bolt.

Sweat dripped from the wounded man's face as he screamed in pain, cursing them all. As soon as the bolt was out, he fell unconscious. Others began tearing cloth from the shirts of some of the dead as blood gushed from the wound. The healers tried to stem the flow by wrapping a piece of cloth tightly around his arm above the wound and applying pressure directly to the wound. As soon they finished, they moved away from their commander, who lay with eyes closed flat on his back.

Albert moved in closer to get a look at the man. "By the Virgin Mary!" he cried aloud as he recognized the face of his longtime friend. "Wat!" he yelled. "Wat Tyler!"

He stared openmouthed as he lowered himself to his knees.

Wat's eyes opened and looked back at Albert just as surprised. "Albert, you bastard!" he yelled. "What in hell are you doing here?" A grimace crossed his face as his arm began to throb.

"It was you then!" said Albert.

"Yeah, friend, that's right, it was me! But what was me?" he asked.

"It was you who Lord Buckingham summoned to bring order to this crew of rustics!" replied Albert.

"I've been here for some time now," said Wat.

"I wondered who was responsible for their skill and organization," said Albert.

"Yeah, that was me, and it wasn't any easy task!" Wat replied.

Albert told him of his chance encounter with Elizabeth; as he did, Gilles stood nearby, listening to the conversation.

"Who is Elizabeth to you?" Gilles interrupted.

Wat stopped short and looked at Gilles intently. "Who the hell are you, and what business do you have to ask me about my sister?"

Gilles immediately backed off.

"Ahhhh!" yelled Wat. "The bloody bastards tied these damn bandages too tight!"

Albert began to loosen them for him.

"Well," yelled Wat, recovering and looking at Gilles. "You haven't answered my question; who the hell are you?"

"Gilles Marshall, squire," he mumbled.

"Ohhh, squire!" said Wat, rolling his eyes sarcastically and smiling at Albert, who thought it best to remain silent. He was not about to get between Gilles and his comeuppance, but he smiled back at Wat. They were informed by two soldiers who were carrying a litter that Wat would be taken to the encampment that had been erected. He yelled obscenities as they lifted him onto the litter. Albert had to laugh at the looks on their faces as Wat turned the air blue. They walked slowly, carrying him as Albert and Gilles walked alongside the litter.

As they arrived, Albert gently gripped Wat's forearm and looked into his eyes. "My prayers are with you, friend," he said. "I will be back to visit you in camp."

"Right, go with care," he answered.

Albert turned and walked away with Gilles following. They began searching the rich grassy areas for their steeds. After giving their animals time to feed, they mounted without words. They rode down the dust-choked roads, dodging the weary infantry and carrying their wounded to the campsite. As they rode, Albert scanned the area were the battle had taken place earlier. He watched as many rustics and a handful of squires and even a few knights were stripping the lifeless bodies of the dead of all their belongings, but the noble of heart brought their fallen comrades to the encampment so that the scavengers could not savage them and so that they could be put to rest with dignity.

As soon as the encampment was completely erected, the soldiers began slaughtering the pigs they had confiscated from a nearby farm, and some foraging was done in the towns they had passed through. However, most of the supplies were brought along with the expedition. While the pigs were being slaughtered, the battle weary troops began to build spits and fires to cook the beasts. A holiday atmosphere prevailed as they readied to celebrate their victory.

When Albert and Gilles finally arrived, the party had begun with feasting, dicing, and playing card games. And there were females of all ages who had been captured and used for the darker pleasures of the expedition's elite, including the one so close to Jesus himself, the army's priest, after which he would then take up his crop and beat himself bloody, lamenting and purging himself of his evil ways. And as Albert and Gilles passed through the encampment, they witnessed the unsavory activities between some of the squires and their knights.

This was particularly strange to them. Gilles stopped to stare in morbid fascination, but Albert just wanted to pass quickly and get on with their search for their comrades. The rustics, who had been kept in order up until now, had finally relapsed into iniquity after their commander was wounded and had begun drinking heavily and fighting with anyone who was unfortunate enough to cross their paths. As they continued on through the camp, some of the men, both rustics and squires asked if they would like to buy some of the goods looted from bodies of the dead and dying.

Albert, disgusted by this practice, drew his sword and chased a few of them away. "To hell with you!" they yelled back as Albert's horse reared up on its hind legs. They scattered in all directions.

Finally, they arrived at their destination and found their comrades on a grassy knoll that sat at the very edge of the encampment. This location overlooked a glorious view displaying a multitude of colors that hid a hideous multitude of sin. The troupe had two tents, one for squires and one for knights. Albert and Gilles dismounted and undressed their horses, leaving the beasts many pounds lighter. They tied them to a makeshift hitching post where there was some late summer grasses to graze. Each horse needed to be watered, for after a day of battle, they were as hungry and thirsty as any soldier.

Afterward, they entered Sir William's tent, where the knights were gathered. The mood inside the tent was very somber, a stark difference to that of other parts of the camp that they had encountered this night.

"Why are we not celebrating our victory?" asked Albert.

Sir William raised his head and looked into Albert's eyes. "We've lost Thomas this day," he said.

Albert stared back at him in shock and disbelief. "How could that be?" he asked, placing a hand over his brow. "My God, not Thomas!" he cried.

"I am sorry," said Sir William. "I know how close you were to him. He was a wonderful friend to all of us."

"Where is he now?" asked Albert in a quivering voice.

"His body rests in the squire's tent," replied Sir William.

Albert turned to go, and Gilles followed. They found Thomas lying upon Sir William's tunic in quiet and reposed, still dressed in complete battle attire. The only sign of violence was a trickle of blood running down the length of his surcoat's arm on the inside. Albert knelt beside the lifeless body with Gilles standing behind him. He put his head down and wept openly.

"Where are you, dear Thomas?" he cried, holding his hands out to his sides. "Where has this journey taken you, my dear friend?" He wanted so much for answers, but there was only silence.

After a time, Gilles left, but Albert remained with Thomas, deep in prayer until the early morning hours. He left the tent in deep despair and walked out to where the horses were tied. He gazed up into the dark, starlit sky with his hand stroking his horse's neck.

"Rest in peace, dear friend," he whispered. He called on Jesus to recognize Thomas for his piety and take him into heaven with him. Although he had fully accepted Thomas' death, he still wished with all his might and heart that Thomas would come back. He walked out beyond the encampment and lay in the grass. He both prayed and cursed God and the church at the same time.

He was deeply saddened and confused by Thomas' death. "Why would God let this happen after all the years of loyalty and faith Thomas has shown?" he asked himself. "This is all there is," he said to himself. And now things began to fall into place as he watched the dawn break on the horizon. He knew now why there was a lust for power and greed deep within some men's hearts. They too knew that this was all there was.

So, they would use these good men for all their worldly possessions, including their very lives, telling them it was a right of passage into heaven. *This is where Thomas' faith had gotten him,* he thought sadly. His thoughts turned to Wat and all the things he had said about the church and so-called pious men. He understood his anger and his want for change. Albert turned, wiping his eyes, and walked back to camp, feeling an urgency to find Wat.

He searched for some time until he finally found him in a makeshift infirmary where scores of soldiers lay wounded. The loud sounds of celebration could be matched by the painful screams of those that were bleeding out or having limbs removed. Albert walked through looking for his friend. He found him sleeping through the racket and commotion around him. He looked down into Wat's face and gently touched his shoulder. Wat's eyes opened, much to Albert's relief, for when he first looked at him he thought he was dead, and he wasn't ready to lose two friends in the same day. He looked up and grinned at Albert.

"I knew you'd come," he said.

"Yes, it just took a little time to find you. How are you faring?" asked Albert.

"It hurts!"

"I owe you my life," said Albert, looking into Wat's eyes.

"You'd have done the same," said Wat, waving his hand. "We are being taken back to Calais," he continued.

"Yes, I would expect you would," replied Albert.

"It's for the best," said Wat. "You know we would only slow the campaign."

Albert sat with Wat for a long time as they talked

about things they had done since their last meeting. The foremost topic was about Elizabeth. Albert told of his chance meeting with her at the lord's manor.

"How is she faring these days?" asked Wat. "I haven't seen her in a very long time," he continued, looking down at his feet.

"She is well, I'm happy to say," replied Albert. *And more beautiful than ever,* he thought to himself. He confided in Wat about their plans to marry when he returned to England. He took the ring from his pocket and showed it to Wat. "Do you remember this?" he asked.

Wat's face lit up. "I surely do!" he said, looking into Albert's eyes. "I'm glad she wants to marry you, my friend. I cannot think of anyone else I would want to call brother."

Albert smiled. "Thanks," he said. "When you get back to England, I would appreciate it greatly if you would watch over her until I return."

Wat gave Albert his word, and they clasped hands. There was a pause in the conversation as Wat maneuvered himself into a sitting position. He looked up at Albert and motioned him to move closer.

"I've heard there is much unrest in England," he said in a quiet voice.

Albert looked a bit puzzled. "How could you know that if you've been in France all this time?" he asked.

"Well, you being a merchant's son, you should know," he said. "I got the news regularly from the merchant ships that sail in and out of Calais. Those seamen know what is happening all the time. It's their business to know as there are many events that can dramatically affect the trade," he continued. "And the talk of revolt would surely devastate trade."

Wat talked to Albert at length. He spoke of a man called John Ball, the fiery preacher who gave sermons that were opposed to the church and the nobles. "I spoke of him years ago, Albert," he said. "Do you remember?"

Albert nodded.

"Well, he has gathered a large following since, but now he sits in the archbishop's dungeon. Because of him, people are beginning to take notice of the injustices perpetrated by some nobles and clerics," he continued. "They are tired of paying the unfair taxes imposed by the rich and the righteous. And now there is this new poll tax that has been proposed to pay for Lord Buckingham's expedition."

"What do you think is going to happen?" asked Albert.

"Well, there is nothing else to do but overtake the king and his ministers," Wat replied.

Albert looked startled and concerned. "You realize that your statements could be considered an act of treason," he said, "so be careful, my friend."

Wat looked at Albert in all seriousness. "I am well aware of my statements, and I know you are in agreement," he said. "When I return to England, I plan to take up John Ball's cause."

Albert worried that Elizabeth would be caught up in the struggle and pleaded with Wat. "You will be in England before me; I beg you take care of Elizabeth. Please protect her from danger and make sure she stays with the good sisters until my return."

Wat promised he would but was a little offended by the statement. "Do you believe I would risk my sister's life?" he asked. "Do you not have faith that we will prevail?"

"Yes! But—" Albert couldn't finish.

"Do you not still agree that something must be done?" said Wat.

"I don't know," said Albert, looking down at his hands.

"Albert, my dear friend and confidant, I know that you believe that what I say is true and right, so why deny it?" said Wat with a sympathetic smile.

Albert looked into his friend's eyes. "I don't know what to believe anymore. I just want to get this campaign over with and return to Elizabeth," he said. "And most of all, I don't want to lose any more friends to a battle."

"Forgive me," said Wat in a softer voice. "I heard about your friend Thomas. It's a sad shame we must lose the good men to this, but that is the price of change. I'm sorry about Thomas, though. I know that if you loved him, he must have been a good man."

They sat silently for a few moments, each in their own thoughts.

"Albert," said Wat finally, "I love you as a brother. All I ask is that you keep your eyes and heart open. And remember Brother William and all those who have suffered as he did."

Albert stood and stared at the ground. "You are right, Wat. I shall never be able to remove that scene from my mind."

"Please consider all that has happened and continues

to happen," said Wat. "I know you will make the right decision."

Albert nodded, feeling more unsure than ever. He clasped Wat's outstretched hand.

"I shall see you in England. I pray you will be safe and come home to marry my sister," Wat said with a grin.

Albert grinned back. "God go with you, my friend," he said.

"And with you, Albert."

Albert walked back to where his comrades were camped. On his way, he heard talk from the other squires of how Lord Buckingham was to knight all the squires in the morning. At first he was excited and happy about finally becoming a knight, but his thoughts grew more worrisome as images of Elizabeth and an uprising in England raced through his mind. He was so very torn between his love for her and all the ideals his father had wanted for him.

Then he thought of Thomas who more than deserved to become a knight, and now he never would. And it galled him to think that a coward such as Gilles would have that glory. The conflicts in his head made him feel weary and discouraged. He didn't know if he could hold his tongue when he arrived at his tent.

When he entered he saw Gilles sleeping, mouth open and snoring like a hound. He looked over at Thomas' body lying cold and still. They would be burying him in the morning. *While we're celebrating a joyous victory, poor Thomas will be laid to rest with a much sadder ceremony,* he thought as he lay down to sleep. Soon physical and mental exhaustion took over, and he drifted off.

Chapter Seventeen

The next morning, he woke to the clamor of soldiers walking past his tent. He jumped to his feet and looked around. Thomas' body had already been removed, but Gilles continued to snore. He walked over to where he slept and gave him a nudge with his boot.

"Get up!" he said. "It's morning."

Gilles snorted and sat up as Albert left the tent. He walked out to the field where he could see them burying the dead. He wanted to make one last visit to Thomas before they put him into the mass grave. It seemed so undignified for such a man to be forever interned with others—some of whom were unworthy of sharing a grave with him.

He stood by the edge of the grave as tears welled up in his eyes. He looked down to see his friend being lowered into the ground. He heard the words of the priest and the others praying for the souls of the honorable dead, and he prayed too. *I will miss you, dear Thomas,* he thought sadly. *And I shall never forget you.*

Immediately following the burial, Lord Buckingham preformed the ceremony for knighting all the squires. As the rustic troops dismantled the campsite, nobles and knights gathered on the flattest ground where the lord's tent had been the prior evening. Here, the squires knelt as he passed with his sword.

"The order of knighthood is noble that he who is a knight should have no dealings with anything or anyone of low morality and who is afflicted with cowardice. He should be strong and proud, a protector of the weak and loyal to the king," he said as he dubbed each one.

Albert bowed his head as he was knighted; then, when the lord passed to the next, he looked over at Gilles, who was now being knighted, and he lowered his head again in disgust.

During the ceremony, the wounded were being loaded onto wagons to be taken to Calais. They would be accompanied by an escort of knights. Among them would be Sir Godfrey and the newly knighted Sir Gilles, which gave Albert a small measure of relief in knowing that his cowardice could not jeopardize the lives of the brave men at arms. He was hopeful too that he would not have to lay eyes on the coward again.

With the wounded out of their way, the army proceeded onward. Whatever beautiful countryside there had been was now being left behind as they began to march through the villages that were put to the torch, people put to the sword, and a once peaceful land left in ruin.

All the while, as they rode, fought, and destroyed, Albert's one dream was to return home. He wondered about his beautiful Elizabeth and if she would tire of waiting for him. Also, he worried about his parents, and whether they would still be there when he returned. He knew they were getting on in years, and he was just beginning to realize their mortality. He feared too that the rebellion Wat spoke of would take place before his return, and he would not be there to protect them. After all, they were merchants and could suffer the same fate as the nobles and churchmen if such an uprising took place. It was a frightening thought, for he could not imagine his life without them.

The army continued fighting through every day, one in Champagne, the next in Orleans, the following day in Anjou and Brittany, and finally, where the ultimate prize laid, the city of Nantes. At no time, however, during the grueling march did the French forces ever give all-out battles. They fought in small skirmishes and harassments, but yet killing and wounding countless Englishmen. Finally, Nantes was in their sights.

This was the finale that Albert had waited for. If he lived through this battle, home would not be far off into the future. However, the attack would never come as Lord Buckingham deemed his forces too weak after the many skirmishes and ambushes that depleted and drained the army. The only alternative was to lay siege to Nantes, which did not last long as they were too weak to complete even this mission. The French had persevered, and the English left accomplishing very little compared to the blood and fortune that had been wasted.

Wat had returned to an England that looked much the same as he had left it except discontent and discord was the order of the day for the common folk. Taxes and incompetence had been the tools of the rich, who were going to get whatever they wanted despite all the calamities that befell their subjects. The atmosphere was akin to a pot filled to capacity over a fire that raged out of control, forcing the pot to explode and overflow with disaster, death, and destruction.

The merchant vessel, *Our Lady,* docked at Paul's Wharf. Along with her merchant cargo were the wounded from Lord Buckingham's campaign. Wat was among them and came ashore, sporting a sling that supported his wounded arm. He hoped he would soon meet up with fellow tradesmen that would be willing to transport him to St. Avery in Southwick. The first place he visited was an old haunt where he found some of the friends he had kept company with before going to France.

After a few drinks and some embellished stories of his whereabouts, one friend agreed to take him to St. Avery's to see his sister. Soon, he was standing at the convent door with his helmet in his hands. A tiny nun opened the door.

"State you business!" she demanded.

Wat almost laughed but held back. It seemed to him that such a tiny, frail-looking, little nun would have a tiny voice to match, and he found this contrast quite funny.

"I've come to see Elizabeth," he said, smiling.

"And who are you," she asked.

"The name is Wat Tyler," he replied. "Elizabeth's brother."

Without another word, she turned and motioned him to follow. She led him through the vestibule and up the stairs to the prioress' chamber. The nun gave the door a tap before opening it.

The prioress turned from the window as they walked in.

"This gentleman has come to see his sister Elizabeth, Prioress," she announced.

"Thank you, Sister," she responded as the nun turned to leave. "Sit down, sir," she said to Wat. "Sister Maria will fetch Elizabeth and bring her to us."

"Thank you," he said.

Within moments, Elizabeth appeared with a wide grin, which diminished when she noticed her brother's wounded arm. She touched him gently on his other arm and asked about the wound. She kissed his face as her eyes filled with tears.

"I prayed for your safety, dear brother," she said as he put his good arm around her.

"Dry your tears, sweet Elizabeth," he said good-naturedly. "I shall not be leaving again for a long time," he continued. "For I have much business to attend to right here."

She looked into his eyes and knew what he meant. She had gotten wind of a rebellion, and the thought of his being caught up in it frightened her.

"Please, Wat, don't do anything that will cause you to get into trouble," she begged.

He could see that this talk was upsetting her, and

he changed the subject. "I have news of someone," he said teasingly.

"Who?" she asked as she began to undo his bandages. She wanted to see how his wound was healing.

He grimaced as she pulled the bandage from the wound. "Dear sister, have mercy!" he said as he looked down at what she was doing.

She took a clean cloth from her apron and dabbed the wound gently, checking it for infection. It seemed to be healing well despite the dirt and sweat.

"I must clean this wound," she said.

"Sweet sister," he said as she began to replace the bandages with clean linen. "I'm visiting for only a short time."

She stared at him sadly.

"Oh, don't look at me in that way, love! I will be going to Maidstone," he cried.

The prioress, who had been standing by and listening to the conversation, had become assured that this was indeed Elizabeth's brother and excused herself from the room, leaving the door open as she left.

"I wanted tell you that I met your lost love on the battlefield just outside of St. Omer," he said smiling.

"You saw Albert there?" she gasped excitedly.

"Yes," he replied, laughing. "He asked me to look after you."

"Well, how can you do that if you're going to Maidstone?" she asked sarcastically.

"I will keep in touch," he said. "You know, he has become a knight. Sir Albert!" he said proudly.

"I can very well imagine Albert as a knight," she

said, beaming. "With God's help, his mission will be completed, and my knight will return home to me."

Suddenly, Wat's manor became serious, and he drew closer to her. He spoke in a low voice so that he could not be overheard. "I wanted to warn you, my sister, that there is great unrest spreading among the common folk. There will soon come a time that it will become dangerous for some of us." He continued, "Even before I came here, I spoke briefly with some of the conspirators in London. I will be with them when this thing erupts."

"Dear brother, please don't speak of such things," she begged. "You know that such talk is treason against the crown. I fear you will find yourself dead or in jail," she cried.

"I will find myself facing the king and—" The look in her eyes made him stop and hold her close to him. "Elizabeth," he said, "you have to know that I have waited for this chance all my life. I could not stand by and watch as others fight for a cause I truly believe is right and good."

She stared at him disapprovingly. "I cannot stop you, Wat, so I will pray that you will call on your good senses when the time comes."

"I must go, love," he said abruptly. He stood looking at her for a long moment.

"Promise me you will return to me, brother," she said.

"Have cheer. I shall. Dry your tears now, and think wonderful thoughts about your knight!" he said. He kissed her forehead before reaching into his pocket and pulling out his money satchel. "Is there anything you are in need of?" he asked.

She shook her head and smiled.

"I supposed they paid you well in France," she said. "I hope that you will spend it wisely."

"Of course," he answered. "I will visit old friends in London and have a few drinks to celebrate my homecoming before going on to Maidstone," he said.

She gave him a skeptical look.

"Fear not, dear sister. I will return," he said.

"Look me in the eyes, Wat," she ordered.

He did so without a blink. "I promise," he said, knowing it would be quite some time before he could keep his promise. She reached up with her hand to touch his face and kissed him.

When she drew back, she noticed the tears in his eyes. "What?" she asked.

"Nothing, I'm just happy to see you," he answered, quickly wiping his eyes. "I must leave," he said again.

He lifted her hand, kissed it, and without another word, turned and walked away. Usually, he would turn and wave as he walked out the door, but this time he didn't look back.

He made his way to Maidstone where he joined the other leaders of a coming rebellion that could change the destiny of England.

Chapter Eighteen

It was a warm summer's day of brilliant skies and favorable winds that allowed Lord Buckingham's weary force to set sail for home. Earlier, royal dispatches reached France with talk of unrest at home. Word passed quickly among the troops. Hearing the news made Albert feel depressed. He knew it had to be the beginning of the rebellion, and he wondered how widespread it could become. He spoke with many of his friends about the possibility that they may have to fight again when they arrived home.

"From what is being reported, there is a huge following of the rebels, and it grows by the day," Sir William told Albert. "You see, they seem to have a large association that traverses over all of England," he continued. "It appears nothing has begun yet, but something is definitely in the wind."

Albert listened, but his mind was on Elizabeth as well as his parents.

"I worry about my parents and a maiden that might be caught up in the uprising," he said.

"The maiden you speak of would be Elizabeth, yes?"

"Yes," Albert replied.

"Never fear, my friend. We will soon be there to crush this thing before it has a chance to threaten anybody," said Sir William.

"There's more to my problem," said Albert, shaking his head. "You see one of the rebels is Elizabeth's brother." He looked intently at Sir William and waited for a reaction. However, he wasn't very surprised to learn that Sir William felt the same. As he knew, many other knights had Lollard sympathies also.

It was common knowledge by this time that the nobles and the clergy were about to clash. The cause of this conflict was because of the collections of funds from English parishes for a French Pope and an overwhelming French college of cardinals. And they were, after all, at war with France. He understood why his comrades would support the conflict, but he still questioned their intentions toward the hardworking, poor folks who more than deserved a chance for a better quality of life.

"I see that your young lady may be one of those who belong to the peasantry."

Albert lowered his head momentarily and then quickly raised it back up, looking Sir William in the eyes.

"Yes," he said. "Her brother is Wat Tyler, who has been a longtime friend and confidant of mine. I have seen many injustices done to them and others of their station by the nobles and the clergy," he continued. "I believe they have a just cause against all those who oppress them," said Albert.

"Yes, my friend, I too believe they do. However, we must remember our place in the scheme of things." William replied. "We are knights and members of the nobility who are despised by the peasants, and there is little we can do to alleviate their suffering. I'm sure of one thing, though; rebellion will serve no purpose. They are sure to be put down almost as quickly as the can rise up. Whatever has to be done to put the rebellion down is what we must do."

Sir William's thoughts were troubling to Albert and drove him deeper into a state of indecision. He was torn between his friendship with Wat, his love for Elizabeth, and his family values. In his mind, they represented two separate ideologies, which conflicted and tore his loyalties in two.

Suddenly, the sky became gray in a matter of minutes, and the seas began to swell as he stood on deck and gazed trancelike over the water. The seas began to toss the ship and sent waves over the side of the vessel. Everyone began to rush toward the rear to shield themselves under the castle. They grasped tight to anything that would keep them from being washed overboard. As Sir William rushed with the others, he called to Albert to abandon his position and join them, but he just stood still as the storm strengthened.

Just as he turned toward Sir William's voice, a large wave overtook him and carried him off across the deck. His lungs filled with water as he struggled to breathe for what seemed like an eternity until a strange calmness took the place of his panic, and he fell limp. He felt himself floating peacefully as the muffled sounds of rushing water and people screaming melted into the air and was replaced by the sweet voice of Elizabeth calling to him. He envisioned her wearing a lovely white gown and beckoning him to come to her. Suddenly, the vision changed to one of darkness, and he could hear his mother crying. He woke abruptly to a heavy pounding on his chest and a terrible, sick feeling in his stomach. He retched violently before reluctantly opening his eyes. Salt water and mucus poured from his nose and mouth as William pumped furiously on his chest.

"We thought we lost you, friend. God be praised! But why didn't you follow me to the rear of the ship?" he asked, with a hint of anger.

"I know not," Albert replied, shaking his head sadly.

"If it had not been for Reginald, here, pulling you back from the sea, you surely would have been swept overboard," Sir William said, pointing to the burley, dark-haired man standing beside him.

Albert, quite embarrassed by his own carelessness, thanked the gentlemen as well as anyone else who had helped in rescuing him.

He was ashamed that he hadn't taken better care and was almost tempted to let himself go to the sweet peacefulness of death. It was a most cowardly act, he thought, and unbecoming of a knight to disgrace the code of chivalry in such a manner. He decided he must face whatever problems come his way and do his best. He prayed to God for forgiveness and strength.

Henry, who had not been able to go to France, was kept informed of the progress of war. Whenever he had news, he always passed it on to Elizabeth as he did this day. When he arrived at the convent, he saw her walking toward the horse stalls.

"Elizabeth!" he called, dismounting and catching up to her. "My dear lady, I have news of the royal fleet. A storm has hampered their landing in London. Word has it that they will dock in Dover."

To Elizabeth, it meant another two days before Albert's arrival.

"From there they will march to London," he continued.

He looked at her for a long moment. "Is there anything else?" she asked, concerned.

"Yes, miss. It does look as though a rebellion has broken out near London, and the royal fleet will most certainly be involved in putting it down," he explained.

"It has started already," she said. "Well then, I must reach Albert right away!"

"Yes, miss," he said. "I too have been called to London to join my comrades; if it pleases you, I can take you along to the wharf where you can board a vessel to Dover." He reached into his satchel and handed her several florins. "Take this," he said. "It will pay your passage."

"I don't know how to thank you, sir," she said, taking the coins. She stood on tiptoes to kiss his cheek. "It is most appreciated," she said, smiling.

Henry bowed his head shyly as his cheeks turned

pink. "Yes, miss, you're quite welcome. Now, dear lady, we must be off," he said, regaining his composure.

"Right away, sir, but I must tell the prioress."

She went directly to the study where she found her deeply rapt in the reading of a manuscript. "My lady," Elizabeth said softly.

The prioress looked up from her reading. "Yes," she replied.

Elizabeth went on to explain her situation, and the prioress understood completely.

"Take heart, my dear," she said. "Everything will be fine. I wish you a safe trip and hope you find what you are looking for, and remember, my dear, should you find you want to return to us, our gates and our hearts will always be open to you."

Elizabeth bowed her head in gratitude and thanked the prioress for her understanding. She stopped by her cell to pick up a few belongings. She took only what she needed to make the trip, and the rest would be left, as it was donated to her by the convent. Finally, she was ready to leave and walked out to meet Henry. He lifted her up onto his horse and then mounted behind her.

Watching from the window as they left, the prioress thought back to her own sadness and said a silent prayer for both of them. She remembered the heartbreak of losing her dear husband to the war in France some years ago. Being childless, she came to the priory to devote her life to prayer. She knew that if the Lord wanted Elizabeth, he would call her, but for now she must follow her heart to wherever it takes her. She also knew her sweet presence would be sorely missed.

The wharf bustled with its usual commotion when Henry and Elizabeth arrived, but she was lucky enough to get passage to Dover. Before boarding, she turned to Henry and kissed him on both cheeks. "Farewell, dear friend," she said. "And, again, I thank you for your kindness."

"God's speed, dear lady," he replied. "And do give my regards to Sir Albert," he said, mounting his horse.

"Of course, sir" she replied.

As she stood and watched him ride away, he turned to wave. She smiled and waved as she turned to walk up the wooden plank to the ship's deck where she met with the large, barrel-chested master who held up six fingers of two savagely disfigured hands, indicating the cost of her passage.

"Do you have the fare, my lady?" he asked.

She handed him the fare and smiled.

"Many thanks, miss," he said. "And welcome aboard. Please step to the stern," he directed.

Elizabeth walked up the deck to the cargo area where the merchants sat. Polite smiles came to their faces as they shifted around in an effort to allow her enough room to sit. She nodded a thank you and took her seat. She was the only woman among all the men whose previously foul-mouthed talk was quelled by her presence. Again, they smiled at her and began to talk in a more seemly manner so as not to offend the lovely young maiden who had graced their midst.

As the cog set sail, Elizabeth, completely exhausted, fell fast asleep. The vessel passed Wargate and remained within eye's distance of the coast. Farther out at sea was the royal fleet, which was following its original plan to dock in London.

After a short and uneventful journey, they reached Dover with Elizabeth still fast asleep. Finally, the master noticed her and gently shook her. She awoke, startled, and jumped to her feet.

"Sorry, miss," he said as she rushed past him and looked out from the deck. "What are you looking for, miss?" he asked.

"The royal fleet," she replied. "I thought it was due to arrive here this day."

"I'm sorry, but I don't know and have heard nothing of it," he said. "My suggestion would be to go ashore and ask about it. I'm sure you will hear some news."

They walked toward the gangplank, and he took her hand as he helped her down. She thanked him politely and looked around worriedly.

"Will you be fine then, miss?" he asked.

"Yes, thank you again, sir."

She hadn't waited very long when two more merchant cogs docked. She asked the master of one of them about the royal fleet.

"Yes," said the small rotund mariner. "It has docked in London. It was able to dock there after all."

"I see," she said. "Thank you, sir."

"It was a pleasure, my dear," he said with a flirty smile.

With evening fast approaching, Elizabeth hurried to leave the wharf to the safety of the nearest convent. There she found a clean, warm bed and kindly nuns who provided some nourishment before she settled in for the night.

At this time, the royal fleet had made its way to London, where there were no immediate signs of unrest among the populace. To greet Sir William and the veteran knights, Sir George and Sir Albert, were their fellows Sir Robert, Sir Godfrey, and Sir Gilles, along with the very nervous Squire Henry. With all the formal greetings aside, Lord Buckingham's force disbanded to their respective villages to put down reported sporadic skirmishes created by bands of peasants. Sir William's retinue rode to Lord Stafford's manor with his men behind him. Henry rode at the rear with Sir Albert and hesitantly informed him of Elizabeth's departure to Dover.

"Why would she go there?" he asked, surprised.

"Well, I advised her, sir. I'm so sorry, but the last we heard, your ship was detoured there," Henry explained. "I am truly sorry."

Albert rode up close to him and placed a hand on his shoulder. "No need to be sorry, my friend, and I thank you for providing the fare for her passage. I know your intentions were good."

Henry looked up and smiled at him. "You are quite welcome, sir," he said.

Lord Stafford greeted them as they arrived. He held a dispatch in his hand. "We have word that the rebels have begun rioting all over the south. We will remain on standby, and if needed, we will be quick to march."

The announcement brought up a dilemma for Albert. With all his heart he wanted to be with his brothers in arms, but with the same intense desire, he wanted to be with Elizabeth in Dover. He spent the evening lost in thought over his quandary, and in the end he decided to leave for Dover no matter the consequences. Love for his lady had won out, and so he would wait until the right moment arose to make his leave.

The following day, Lord Stafford ordered his retinue back to London to await any further news of the rebellion. Not taking this very seriously, he allowed his men to indulge themselves in recreational activities in the city. Albert and Henry rode off together to find a quiet tavern to refresh themselves and talk.

His decision to go to Dover weighed heavily on his mind, and he trusted his friend enough to confess his plans. "I must go to her as it may be the last chance I get to see her," he said. "I love her very much."

Henry looked into Albert's eyes and nodded. "My friend, you do realize the gravity of your actions?"

"Yes, I would be deserting you and the rest of my comrades."

"Yes, that's true, but I have to say, I would do the same had I ever been fortunate enough to fall in love," said Henry, putting his hand on Albert's shoulder. In the spirit of friendship, they raised their mugs to one another. "To love and war," said Henry,

"Yes, to love and war."

After they had drunk their fill, they mounted their horses, bid their good-byes, and parted company. Albert headed toward the docks, thinking this would be the quickest way to Dover, and he didn't want to take the chance of using the roads as he might be stopped and sent back. He looked around and found a master who was preparing to set sail.

"Are you sailing for Dover?" he asked.

"No, sir," said the master, pointing to another ship. "But I believe that vessel is headed there."

"Thank you," said Albert as he led his horse in the direction indicated.

He approached the master. "Sailing to Dover?"

The master gave a nod and held up eight fingers, indicating the fare. Albert agreed as he reached into his satchel and handed the man the coins.

He proceeded to board, but the sound of a very raspy voice brought him back. "That was for you, Sir Knight," the voice insisted sarcastically, "not the horse."

"I don't like your tone, sir," replied Albert.

"I don't care what you like or don't like. You must pay for your horse!" said the man, stepping toward him. Albert immediately drew his sword, and the man backed off slightly but still held his ground. With one large step forward, Albert grabbed the man by his collar with his free hand and drew him face-to-face.

"I will surely run you through that fat stomach and relieve you of your innards, my surly friend."

The crewmen who were watching came quickly to their master's aid.

"Enough, mates," said the master. "I was a bit hasty, sir. I apologize."

The men backed off immediately as they all knew the consequences of killing or merely injuring a knight of the king. Albert unhanded the man and drew back, looking suspiciously around at the crew, and started up the gangplank.

Within a short time, the merchant cog set sail. Albert could only hope and pray that he would find Elizabeth before the country broke out into civil war.

As he sailed, he gazed out over the ocean, thinking of days gone by and praying that fate would be kind. A loud whinny from his horse brought him back to the here and now. He reached up, pet the white patch on its snout, and marveled at its beauty.

"I pray we are doing the right thing, friend," he sighed.

The horse responded with nodding as if it understood and approved. Albert smiled as he stroked its long and shiny, black neck.

He looked up into the sky as darkness approached, and the crew began lighting the torches. Soon they were making their way into Dover, and Albert and his steed disembarked with nightfall upon them. He knew there would be little chance of finding Elizabeth that night. The only thing to do would be to find lodging and begin searching in the morning.

Chapter Nineteen

Early the next morning, Elizabeth left the convent and walked down to the waterfront, where she asked various seamen about the royal fleet's arrival. She was told that it had not landed and that it would not because it had landed in London. With this news and no money left to make passage, she returned to the convent. She had to think about how she was going to get back to London. She decided that she would travel with a group of pilgrims to the shrine of St. Thomas in Canterbury. From there, perhaps, there would be a group that would be heading north and could bring her to London.

As she left Dover, Albert began to search the waterfront, barely missing her by a few moments. He talked to many sailors who claimed they had not seen her. Now, in desperation, he thought of searching the nearby convents. He was sure that was where she would go if she couldn't find him.

As he left the docks, he confronted one last seaman and questioned him.

"Yes," the man said. "I spoke to the young women this morning, sir. She said she was looking for the royal fleet. Of course, I told her it was docked in London."

"Did she say she was going to London?"

"She did not, sir," replied the seamen.

Albert thanked him and was on his way.

The pilgrim cart rolled along the road toward Canterbury. As it traveled farther away from Dover, there were noticeably more commoners taking up arms and on the road. Farther on, they were forced off the road by a fleeing justice, and his commissioners followed by a band of wild-eyed rustics who were hurling stones at anything that moved. The pilgrims stopped and hid behind the wagon until they all passed by and it was safe to continue. The friar in charge assured them to fear not, for those that were being pursued were the collectors of taxes and had little concern for religious pilgrims. However, as they continued, the road seemed dense with ruffians.

Up ahead was a roadblock where some commoners were stopping all intruders and searching them. When the pilgrims approached the roadblock, they were ordered out of the wagon. They were roughly handled as the men searched and questioned them.

"This is a pilgrimage," said the friar indignantly. "We are on our way to the church of St. Thomas à Becket."

Within seconds, a large, burly man bounded up to

the friar, and with one blow the friar fell to his knees. "Shut your mouth!" the man yelled.

The friar reached into his robe for his rosary. He held it up to the man evidence of his mission as the blood spilled from his nose. The man ripped them from his hand and wrapped them around the friar's neck. He began to tighten them as he grinned into the friar's bloody face. The friar began to feel faint from the loss of air and blood, and just before he succumbed to the abuse, the man let him go, shoving him roughly to the ground. The clergyman gulped and gasped for air as he lay there.

As the others were being interrogated and relieved of their belongings by the rustics, Elizabeth stood and watched in horror. No one seemed to notice her at first, but suddenly someone grabbed her from behind. A man swung her around to face him and gripped her wrists tightly. She found herself staring into the man's dark eyes. He was just a few inches taller than her and was strongly built. He sported a trimmed beard, and his hair was dark and curly. Some might have thought him handsome, but his eyes were cold, and his lips curled up in a cruel smile.

"Unhand me, you brute!" she demanded.

"I'll not let this pretty little piece of fluff go yet, my love," he said, leering at her in a way that struck fear into her heart. "What is your name, love?" he said with mock politeness. The thought of what might come next raced through her mind, and she had to think quickly.

"My name, sir, is Elizabeth Tyler," she said indignantly, pulling her wrists from his grip. "I am the sister of Wat Tyler, and it is he I am traveling to meet! If you release us now, without further harm, I will not report this incident to him. Do I make myself clear, sir?"

The man stood for a moment, staring at her and trying to process what she had just told him. "Oh yes, miss," he said, suddenly humbled. "Let them go!" he called to the others, "They are to meet Tyler in Canterbury," he explained.

All the pilgrims were immediately unhanded and helped back onto the wagon with their belongings retuned to them—all, that is, except Elizabeth.

The cart began to pull away, everyone looking at Elizabeth in shock as they passed. A thousand dreads went through her mind as she wondered why she had not been released with the others.

"Please come with me, miss," said the leader of the group politely.

Elizabeth looked around suspiciously and followed him. He took her back up the road through various groups of people who were walking in the opposite direction. Some were carrying clubs, pitchforks, axes, or any other kinds of object that could be used as weapons. She still had no idea where he was leading her and could only hope that she was being taken to her brother.

As they made their way, she could see a group of men in the middle of the road a short distance away. She could not quite make out what they were doing, but as she got closer, she could see that they were tossing some sort of object to one another and laughing outrageously. It wasn't until they had started past the group that she realized the object they were playing with was in fact someone's head. The realization made her feel faint and her knees grow weak. She turned from the gruesome scene, holding one hand over her mouth and the other on her stomach, willing herself not to vomit.

"I'm sorry, miss," the rustic leader said. "But there was good reason for killing him, you see. He was one of the king's sergeants at arms. Those men asked him to swear allegiance to our cause—he refused. So, there was no other alternative," he explained, shrugging helplessly.

Elizabeth closed her eyes and stood unsteadily as she whispered a short prayer for both the sergeant and the rustics who had killed him.

Finally, they reached a manor that was being ransacked and torched. She followed the leader to a man who was busy with his destructive handiwork. He spun around quickly when he sensed their approach and was immediately captivated by Elizabeth's loveliness.

"Hello, love," he said mockingly.

Her escort frowned and cleared his throat indignantly. "This is Elizabeth Tyler," he said. "She is in search of her brother, Wat Tyler."

The man held out his hand to her. "The name's John, miss," he said respectfully. "You must forgive my clumsiness and let me make my apologies for being crass," he continued, bowing his head. "I must say, he is quite a distance away from here, in Rochester. However, I will have a guide lead you to him."

"Thank you, sir," Elizabeth responded politely.

John led her to where a man was tying up the horses. "This is James; he will be your guide, miss." John watched as the two mounted. "God's speed, Elizabeth, and give Wat my regards."

"Will do," she said. "And thank you again, sir."

They arrived very late to Rochester Castle where the air was thick with the smoke from the burning buildings. Riding toward the castle, they had to dodge the scattered debris and a few bodies with people kneeling beside them on the road. As they moved closer to the castle, the crowd of commoners began to thicken. Elizabeth had never seen so many people on the road at the same time before.

They pushed the tide of human misery aside as they forged ahead. As they did, Elizabeth began to realize that these were people who had risen from the depths of squalor and degradation and now tasted the power to pass judgment on their oppressors, a power that might very well drive the monarchy to the brink of disaster if its demands were not met. Looking at the chaos around her, she knew that everything that Wat had predicted was about to come to pass. The thought was frightening.

At the castle Wat and his many followers were celebrating their conquest. They had freed the prisoner who had been jailed earlier in the week for his lapse in payment of his taxes. The former occupants, a constable and a small garrison, were overtaken and made to swear an oath of allegiance to the peasant cause and were set free with only the clothes they wore and nothing more. Elizabeth and her escort entered the castle grounds where Wat was congratulating some of his men for a job well done.

Sitting atop a horse, he could see his sister's approach.

He immediately stopped speaking and called her name. She heard his voice but could not see him through the crowd. Suddenly, the mass of people began to part as if they were the Red Sea parting for Moses, and she was able to see her brother walking toward her. She ran to him, throwing her arms around his neck. He held her for a long moment, looked at her, and kissed both her cheeks. The crowd formed a circle around them and cheered.

"What is happening here?" she asked. "I fear much for you, dear brother."

"There's no reason to fear," he said, hugging her. "'Tis justice! Why did you not stay at the priory as I asked you to?" he asked with a look of disapproval.

"I . . . I . . ." she stammered.

"You could have been waylaid on the road," he said.

"I didn't intend to come here. I was headed for London to find Albert. He was with the royal fleet, which had first been redirected to Dover and then back to London," she explained.

"Well then, how did you know to find me here?"

"I didn't know. I joined a pilgrimage that was going to Canterbury from Dover, and we were seized by a band of rustics on route. They let the pilgrims go, but I was detained."

"A wasted journey on such dangerous roads," he said, shaking his head.

She looked down at the ground sadly and then brightened as she looked back at her brother.

"Not all wasted," she said cheerfully. "I was given the opportunity to see my dear brother."

He smiled down at her and hugged her again.

They shared the evening meal and retired for the night. Elizabeth rose before dawn and prepared to leave for London with her escort, John. "When will I see you again?" she asked Wat.

"I will see you in London," he assured her.

She gave him one last hug. "I shall pray for you, dear brother."

"God's speed, and give my regards to your shining knight," he said.

She smiled and nodded. "Be safe, my brother," she said as she rode away.

As the large contingent prepared their advance on Maidstone, Wat, who was leader of a small faction, was now chosen supreme leader of the revolt. The election gave him cause to address the large multitude that was swelling in numbers by the day. Wat bellowed out his message as the crowd grew deathly quiet.

"This is not to be the average uprising. It will not take place in just one small area. No, my friends, it shall in fact encompass the whole of England," he shouted. "As this band of commoners march out for the common good to show its opposition to the unfairness of the laws, it shall not do injustice to those who have not practiced it. Let only those who are guilty of such injustices be punished accordingly! This force will not be a band of untamed rabble-rousers, but a trained and organized army of soldiers," he continued.

"Organization is the key to our success. So today we set out on this momentous journey from which some of us will not return. We go with the intent to breathe new life into our church, our country, and most of all, ourselves. From this day forward, in our country, I deem slavery dead forever!"

A loud cheer rose from the crowd at the end of his speech as they began to celebrate for the last time before going forth into the battles that lay ahead of them.

Albert, not knowing Elizabeth's whereabouts, searched the wharf for someone who may have heard of ships that were diverted or were about to dock soon. No one seemed to know anything. As he walked up from the shore, he decided the best places to check would one of the nearby convents.

Of course she would go there if she needed shelter. He mounted his horse and rode to the convent of St. Mary de Castio, which sat high on a hill above the town. There, in the confines of the tranquil retreat, he finally got the information he was looking for.

"Yes, a young woman by the name of Elizabeth stayed last evening, but she left early this morning with a group of pilgrims who were headed for Canterbury."

They also told him of the uprising in the Maidstone area. He thanked them for their kindness and left for Canterbury. Usually, the road would be choked with pilgrims, but today Albert found it surprisingly vacant with the exception of a few merchants and pilgrims traveling in the opposite direction.

He rode into Canterbury, finding an unusual number of commoners carrying various weapons and milling about as if they were waiting for something to happen. He continued up to the cathedral where a few pilgrims were praying. In his effort to show respect, he waited outside St. Thomas' Shrine until their prayers ended, and they were led out of the chapel by their friar. As they exited, Albert questioned one here and there.

No one he questioned had any information for him, but one asked to employ his services as a knight for his journey home, to which Albert had to decline. As he spoke to the pilgrim, the friar of the chapel walked by, catching his eye. He made his excuses to the pilgrim and hurried off into the crowd. He dismounted and led his horse through the crowd that had gathered until he found the friar. He called out, and the friar turned around and saw a young knight walking rapidly toward him. Albert asked about Elizabeth, and the friar told him of the ruffians who had apprehended her.

"I'm sorry, but I know not what became of her. However, she seemed to know some of the men as she mentioned a name, and we were immediately released. If my memory serves me, I believe she said a man by the name of Wat Tyler was her brother."

Albert thanked him, quickly mounted his horse, and made his way through the crowd. He knew that he would need to go to Maidstone where the uprising had started. That's where he would find Wat, and hopefully Elizabeth would be with him. It was now late afternoon, but he still had a few good hours of sunlight left.

As he rode, there were a few areas in which great movements of peasants, farmers, and other commoners became hostile and threw stones and other missiles at him as he passed through at a gallop. In other areas, the road was completely empty of any traffic at all. He reached the village of Bredgar as night was falling. As he entered, he could hear the loud voices of people lighting torches, and he could sense trouble in the air. He wondered if he should just slip away into the night or take a chance and hope that by mentioning Wat's name he would be safe for the night.

He decided his only chance of finding Elizabeth would be his second choice.

He knew she would be among the commoners, and more than likely she would still be with Wat. He rode into the village and toward some rustics, who quickly surrounded him and began to question his presence there.

"Are you a sergeant of arms?" one of them asked. "Why are you here?"

"I'm looking for Wat Tyler," said Albert. "I must get word to his sister and him. You see, I am her intended," he said. "We were planning to meet in London, but the royal fleet was diverted because of a storm."

The group of ruffians looked around at one another, not sure whether to believe him or not, but the man who seemed to be in charge nodded to the rest.

"What is Wat's sister's name then?" he asked.

"Elizabeth," replied Albert.

"Let him pass, I believe he's telling the truth. Wat is at Maidstone at this moment," he told Albert. "He should be there for some days. I would advise you to leave here in the morning in order to catch him before he moves on."

"Thank you all," Albert said to the group, "for your understanding and information. Good-night to you, gentlemen," he said, bowing his head.

Although darkness was starting to descend, he

decided to press on as far as he could now that he knew where to find Wat.

Upon leaving the town, a light drizzle began to fall and soon became heavy enough to stall his journey. The only thing to do would be to find shelter. So he headed for a nearby forest where he made camp under a very large oak, but it was not long before he became soaked. Despite the discomfort of his wet, woolen uniform, he laid himself down against the thick trunk of the tree and fell fast asleep.

The morning brought dryer, calmer weather, and he awoke before the sun rose. Stretching and breathing in the morning air, he began to saddle his horse. Soon he mounted the steed and rode off toward Maidstone.

A few hours later, he arrived at his destination. As he rode through, he glanced around the village and noticed some damage, but the rustics were preoccupied with the archbishop's jail. They had encircled it but had not yet attempted to storm it. As Albert slowed his horse to a stop, he was surrounded by a band of peasants.

"I'm looking for Wat Tyler. I got word that he was here," he said to the group.

"He is at Rochester Castle," one man called out as the rest began closing in on him to get a better look. He began to feel a bit uncomfortable with the nearness of these men.

"What business do you have with him?" another asked rudely. Suddenly a hand shot out grabbing his leg and pulling him off his horse as others began to flaunt their weapons threateningly.

A staff, which one ruffian was waving about, hit

Albert's horse in the leg, causing him to rear up. The crowd let out a collective yell as some tried to calm the horse. Albert immediately grabbed the horse's reins and pulled him down giving one man the opportunity to mount. Albert, still holding the reigns, prompted his horse to run, trampling those who were not quick enough to remove themselves from the horse's path. As the animal took off, he maintained his grip and pulled himself up onto the back alongside the ruffian.

The two rode at a full gallop as they struggled to push one another off the horse. Albert gave one hardy shove, and the peasant lost his seating but stubbornly hung on to the saddle for dear life. Finally, Albert drew his sword and gave one blow to the man's head, and he quickly tumbled off onto the roadside. Albert galloped away toward Rochester without looking back.

Chapter Twenty

As Albert neared Rochester Castle, he slowed his pace and could hear sounds of a large group of people yelling in the distance. Soon, the sound of marching became clear, and as he reached a clearing, he could see the advance column of a large peasant force moving toward him. He stopped and looked with astonishment, his heart racing. It was a well-organized army, convincing Albert that it must be Wat who was in charge.

As he came within a few paces of them, a small group broke ranks and surrounded him while the others remained in formation.

"Where are you bound, Sir Knight?" asked one shabby rustic who was holding a large ax at the ready in case the answer was not to his liking.

"I'm looking for Wat Tyler," Albert replied.

"Come down off your horse, and address me face-to-face," the man demanded. Two men grabbed Albert's arms and immediately tied his hands behind his back.

They removed his armor and tied a noose around his neck. The group began jeering and hurling insults at him.

"Are you one of the constable's men?" one shouted as he jabbed Albert's side with his staff.

Albert swung around and gave the man a searing look. "I'm a friend of Wat Tyler's," was all he would say.

"He lies!" one man screamed. "Hang him! Hang him!" they all taunted as the group erupted into chaos.

Pushing and shoving him and each other, they led him to a large, oak tree that stood at the edge of the forest. Albert tried to attack those who were closest to him and make a break for it, but a hard blow by someone's club quelled his efforts. He dropped to his knees in a daze. Two men pulled him to his feet and dragged him to the tree. One man, who had been holding the end of the rope, climbed to the nearest strong limb, threw the rope over to another on the ground, and pulled the rope taught, causing the noose to tighten around Albert's neck. He tried to speak to tell them that they were making a mistake, but the words stuck in his throat as he coughed and gasped for air.

Barely conscious, he could hear the remainder of the peasant army passing and taking little notice of what was happening. They were all too familiar and even a little bored with the hanging of knights as it had become an everyday occurrence of late.

The crowd cheered as Albert was hoisted off the ground. He kicked his feet wildly as the rope tightened. He tried with all his might to wriggle free. But soon his legs slowed, his struggle waned and, within minutes, he hung limp as his face and hands turned from a reddish-blue color to deathly gray. Suddenly, the limb gave way under the weight and crashed to the ground with Albert still tied to it.

A few rushed over to him and checked for signs of life—there were none. As he lay on the ground, lifeless, a few of the ruffians argued over his belongings. Finally a fight broke out among them, drawing the attention of the leader of the army.

Wat turned and looked back to see what the commotion was. He saw the body crash to the ground and the fools fighting. He raced back to see what it was all about.

"What in hell is going on here?" he demanded, standing between the two that had come to blows over Albert's gold spurs. "Our march is being delayed, and you bastards are fighting over trinkets?" he yelled. He looked around at the troublemakers and ordered them back to the ranks. He stood staring at the rest of the group, the ones he knew he could get through to.

"Gentlemen," he said in a calmer voice, "let us not forget our mission. Our goal is to rescue John Ball, and you are wasting our time with the hanging of some poor bastard just for his gold spurs! We must not forget—" he continued as he turned to look down at the face of the hanged man. "My God!" he screamed, as he rushed to Albert's side.

Wat removed the rope from his neck and tried to find signs of life. He placed his head on Albert's chest and found it still and silent. He looked at his childhood friend as the tears welled up in his eyes. Everyone stood motionless as they watched their fearless and brave leader weep like a child. "How could this happen?" he sobbed. "How will I tell Elizabeth?"

He looked up at his men. "Go and see if there is anyone with medical knowledge, and bring him to me," he said. Two of the men ran toward the now halted army and searched the ranks. They returned with three other men; one of whom was a former priest.

"He has expired, sir," he said upon examining the body, "I'm very sorry."

Wat hung his head as the tears rolled onto the ground. He whispered a silent prayer for his most, dear friend and looked up at the group.

"I want all those who were responsible for this to be sent to me immediately," he demanded, regaining his composure.

The large peasant force that stretched through the forest was brought back to the field where it would camp for the night. The guilty parties involved in the hanging were beaten and hanged at Wat's command.

During that evening, Wat and some of his trusted confidants planned for Albert's burial. Later, he lay down on the bare ground to rest. Totally disheartened, he spent the sleepless night thinking of his sorrow and loss. His moods changed constantly from despair, questioning his own leadership abilities to outright anger at those who had done the deed, cursing their retched souls.

He felt the fire for the rebellion was flickering, and he wasn't sure he could go on. He found himself digging deep into his soul for the fortitude he had once possessed, and by the time the sun came up, he had resolved the matter. He decided that to give in now would make a mockery of Albert's death, and that thought gave him strength. He knew what he had to do. He rose, exhausted from the night's turmoil, and gathered with his force for the burial.

As he stood before the crowd, he began the eulogy of his boyhood friend. He spoke of courage and valor with his voice breaking now and then. Finally, the grave was ready, and the priest had given his benediction. Wat stood by the open grave as they lowered Albert into the ground. He grabbed a clump of dirt and was the first to drop it in. It landed on Albert's chest, causing the body to twitch. Wat's eyes widened as the next man dropped another clump onto the body. A groan rose up from the open grave. Wat immediately called a halt to the procedure and knelt down at the edge.

The others around him began to back away in fear and bewilderment, and some ran when Albert began to cough and gag. Wat stood in amazement, realizing at that moment that Albert was indeed alive and in need of help. He jumped down into the shallow grave and lifted his friend's head. He yelled for someone to help him lift Albert from the grave. A few, brave souls cautiously looked over the edge of the hole. "Get your cowardly arses moving and help me lift him out," Wat screamed, sending the men scurrying for a rope. He tied it around Albert's waist and sent him up.

Kneeling beside Albert, Wat gently wiped his face.

Albert opened his eyes and looked up at Wat.

"Praise God," said Wat, smiling. "We thought you were called to the angels, my friend!"

Albert smiled back. "You're not having done with me that easily," he replied.

"Elizabeth will be glad of that!" Wat chuckled.

Word spread through the troops that a miracle had occurred, and Wat was convinced this was true. If there was ever any doubt about their mission, it was now put to rest. Everyone knew that their cause was just and that God had given them a sign from heaven. Wat remained with Albert as he recovered all that day and night, and by the next morning, they were ready to continue their march.

On June 10, the peasant army marched into Canterbury on a path of destruction. They seized and ransacked the homes of lawyers, government officials, and the biggest prize of all, the residence of the archbishop, who fortunately for him, was not present at the time.

They remained in Canterbury for a day and a half before Wat decided that the time was right to invade Maidstone. By this time, Albert had recovered his full strength, and Wat had his armor and other belongings returned to him. He thanked Wat once more for saving his life and inquired about Elizabeth. "I sent her on to London because I'd heard that the king's fleet would be docking there," he explained.

"Yes, of course," Albert replied.

"How did you get here then?" Wat asked.

"Well," said Albert. "You see I've deserted my company. I know I will be pursued if I go to London, but I must find her and take her someplace that is safe."

"Go to the convent of St. Mary's. You will find her there," said Wat. He paused and looked into Albert's eyes. "There is another concern, friend," he said slowly.

"What's that?" asked Albert

"I've heard that there are riots breaking out all over the south, and my concern is with your parents. One report I received was that they were killing merchants in Colchester, and there were a few who were Florentine. I'm fairly sure that they may have attacked Sudbury as well. I fear you mother and father may be in danger."

Albert looked stunned.

"I'm sorry I have to give you such news, but 'tis better if you know."

"Yes, of course, but what shall I do?"

"Before you go to London, you should immediately go to Sudbury," said Wat, "and see to it that your parents board a ship to mainland Europe. They can return when we have finished our mission, and things have calmed down here."

Albert looked at Wat, and they embraced.

"Now, I must go and get a night's sleep, for tomorrow, we march on Maidstone!"

In the morning, Albert awoke early and readied his horse for the journey. He and Wat stood in the field under an overcast sky and clasped hands.

"Take care of my sister, and give tidings to your parents, Sir Albert," said Wat, smiling.

"Yes, and we'll pray for your success, sir," Albert replied as he mounted his steed. "God go with you, my friend," he said.

"And with you, Albert," Wat replied.

Albert left with the feeling of deep concern but confident that he was doing the right thing.

Wat led his army toward Maidstone not absolutely

sure if he would ever see his boyhood friend or his sister again, but he was sure his mission was just, and that gave him courage to go on. His peasant army cut a path of destruction and fear among the nobility; some of whom were put to the sword if Wat saw it was fitting. After the guards were subdued in the dungeon of Maidstone, the peasants released the fiery, religious zealot John Ball. The crowd opened a path to let him pass as they cheered him on.

When the crowd had settled down, he began to speak. He declared that he would join in the rebellion as their spiritual leader and fight alongside them. After leaving Maidstone, they set their sights on London. A network of couriers was in place around England informing all the groups of each other's intended plans. Since Wat's group was the largest, the news of his march would be sent to the other groups in hopes that they would join him there, and on eleventh of June, he began his march on London.

Albert's ride toward London was without major incidents; however, there were a few groups of rebels on the road who were headed for their respective forces. Upon their encounters with him, they would yell hoots and insults at him, but they didn't bother to intercept as they had a more urgent calling at hand. As he neared the city, more and more of the population was on the move. At first, there were a few carts hastily carrying people and goods out of the city. He continued on toward the center as a thickening crowd of refugees made their way out on every mode of transportation imaginable—pulling, dragging, or carrying many of their belongings as fast as they could go.

With this confusion at its peak, he headed toward St. Mary's where the prioress was leading a massive effort to reinforce the priory against a possible attack. Albert rode into the churchyard and proceeded toward the prioress who was in the midst of directing operations.

She led him into her study, and he explained who he was and why he was there.

Her face lit up when he told her his name. "Oh my, so you're Sir Albert!" she said, holding her hand out to him. "I've heard much about you, my good man. Elizabeth spoke of you so many times." She paused in their conversation and looked down thoughtfully.

"Is there something wrong?" Albert asked.

"Oh no, not wrong," she answered. "But I am sorry to tell you that Elizabeth is not here."

"Did she say where she was going?" he asked.

"Again, sir, I'm sorry. I cannot say."

"I see," he said. "I thank you, Sister."

He left quickly with a feeling of urgency. The answers he had gotten from the prioress made him worry.

He hadn't gotten far down the road when he spotted Henry and Gilles riding toward him at full gallop. Henry reached him first and stopped suddenly, kicking up the dust around them. Henry called to him and moved his horse close enough for them to clasp arms. Gilles was a short distance away.

"Well, if it isn't our very own deserting coward," he called, staying at a safe distance.

Albert, immediately drawing his sword, rode toward him.

"Was there something you wanted to say, sir?" he

asked sarcastically. "I couldn't hear you from so long a distance."

Gilles who had drawn his sword when he saw Albert approaching swung it in a frenzied panic as Albert got nearer to him.

As the two swords clashed, Henry looked on without a word. The power of Albert's sword unhorsed his rival, and Gilles sat on the ground with the wind knocked out of him. Albert immediately dismounted and quickly walked toward him, raising his sword, but before he could dispatch the rogue, Gilles put his arms up over his head and begged for mercy.

Henry called out for Albert to stop at the same time.

Albert stood over Gilles for a moment and then lowered his sword to his side. "The Lord was with you today, friend, but don't count on him saving you the next time," Albert said angrily. He walked toward Henry, giving him a look of disgust.

"Cool your head, Albert," he said. "You know very well he's not worth the effort of killing him."

"It would be no effort at all," Albert mumbled.

"Forget about him," said Henry. "I have news of Elizabeth!"

Albert's head shot up. "What news?" he asked.

Henry told him that she came to him asking about the royal fleet and its whereabouts. "I told her that you had boarded a vessel to Dover in your search for her."

"Where is she now?" Albert interrupted.

"I was getting to that," Henry replied. "The last I knew of her, she was riding out of the city with a band of rebels, presumably back to her brother."

This sudden turn of events put Albert in a compromising position. He was very anxious to pursue Elizabeth but more worried about his parents.

"I believe Elizabeth will be reasonably safe with her brother," said Henry, reading Albert's thoughts.

"I must go, Henry," Albert said as turned his horse toward Sudbury. "And thank you for helping."

"God go with you, Albert," he replied.

Albert rode his horse past Gilles who had recovered and was walking his horse back toward Henry. He watched resentfully as Albert rode away at full gallop.

Chapter Twenty-one

Albert rode through Chelmsford, noticing that there was little destruction to the area, giving him hope that they may have bypassed Sudbury as well. However, as he neared his hometown, his hopes were dashed, and he could see signs of trouble. Many of the merchants living in the area were being molested by a growing crowd of peasants. He reached Sudbury in the late morning and quickly made his way toward his parents' home. As he approached, his heart beat furiously in fear of what he might find. A large lump formed in his throat as he tried to hold back the tears.

From a short distance down the road, he could see that the house was nothing but charred ruins. He paused in the road for a moment, bracing himself for the worst. He arrived at what was once the front garden and walked up to the burned-out doorway. He began searching through the rubble and carefully turning over large pieces of debris. He prayed he would not find his parents there and hoped upon hope that they had escaped the terror. Finding not a sign of them, he went to the barn, which had received much fire damage but was still standing. Inside, he found that the animals had succumbed to the smoke and heat.

He looked around sadly and sifted through the burnt hay and ashes, but he still didn't find them. Again he was relieved, but he wondered where they could have gone. He walked out of the barn's back door and through the back garden. As he approached the well, he had a horrible image in his head of his dear mother screaming as they threw his father down the well. His thoughts were interrupted by the sounds of moaning from the other side of the well.

He quickly stepped up and looked around the well wall. His mother sat on the ground with her back leaning against the side of the well with John's head in her lap; she was wiping his face with her apron. Albert could see the large bloodstain and rip in his tunic at the shoulder.

Sara looked up and cried out with a start as Albert approached. "Albert!" she said with great relief. "Help me! He's unconscious, and I fear he will die!"

Albert immediately drew water from the well, held the cup to his father's lips, and then gave the cup to his mother. She took a drink and handed it back to him. Albert lifted his father's eyelids as John let out a groan.

"He coming to," Albert said as he lifted his father off his mother's lap.

He laid him on a knoll of soft grass and helped his mother to her feet. She hugged her son as if she would never let him go and cried. Her face was battered, and her arms were spotted with bruises. "We must tend to his wound before infection sets in," she said.

Albert kneeled down beside his father to get a closer look. His mother was right beside him.

"It doesn't look deep, but I fear he's lost a lot of blood," she said. "Go and get some more water from the well."

Albert moved obediently. He walked into the area where the house once stood and rummaged through the kitchen area to find a cooking pot. He filled it with well water and gave it to his mother. She tore off the hem of her apron, soaked it in water, and washed John's wound. He winced, and his eyes were instantly open. Sara told Albert of the devastation and how bravely his father had tried to defend their home.

"He was as brave as a lion," she boasted.

"Yes, Mother, but why did you not leave?" he asked.

"What?" she said incredulously. "And let them take what is rightfully ours without a fight! Never!"

"But what good was it?" he reasoned. "They took everything of value anyway."

She looked around tearfully. "They didn't take our pride, and we are still alive," she said with determination.

Albert smiled and hugged her. "Yes, that's true," he said. "But it is no longer safe here. You both must go to Calais until things calm down. I will get the cart from the barn and hook my horse up. We can head out for Colchester immediately. I'm sure we can get passage to Calais from there."

Soon, they were riding out of Sudbury in haste and were making their way toward the coast. The roads to Colchester were clear of traffic as most of the population had fled into the safety of the woods or hills, and the rebels made their way toward London. The cart was slow, and it took the remainder of the day before they arrived in Colchester. It was late, and there were no vessels leaving that night. They would have to wait till morning.

That night, they found a ship that was scheduled to sail the next morning. Albert had the funds for the voyage to and from Calais but was lacking enough to pay for the ship's doctor to tend his father's wound. He decided to sell the cart, horse, and even his armor to the first person who would buy and pay the doctor his fee.

By the morning, the weather was more than favorable for sailing, and the time it took to get there was virtually cut in half. They arrived in Calais before darkness set in. The cog docked, and all remained on board for the night. It was just as well because John had remained weak and semiconscious throughout the trip, and staying on board and resting would help him to recover a little more.

With the new day arriving, the wharf bustled with crews loading their cargo onto ships bound for countless countries, except England. Fear of the rebellion that had started a day earlier was stifling commerce. All the passengers were awakened by the crewmen. The passengers would have to disembark before they could unload what little cargo they had brought from England.

Sara had been awake a long while before everyone else. She fretted much over John's condition. He should have been recovering more quickly, and he was not showing signs of his usual alertness. It alarmed her that he was still asleep when everyone around them was preparing to disembark. They brought him to the ship's doctor below deck and asked to leave him until they could secure a place to stay and borrow a cart. Sara remained by her husband's side as Albert left the ship and headed for the home of William Paxton, one of the homes that John had stayed in while on business in Calais.

William was a very good friend and welcomed Albert with open arms. Albert explained what had happened to his father, and William loaned him his wagon and horse to go and fetch him. After his parents were settled in, he informed them that he would have to return to London. Sara put her hands over her face and began to weep. It was too much for her to take.

"How can you leave with your father so ill? We need you, son, and I'm afraid to have you go back . . . I . . . I . . . " She hesitated. "I'm afraid!" she sobbed.

"Why must you go back?" asked William's wife. "Look at your poor mother!"

He tried to explain to them that he had deserted in order to come back and make sure his parents were taken care of. He didn't mention that he could be executed for desertion if they caught him and that he was going back to find Elizabeth.

Finally, he had to leave. His mother had calmed down, and his father was resting comfortably under her care. Kissing them good-bye and thanking their hosts, he and William left for the wharf. When they arrived, he bade William farewell and asked him to watch over his parents until his return. William promised he would and loaned Albert money for passage. Albert expressed his gratitude, embraced William, and jumped down from the wagon. William waved as Albert bounded up the gangplank.

"God's speed, Albert!" he said.

Albert turned and waved back.

Wat had already begun his march, leading his peasant army on London while all across the country uprisings were occurring in Norfolk, Suffolk, Cambridge, Beverly, and Bridgewater to name only a few. There was nothing sacred left. Even churches were being destroyed, ransacked, and looted as the half-crazed peasants purged the surrounding towns and villages. Most people had fled the terror, but there were some who stood strong and refused to be driven out.

In Bury St. Edmunds, the prior of the abbey refused to denounce feudalism. He was promptly taken out and beheaded, as were so many others who were loyal to the nobility and the church.

By June 13, Wat's southern peasant army reached Southwark. Resistance was sporadic at best, but Wat thought it better if Elizabeth returned to the convent until the danger subsided. In spite of her protests, she was escorted by one of his trusted scouts to the nearest intact convent. He promised that Albert would join her there as soon as possible.

They reached London to find that the mayor had closed all the gates to the city. His efforts were in vain as the peasants living inside were taking over, and they opened them, allowing an onslaught of destruction and murder the likes of which was never seen before. Wat led them through, but he no longer had control of the mob.

The first to be plundered was the palace of John Gaunt. After they had completely sacked the place, they put it to the torch and cheered as the entire interior burned out, leaving nothing to salvage. They went from there to the temple, which was the bastion of the lawyers, set afire all records of servitude, and burned the building to the ground.

While this was taking place, Wat took the opportunity to contact King Richard through messengers, but his request for a conference was rejected. He ordered his army to the jails of Newgate and Fleet where they freed the unruly rabble to join the peasant ranks. Together they sacked and torched the prisons.

The peasant army took out all their frustrations and anger on London, and its fate rested in the hands of their leader. There were nobles and knights who had tried to protect the city, but their numbers were too small to be effective, and they were easily overwhelmed.

The king controlled little more than the castle and the tower. In his presence was a small force led by the mayor, Lord Wadsworth, along with two of his chief ministers, Robert Hales and Simon Sudbury, Archbishop of Canterbury, and a few of the lesser-ranked ministers.

Wat was persistent in his request for an audience

with the king, and finally he was accommodated. A council was called by the king, realizing the gravity of the situation, and he agreed to a meeting with the peasant leader. The messenger was sent to inform him of the king's decision to confer. Wat's face broke out into a wide grin when he got the news, and on the 14 of June, the meeting took place at Mile End.

Here, with all his ministers, King Richard listened patiently to the demands put forth by the peasant chief, Wat Tyler, as scores of clerks recorded: All serfdom would be abolished, all feudal dues and serves were to end, and a general amnesty was given for all those who took part in the rebellion with the handing over of the royal councilors to the peasants immediately following the meeting.

All the demands the king was willing to abide by except for the handing over of councilors, which would include Robert Hales and Archbishop Simon Sudbury.

Wat abruptly terminated the meeting. "All the demands must be met, or the terms we have reached thus far are invalid!" he said, impatiently. He left the meeting in a huff, turning his back on the king, which was an act of defiance and disrespect. All those present buzzed about how rude and indelicate the loathsome peasant leader's manners were.

"The habits of low breeding!" one minister proclaimed.

Wat and his men returned to London where he ordered his army to seize the king's chapel. When they arrived at the front gate, they were met by Robert Hales, who they swiftly dragged into the courtyard and beheaded. With Wat in the lead, they stormed the chapel where the archbishop was leading the mass.

Bursting through the door, Wat swiftly bounded up to the altar. The archbishop shook with fear as beads of sweat formed on his forehead.

"Do you remember me, Simon?" Wat asked with an evil smile.

The archbishop shook his head mutely in denial. He most certainly did remember Wat and his lovely sister but was too frightened to speak.

"Let me remind you then," Wat said in a low voice. "It was in the town of Sudbury some years ago," he continued. "When you tried to seduce Elizabeth, and she made a fool of you! Does that sound familiar, Your Eminence?" he sneered.

Simon stood speechless as the sweat from his brow tricked down the side of his face. He continued to shake his head in the negative. "Have mercy, please!" he cried.

Wat looked him in the eyes but was not dissuaded from his wrath. "And perhaps you remember one of heaven's good souls who tried and failed to expose you for what you really are," he said as Simon began to shake uncontrollably. "At the time, you seemed to get much pleasure from watching him burn at the stake."

"I . . . I don't . . . " Simon stammered.

"His name was Brother William!" shouted Wat. "Do you remember now?" he screamed.

Simon felt faint, and his knees buckled under him. He dropped to the floor like a sack of rags.

Wat and two of his men grabbed him by the arms and hoisted him to his feet. His large miter had fallen from his head. Wat called for one of his comrades to retrieve it. As the peasant handed it to him, Wat asked him to find spikes and a mallet. They dragged the frantically blubbering archbishop out to the courtyard and forced him to his knees. Simon looked around and saw the body of Hales lying nearby without its head.

By this time, the peasant had returned with a spikes and a mallet.

"Your Eminence," said Wat with mock politeness. "I have the perfect solution to the problem you have of keeping your miter from falling from your holy head." He roughly replaced the miter on the archbishop's head. Simon began to scream like a woman as Wat pushed his head down on the wooden bench standing beside him. With his men holding Simon down, Wat proceed to drive the spike through the miter and into the archbishop's forehead.

With one mighty blow, the blood spewed everywhere, forcing many of the onlookers to step back.

They turned the archbishop's limp body face down and sent a second spike through the back of Simon's head. Wat then picked up his battle-ax and brought it down on the back of his neck, severing his head from his body. They placed the heads of both Simon and Robert onto wooden pikes that had been fashioned from tree limbs and held them high above the cheering mob. They then headed for London Bridge where the bodies were hacked up and thrown into the Thames while their heads watched with dead eyes from high atop the bridge.

With all the excitement, the crowd was in a murderous mood and no longer satisfied with the mere destruction of property. Their next target was the foreigners of London, particularly the Flemmings, who were highly resented because of the stiff competition they presented to English tradesmen. The attack on these people was swift and overwhelming, giving them no time to mount a defense.

The peasant army swooped down on their shops, and without hesitation dispatched all to the last one. From there, they went on to seek out all the lawyers, hacking off their heads as they tried to run. No one was exempt from the massacre. Bankers, moneylenders, priests, tax collectors, and even some of their own were put to the sword.

The streets of London ran with blood as scores of dismembered corpses lay rotting in roadways, alleys, homes, and public buildings. Hearing of the atrocities and learning that two of his closest ministers had been murdered, King Richard sent word to Wat requesting another meeting. Wat laughed out loud when he got the message.

"Now, it's his turn to beg!" he said to the herald. "Well, sir, you can tell him I accept."

The king was apprehensive about facing Wat and his large contingent. Not knowing whether he would return alive, he went to visit his mother for what he feared would be the last time, and before leaving, he went to the chapel to receive absolution and his last sacraments.

Chapter Twenty-two

On the fifteenth of June, King Richard met with Wat in Smithfield, which was located outside of the town of Aldersgate. King Richard arrived with a retinue of two hundred men. Wat met him with only an associate, but his peasant army was not far away in the event of treachery. This time, Wat had made many new demands, one of which concerned church property and was quite extensive.

He proposed that large amounts of property be liquidated, and the proceeds be divided amongst the poor. This proposal outraged the king and his men, and an argument ensued. A member of the royal party yelled that Wat Tyler and his army were no more than a pack of thieves.

Infuriated, Wat commanded his aide to promptly dispatch the loudmouthed noble, but Mayor Wadsworth quickly blocked the aide's dagger. Wat immediately drew his own dagger and thrust at the mayor, striking a blow that was blocked by his armor. Wadsworth then drew a small cutlass, wounding Wat and causing a melee to break out. Another royal drew his sword and swiftly ran Wat through not once but twice, severely wounding the peasant leader. He then, just as quickly, dispatched the aide.

After the melee, Wat, critically wounded, rode back to his army, claiming treason. Within moments of his arrival, he fell from his horse. His comrades ran to his rescue, and one friend held his head in his hand.

"Tell Elizabeth I love her and Albert to stand strong and take care of her," he gasped. His comrade lowered Wat's head from his hand and stood.

"He's dead!" he called to the crowd.

There was a long moment of shocked silence.

"We've been betrayed by the king!" he yelled, causing outcries of injustice from the crowd. Some rose whatever weapons they had and began to organize themselves for an attack on the king's men as others remained silently stunned at the unexpected turn of events.

Sensing the peasant army had been demoralized, King Richard rode out to meet them. Everyone watched his approach with shocked silence as he came to them without his protective entourage. He stood alone and to their surprise was a mere boy. Some stood ready to defend themselves if need be, but others stared in awe.

With each step he took, Richard gained more and more confidence. He finally stopped in the midst of the hostile crowd. "Are you ready to kill your king?" he asked. "If not, then follow him, and fear not, for all that you have asked for will be granted!" A loud cheer went up, and the peasant force fell into line behind the king.

At this time, the mayor of London rode off into the city to gather all its aldermen and men at arms, which would include Albert's fellow knights of the Lord Stafford manor.

Now with thousands of men at arms, Wadsworth led them to the field where the king had made his peace with the rebels by an extraordinary show of courage. Wanting to destroy the rag-tag group, Wadsworth readied his men for the attack. Seeing this, the king forbade it and let the rebels disperse peacefully. Angry over the king's betrayal, they swarmed through London wreaking havoc on the already devastated city. There was widespread burning and looting of all private homes and public establishments in the surrounding villages, and in their path of destruction, was the church of St. Avery in Southwick.

Elizabeth had remained in the priory through the violence with the thought that when the rebellion was over her victorious brother and her Albert would come for her. Sadly, she was not aware of Wat's fate and that the church was now open to plunder by the renegades.

As she prayed with the nuns, a loud thud interrupted the silence. They all looked up at the chapel entrance. Again, there was loud banging and voices yelling. Elizabeth stood up straight. She was sure it was Wat's army come to rescue her. All the nuns stood too and looked at her expectantly. "Do not be afraid, Sisters.

'Tis only my brother and his men," she announced, heading for the door.

Once outside, she observed a mob of angry men destroying the garden and statuary with crudely made weapons and setting the barn on fire with their torches. Wat was nowhere to be seen, and her heart leaped in fear. They were about to set the chapel on fire when they noticed her standing at the door.

"Stop!" she cried. "You must not! There are several sisters praying in this chapel. Have you no respect for the sacred?" she screamed. "Where is Wat Tyler?" she demanded.

"Who wants to know?" one man yelled.

"I do, sir. I am his sister, Elizabeth Tyler. Now answer my question," she demanded.

One of rustics recognized her and pushed his way through the crowd to where she was standing. "She speaks the truth!" he said, turning toward the crowd.

Everyone lowered their weapons and began to leave the premises.

"I'm sorry to say, miss, but your brother is no longer with us," the man said softly. "He was murdered by the king's men."

Elizabeth gasped, placing her hand to her mouth as the tears filled her eyes.

"No, you lie!" she cried.

"I'm so sorry, Elizabeth, but 'tis true," he whispered. He put his arms around her in comfort as she covered her face and wept.

"No, no, no! It can't be true!" she sobbed. But she knew it was.

The prioress and the nuns stepped out of chapel

door cautiously and looked around in horror. They immediately tried to save the barn as others rushed to rescue the livestock inside. Elizabeth gained her composure and helped them to put out the fire. She told the prioress what had happened to her brother.

"I am so very sorry, my child," she said, taking her hand. "What will you do?" she asked.

"I must leave." Elizabeth sobbed. "I must go and find him."

"There is nothing out there but heartbreak, child," said the prioress. "Do stay here where it is safe and peaceful."

But Elizabeth felt her life was in ruins, and she knew she must find Wat to make sure he was buried in the Christian faith.

Her thoughts turned to Albert. She had no idea where he was or even if he was still alive. And if he was, did he still love her?

She made up her mind to remain on her own from this day forward. She would earn a living somehow and make her own way in the world. She had many skills in brewing, cooking, and medicine, which she could use to her advantage.

"Alas, I must go, but I am most grateful for all your help and kindness over the years. I shall never forget you, Prioress," she said, hugging her.

Elizabeth walked to the gates, turned, waved, and headed toward the city.

As she neared the city, she could hear the screams and sounds of destruction getting closer. As she reached London Bridge, scores of frantic, frighten people fled past her. She had almost gotten to the opposite side when she stopped.

There, impaled on two pikes were the heads of Jack Straw and beside him was that of Wat Tyler. Tears welled up in her eyes as she approached the grisly scene. She fell to her knees before them, hung her head in sorrow, and lifted her hands in prayer.

"Oh, Jesus, have mercy on their souls," she prayed. As she knelt, many of those pursued by the king's men ran past her, some almost tripping over her in their attempt to flee. She paid little attention to them as they brushed past, but a woman ran right into her, knocking Elizabeth to the ground. The woman soon recovered and continued to run. Elizabeth sat up, holding her head. Suddenly, she felt a hand on her shoulder and jumped to her feet. She turned quickly and found herself looking into deep blue eyes. She recognized him immediately.

"Henry!" she cried a she grasped his arm. "Thank God it's you!"

Squire Henry held out his hand to steady her. "Yes!" he said, pointing to the squire who had accompanied him. "We're here to escort law-abiding citizens safely out of the city. What are you doing here, miss?" he asked.

She began to cry and pointed to the pikes. "Look what they have done to my dear brother and this other poor soul!"

Henry took her in his arms without looking at the horrible display. "Come, Elizabeth, we will see to it that he gets a proper burial." He helped her mount his horse and climbed on behind her. She leaned against his strong, muscular chest and sobbed as he tried to comfort her with reassuring words.

"I must find Albert's body," she cried.

There was a long pause, and she craned her neck to get a look at his face. "What wrong?" she asked.

He looked into her eyes with a flicker of a sad smile.

She frowned at him, and his smile widened a bit.

"Albert is not dead!"

"My God, Henry, where is he then?" she asked excitedly.

He told her that he had seen Albert only days ago. "He was looking for you at the convent, but the prioress told him you had gone with your brother, and he went off to look for you. That's when I had a chance meeting with him. He decided that you would be safe with your brother protecting you, and if the situation became dangerous, he would send you back to the convent. I advised him of the danger in Sudbury. The last I spoke to him, he had planned to go there to rescue his parents and help them get to Calais."

Henry snapped his reins and rode down Thames Street towards St. Paul's Wharf.

"Henry!" called his comrade from behind. "Look down there!" he said, nodding in the other direction.

Henry turned his horse to the rear and saw three men riding at a quick pace toward them. He and the other squire quickly snapped their reins, bringing their horses to a full gallop.

They were close to Paul's Wharf when Henry decided it was too risky to take Elizabeth any farther. He knew the king's men would not look kindly on the sister of a rebel. If there was going to be a fight, he wanted her out of the way, so he dropped her at the wharf.

"Go and hide in the alleyway until I come back for you," he said.

She quickly dismounted and headed for the alley.

As the three horsemen came closer, Henry recognized one of the three knights as Sir Gilles. "Did I see someone riding with you, Henry," he asked, to which Henry denied and his comrade confirmed. Gilles gave a knowing smile and commanded them to follow him. They did so without protest, but Henry worried for Elizabeth. He would have to find a way to get back to her, and he assured himself that he would, no matter what happened.

On thirteenth of June, Albert tried to get passage back to London but to no avail. Merchant vessels were not sailing to England on news of the revolt. Word had reached Calais of the deaths of seamen and severe damage to their ships caused by the violence there. Deeply depressed, he returned to William Paxton's home, where his parents were recovering from their ordeal. He would remain there for two more days when finally he got word that the worst was over, and the king had retained power.

The rebel armies had disbanded and most peasants were either killed or had fled to the safety of the countryside. One sailor told Albert that some of the rebel leaders had been executed, and he worried about Wat and Elizabeth. He hoped and prayed that his friend was not among the dead, but if he were, he would have sent his sister to safety of the convent before he saw such violence.

Albert managed to buy passage on *The Mary*, which the brave Master Simms commanded. Albert had had much trouble trying to purchase passage as many were still afraid to go to London, but Simms was a hearty and experienced sailor who would not be deterred by a "little skirmish in London," for he had fought in his share of battles with the French, the Castilians, and the Genoese in days past. The tranquil seas made for a swift passage, which began early in the morning, and they reached London by the end of the day.

"The city is ablaze, sir! I cannot unload the cargo, but I will set you ashore." Albert clutched the rail as the sweat dripped from his face and palms.

He was not listening. The screams and bloodshed mesmerized him as he stared at the chaos that was taking place before his eyes.

"Sir Albert," shouted Simms. "We are nearing the wharf!"

Simms's shouts brought Albert back to his senses. Coming out of his daze, he turned and looked at him. He reached into his satchel, took all the coin he had, and handed it to Simms.

"Take this, and await my return if you can. I must go and find Elizabeth and her brother, but if you find yourself or your ship is in any danger, by all means, sail away immediately."

Simms stepped forward and placed his strong hand on Albert's shoulder. "I will try to maintain as long as I can, and God be with you, sir."

Albert thrust his hand out to shake the seaman's hand. He thanked him and started down the gangplank. His heart pounded, and he sweated profusely as he looked around nervously. He was well aware that the king's men would be searching for him, but that wouldn't keep him from his search.

From Paul's Wharf he ran up Thames Street. The stench filled the air with a vile odor as he passed mangled, lifeless bodies and bits of body parts that littered the streets and alleyways. His pace slowed as he approached Castle Bayard, and he stopped now and again to examine various corpses of the indiscriminate dead. He was hoping he would not find any loved ones among them, especially Elizabeth. Merciful God! He prayed that he would not find her among the dead. He continued to search as ragged men, women, and children rushed past him, fleeing for their lives. As he bent down to examine the body of a woman, a shrill cry got his attention, and he looked in the direction of the sound.

Just as he stood to get a better view, he heard a groan coming from the same direction, and he moved toward the body he thought the cry had come from. He stood above a man lying face down. As Albert knelt down beside him, he saw the man's fingers move. He gently turned the dying man over and gazed into his eyes. Albert looked down and noticed the huge gash in the man's stomach, exposing some of his innards. He knew from his experiences in battle that this was a slow and excruciatingly painful death.

"Please, sir," the man cried. "Finish me!"

With pity, Albert looked back upon the battered face.

"Please, sir," the man begged. "In the name of our beloved Savior, end my suffering!"

Albert slowly drew his dagger. He hesitated for one moment, looking into the man's face and hearing him whisper, "Please!" Taking a deep breath and placing his dagger on the man's chest, Albert closed his eyes and whispered a prayer as he plunged the dagger into the man's heart. He felt the cracking of ribs as blood spurted out, covering his hands. He heard the man's final gasp of air as he withdrew his dagger. As he rose, Albert looked down at the man's face again to see that he was finally at peace, and Albert felt a rush of relief for him. He stood, wiping the blood from his hands with his sleeves. He made the sign of the cross and began to walk away, resuming his search.

He arrived at Black Friars Convent noticing that its sanctuary had been destroyed, presumably by an angry peasant mob. He passed St. Paul's to West Cheap Street where he encountered a small group of fleeing commoners. Believing Albert was one of the king's knights, they knelt down at his feet.

"Have mercy, my lord," one cried.

Albert motioned them to rise. "I am not one of the king's men. You have no need to fear me, but I'm hoping you can help me. "I'm looking for Wat Tyler. Does anyone here know of his whereabouts?"

One man stepped forward to speak. He looked at Albert with sad eyes, and Albert steadied himself for bad news.

"His head rests on London Bridge with that of Jack Straw's," the man replied.

"Oh God," Albert cried softly. His eyes filled as he

lowered his head. In an unsteady voice he asked, "What of his sister? Does anyone know what became of her?"

"We know not, sir," one replied hastily as the group started off again, making their way toward the city gates and the freedom of the countryside.

Albert turned and continued on his way. His search seemed to last an eternity. Finally, his pace slowed. Feeling exhausted and discouraged, he decided to surrender himself to the king's forces.

After all, he was a fugitive, and with Wat dead and little hope of finding Elizabeth, it was his only choice. He would first return to the vessel and set Master Sims on his way. He began retracing his steps back through the city. Many peasants continued to pass him, running with horse and infantry companies not far behind. Through the fray he walked, oblivious to his surroundings, and by some miracle, not being recognized by anyone in the companies of men who were pursuing the rebels.

Sounds grew distant, and there seemed to be a lull in the action, followed by a momentary silence. He was lost in thoughts of Elizabeth. Tears filled his eyes and rolled down his cheeks as he walked head down toward Paul's Wharf. He feared that the worst had befallen her. He tried to console himself with the thought that perhaps she had escaped and returned to the safety of the convent, but he also knew that she would try to protect her brother and be caught up in the melee. As he passed an alleyway, he heard a soft cry coming from within.

His first thought was to avoid the situation, but as unpleasant as it could be, his conscience and curiosity would not let him walk past. He turned and entered into the darkness, stumbling on what were the bloated remains of some poor wretch. He took a step forward. It was hard to see at first, but as his eyes began to adjust to the darkness, he noticed something at the far end in the corner of the alley. It looked like a pile of old rags, but he couldn't be sure. He waited and called out, but there was no reply. Again he waited, beginning to think that he'd imagined it. As he turned to leave, he heard a whimper and looked back. Someone was there! Albert thought it might be a child, but then he heard the loveliest sound.

"Albert!" called a soft, familiar voice.

Without a word, Albert rushed toward her. He leaned forward to touch her outstretched arms and drew her toward him.

"Elizabeth," he whispered as he held her.

They looked at each other through teary, unbelieving eyes.

"I thought I lost you forever," he cried. They held each other for a long moment. Albert kissed the top of her head. He was relieved to have found her but reluctant to share the bad news about her brother.

In the moments they stood together, holding each other in the dim light of the alley, oblivious to the stinking garbage and the stench of death all around them, Albert thought about a time of hopeful youth.

A distant cry brought Albert's mind back to the present; his arms still around Elizabeth.

"We have wasted too much time here," he said as he took her hand and led her out of the alley.

"Where are we to go?" she asked.

"There is a vessel that awaits us at the wharf, but we must hurry. Wait!" he said. Just as they were about to leave, Albert heard horses quickly approaching. He pulled her back into the alley and out of sight until they passed.

"Henry has promised me that he would return," she said.

"We cannot afford to wait," Albert replied as tugged at her hand. "He would not want you to wait for him if it meant being in danger."

"Yes, of course," she said as she followed him.

They ran toward the wharf. Only a few short steps and they would be free. As they ran, they were spied by a group of knights on horseback accompanied by two bowmen who were passing by. They stopped when they saw the two in flight. "Stop! Stop in the name of the king!" they yelled, but Albert and Elizabeth kept running. The bowman drew their arrows and prepared to fire.

Elizabeth hesitated, but Albert tugged on her hand and pulled her along. The order was given to fire, and arrows flew through the air, none finding their mark save one. It dug deep into Elizabeth's backbone, and her hand went limp in his.

Albert turned to help her as she fell to the ground. He knelt down beside her and pulled her head onto his lap. "Elizabeth!" he cried as the arrows flew past him. He pulled out the iron ring that she had waited so long for from his satchel and placed it on her finger once again. She looked up at him and smiled.

"I love you, Albert," she said as she closed her eyes and drew her last breath.

"No, no, Elizabeth! Please don't die. I love you too!" he sobbed as he held his cheek to hers. The knight who had ordered the attack raced toward Albert with a drawn sword.

Albert immediately stood and drew his dagger in defense. He looked up into the knight's face—it was Sir Gilles. He let his dagger fall to his side, giving Gilles the opportunity to attack. His sword made contact with Albert's chest, his legs gave way, and he fell to his knees beside Elizabeth.

He looked up at Gilles with a jeering smile and laid his body down beside his love. He gently placed his arm around her as life quickly faded from his body.

Albert closed his eyes and saw Elizabeth standing before him. Her eyes had never looked greener, and her skin glowed with the light of goodness. She held out her hand, and he raised himself up, taking it to his heart. The two looked down and felt a lightness of being as they both rose above the scene.

Sir Gilles stood over them triumphantly. He gazed down over their bodies; the smirk on his face slowly faded as he realized he had not taken anything from them that they truly wanted, and in reality, *they* had been the victors.

For the two lovers, it was not the end but the beginning, for their spirits rose high above a world filled with pain and sorrow and into a world of everlasting peace and love.

Epilogue

Although the rebels held London for two weeks and got King Richard's sworn statement that their demands to end villainy would be met, the death of Wat Tyler turned the tide of the rebellion, and the king reneged on his promises. However, the poll tax was never reinstated, and the psychological impact of the uprising paved the way toward the end of feudalism. Many of the participants of the rebellion would gain little for their efforts; however, their forebears would reap the benefits of the accomplishments achieved in those few short weeks.